# Praise for *A Secret to Die For*

"Lisa Harris has done it again! *A Secret to Die For* is a fast-paced romantic thriller packed with twists and turns. High-tension action and well-paced romance—everything you want in a romantic suspense—Harris delivers!"

**Elizabeth Goddard**, award-winning author
of the Coldwater Bay Intrigue series

"Discussions of faith and tragedy add depth and poignancy to an exciting, well-crafted tale of romantic suspense from veteran thriller-writer Harris."

*Booklist*

"With her signature pulse-pounding suspense, Lisa Harris takes readers deep into the heart of fear in this race against the clock."

*Family Fiction*

"Another skillfully crafted novel by a master of the genre."

*Midwest Book Review*

*DEADLY INTENTIONS*

## Also by Lisa Harris

# DEADLY INTENTIONS

# LISA HARRIS

**Revell**

a division of Baker Publishing Group
Grand Rapids, Michigan

Published by Revell
a division of Baker Publishing Group
PO Box 6287, Grand Rapids, MI 49516-6287
www.revellbooks.com

Printed in the United States of America

Library of Congress Cataloging-in-Publication Data
Names: Harris, Lisa, 1969– author.
Title: Deadly intentions / Lisa Harris.
Description: Grand Rapids, MI : Revell, [2019]
Identifiers: LCCN 2018052135 | ISBN 9780800729165 (paper)
Subjects: LCSH: Murder—Investigation—Fiction. | Serial murder investigation—
   Fiction.
Classification: LCC PS3608.A78315 D425 2019 | DDC 813/.6—dc23
LC record available at https://lccn.loc.gov/2018052135

ISBN 978-0-8007-3625-5 (casebound)

Published in association with Joyce Hart of the Hartline Literary Agency, LLC.

19  20  21  22  23  24  25      7  6  5  4  3  2  1

For God has not given us a spirit of fear, but of power and of love and of a sound mind.

2 Timothy 1:7

# Prologue

Josh Solomon had barely slept in thirty-six hours. The call had come in while he'd been eating dinner with his wife. The body of a seventeen-year-old had been found in a dumpster on the north side of town by a store owner taking out the trash. It was days like this when he wondered why he hadn't chosen a different career. But a decade of investigating homicides had given him one thing. A feeling that he was responsible for—at least in part—cleaning up the scum littering the streets.

Still, he was exhausted.

He flipped off the car radio as the news came on, relishing the silence. The last thing he wanted to listen to right now was another depressing news cycle. Olivia wouldn't be home until tomorrow, which meant a night of playing the role of a bachelor. Not that he minded the time alone. As much as he enjoyed coming home to his wife, after the day he'd just had, he could use a couple hours to wind down watching some brainless movie and falling asleep on the couch.

Five minutes later, he pulled into the driveway of their two-story home, reached up to open the garage with the remote, then paused. Two figures wearing dark hoodies ran out the side door of the house. His headlights caught a glimpse of the men as they hesitated, then took off running across the neighbor's lawn and down the street.

Without stopping to think about the consequences, Josh slammed the car into park, jumped out of the driver's seat, and took off after them.

He pulled his phone out of his pocket and put in a call to dispatch. "This is Detective Josh Solomon. I need backup immediately at my residence. Two intruders just ran out of my house, heading north up Washington Street."

He gave the operator his full address, then glanced back at the house, now second-guessing his decision to give chase in the dark. There were always risks with following on his own, and he had no idea if the men were armed. Reacting without a plan—alone—was always dangerous, but this was *his* house. Over the past couple months, nine houses in his neighborhood had been burglarized. So far no one had been hurt in the process, but these guys needed to be stopped.

His internal debate ended. As long as he could maintain visual contact with them, he'd stay in pursuit. He'd ensure they knew he was behind them and let them tire out. If they tried to engage, he'd back off. He had no desire to escalate the situation, but whoever these guys were, he wanted them locked up.

The scenario in this neighborhood had become far too common, but this time they'd messed with the wrong homeowner, and he was going to make sure their string of luck had just run out. The streetlight exposed their position, and he quickened his pace. Unless he kept close, the odds of losing them were high. There were a dozen places they could hide, or even turn the tables and come after him.

Five seconds later, they vanished. Josh stopped at the street corner to catch his breath while he studied the surroundings for movement. A dog barked in the distance, but there was no sign of the intruders.

He'd lost them.

His phone rang. "Quinton?"

"I just heard your call go through. What's going on?"

"Two intruders were coming out the side door of my house when I pulled up. I took off after them, but I've lost 'em."

"What about Olivia?"

"She left yesterday for a medical conference. Won't be back till tomorrow night."

"Don't try to find them on your own. Go back to the house. See what kind of damage they've done. I'm heading to your place now."

Josh started back to his house at a jog, adrenaline still pumping. Something had been nagging at him ever since he'd arrived home, but what? He stopped in the driveway and stared at the front of the house. Then it registered. The upstairs light was on. Which wasn't possible. Intruders wouldn't turn on lights. Olivia wasn't due home until tomorrow, and he knew he hadn't left it on.

He reached into his car, clicked the garage door opener on the visor, and felt his heart go still . . . Olivia's silver Prius was parked in the garage.

How was that possible?

He ran into the garage, then opened the door into the house. "Olivia?"

No answer.

He checked his phone as he rushed toward the kitchen. No messages. No missed calls.

But her coat had been thrown over one of the breakfast nook chairs where she always left it after work. Chinese takeout sat on the kitchen bar, still in the plastic bags. He breathed in the smell of garlic and seared meat and felt his stomach heave.

Why hadn't she told him she was coming home early?

"Olivia?"

The faint sound of sirens wailed in the background through the open garage. He hurried up the stairs while fear swept through him. If she'd been here when the house had been broken into . . . If she'd walked in on the burglars . . . And why wasn't she answering?

This he knew—sometimes people died because they'd been in the wrong place at the wrong time. But not *his* family. Not *his* wife.

He stopped at the threshold of their room. Fully clothed, Olivia lay in the middle of the bed like she was sleeping, her hair spread out across the pillow. A red stain seeped from her abdomen.

He fumbled for his phone as he rushed to the bed. He needed to make sure they sent an ambulance. Needed to know if she was still alive.

"Josh . . ."

His heart stilled. "Olivia . . ."

He caught the pain in her eyes as she continued. "They . . . they must have already been in the house. I came upstairs to change . . ."

He grabbed a shirt from the edge of the bed, found the wound, then pressed the shirt against her side.

"Don't try to talk. You're going to be fine."

With his free hand he punched in 911, praying he'd somehow be able to keep his word.

"I need an ambulance," he said once the operator answered. "My wife . . . my wife's been shot."

"Sir, can you give me your name and address?"

Numbness spread through him as he gave her their address.

"A squad car and ambulance have been sent to your address. Where's your wife right now?"

"I'm upstairs with her, in our bedroom. Third door on the . . . on the left."

"Can you tell me where she was shot?"

"In her abdomen. There's blood everywhere."

"Were you there when it happened?"

"No. I . . . When I got home, two male intruders were exiting the house from a side door."

"I want you to stay on the line with me but keep pressure on the wound. The ambulance is about two minutes out."

Two minutes? He studied Olivia's pale face. She was the woman he'd pledged to be with through sickness and in health. To honor. To cleave to . . . To love . . . He dropped the phone, allowing him to pull her against him and nestle his face in her hair. He couldn't lose her. Not this way.

Olivia reached up and pulled on his arm, as she struggled to breathe, "I'm . . . sorry. So sorry. I came home early . . . because I needed to talk to you—"

"Don't talk. Just lie still. Everything's going to be okay."

Except he knew it wasn't. Blood already soaked through the shirt and onto the comforter she'd bought last month.

"I need you to know the . . . the truth about what happened. Why . . . why . . ."

Her increasing struggle to breathe only multiplied his panic as he struggled to understand what she was saying. "Shhh . . ." He pressed his fingers against her lips. "You're going to be fine. And we'll catch whoever did this."

Sirens wound down in front of the house, the vehicles' strobe lights reflecting against the mirror on the other side of the room. This was supposed to be someone else's nightmare. He investigated the crimes. Husbands murdering their wives, crimes of passion, jealousy. He was on the other side, looking on.

He wasn't supposed to be the victim.

A paramedic entered the room. "Sir . . . I need you to step back, out of the way, so we can help her."

Josh climbed off the bed and stumbled backward as they went to work. The walls were closing in on him. Why hadn't he caught the men who'd broken in? There were no answers. Just questions about the nightmare he'd walked into.

"Josh." Someone grasped his arm and pulled him away from the bed. But he couldn't leave Olivia.

"Don't—"

He glanced up at his partner. Quinton Lambert was two hundred and thirty pounds, with dark skin and kinky hair that had started to gray over the past couple years. He forced Josh across the hardwood floors and out of the way.

"I know this is hard but let them work on her."

Josh stood in the corner of the room while they worked on her, his dress shirt now covered with blood. It was as if he were watching through someone else's eyes. Some late-night detective show. Because this couldn't be real—her pale face staring up at the ceiling, her body limp.

Quinton's hand rested on Josh's shoulder. "Tell me what happened."

"I don't know." When had his mind frozen? He couldn't think. Couldn't remember. He couldn't be a husband of the victim. He was a detective who found the answers. Who never panicked.

"Josh . . . the more information you give me, the more it will help us find them."

"I know."

"Take a deep breath and try to focus on my questions. Did you see the men who broke into your house?"

The words clicked something on in his brain. He knew Quinton. He was trying to distract him. Trying to get him to focus on something he could do rather than on what he was losing. Figuring out who had done this had to be better than this feeling of helplessness. He spent his days tracking down killers. Had learned to shut down his emotions in order to cope. He needed to do the same now.

"I saw them coming out of the house and tried to chase them down. Two men, early twenties. I only saw them for an instant in the beam of my car's headlights when they turned and looked at me. One had a dark beard. The other . . . it was hard to tell. Red shoes. I remember he had red shoes."

He fought to remember the details. "I took off after them, heading north on Washington Street. After about five minutes I lost them in the darkness when they ducked into someone's yard."

"That's when I called you?"

Josh nodded. "I decided to go back to the house like you said. But Olivia . . . she wasn't supposed to get back until tomorrow." Confusion wormed its way through him again. "I don't know why she's here."

"She was here when they broke in?"

He nodded again. "I never saw a weapon, but they must have been armed."

"We'll have officers search the vicinity in case they dumped it."

Josh shifted his gaze back to Olivia. The paramedics were shouting back and forth. Trying to stop the bleeding. Trying to start her heart. The room began to spin again. Two men had broken into his home. Shot his wife. Something that never should have happened. It was his job to protect her, but now . . .

"Josh, I want you to keep focusing on me. You can help her the most right now by helping us figure out who did this."

The paramedics shouted out frantic directives as they continued working on her. He felt his own heart stop. Eleven years of marriage wasn't supposed to end this way. He'd always loved her. Always imagined the two of them getting old and retiring together. He couldn't hear Quinton anymore. Could barely breathe.

"I can't lose her, Quinton. Not this way." Josh started back toward the bed, but Quinton held him back.

"Let them do their job, Josh. They're going to take her to the hospital. If there's any chance at all for them to save her, they will."

He watched the paramedics transfer Olivia's limp body to a gurney. But he somehow knew it was too late. She wasn't coming back. He felt his legs collapse as he leaned his back against the bedroom wall, then slowly slid to the ground. Suddenly everything was clear. This was his new reality. A widower before he turned forty. And Olivia . . .

Life as he knew it was over.

# 1

Caitlyn Lindsey hated the cold. That bone-chilling, icy feeling in the dead of winter that always felt impossible to shake. Cold that had finally compelled her to move from upstate New York to Houston, Texas. Then the weatherman had predicted an unseasonable arctic blast for the next thirty-six hours, with temperatures falling below freezing, forcing her to admit that today, she'd need the scarf and heavy coat she'd shed two years ago.

But facing the chill outside seemed nothing compared to the shock of having to attend Helen's funeral.

She swallowed the lump in her throat as she sat down on the padded seat in the church sanctuary and tried not to cry. Today's funeral had totally thrown her off-balance. She knew Helen. Knew she would never kill herself as the coroner had concluded. It just wasn't possible. For the past two years, nearly every day at eleven thirty, she and Helen had sat in the break room at MedTECH Labs, eating their lunches and chatting about things outside work, like Helen's three grandchildren and the trip she was planning to Vegas next summer. But the final verdict on Helen's untimely death had been strikingly different. She had been on anxiety meds, they'd said, and had been depressed. An overdose of sleeping pills was the official conclusion.

But Caitlyn didn't believe it.

She stuffed down the wave of fear that was getting harder and harder to control as Helen's son started speaking. She didn't have any conclusive proof for any of her suspicions. Not yet. But three recent deaths of fellow employees at MedTECH wasn't something she could ignore. A year ago, Olivia Solomon had been shot in cold blood during a home invasion. Then three months ago, Dr. Abbott had died of a heart attack. At the time, both deaths had been tragic losses, and she'd never even considered they might be connected. Never considered they could be related to their work at MedTECH.

Helen had changed all of that.

Unable to force her mind to settle, she only half listened to Gavin Fletcher giving his mother's eulogy. Instead, she was taking the only approach she knew. Her scientific background required investigative skills that used observation, data, and evaluation from experiments to test predictions. That same approach was how she'd come to the conclusion that Helen's death—and that of the others—was no coincidence.

She leaned back in the cushioned pew and tried to push away the growing panic. Olivia's words from a year ago replayed through her mind like a broken record. Her friend had called her on her way home from a conference and asked to meet her for an early breakfast the next morning. She'd left a message on her voice mail.

*Caitlyn . . . this is Olivia. You're probably at the gym, but I need some advice about some research going on at the lab and wondered if you could meet me for breakfast before work tomorrow. I'm concerned about some of the data from this new project I've been working on . . . Starlighter. We found some anomalies that I'm concerned about. Anyway . . . we can talk tomorrow if you're free.*

At the time, she hadn't thought anything about her friend's

request. It wouldn't have been the first time they'd met for coffee to discuss a project, especially when their team moved into the development phase for a vaccine, before they could be approved for a clinical trial. But the next morning, instead of meeting Olivia, she'd gotten the call that her friend was dead. While her murder had left her and her colleagues reeling, there had been no reason to question the cause of Olivia's death. According to the official police report, two men had broken into a house and shot Olivia when she confronted them.

Now Helen had mentioned the same research project to her, Starlighter, and two days later, her friend was dead. Caitlyn had yet to confirm the project even existed, which didn't make sense. Looking back, she wished she would have pressed Helen to tell her what was bothering her, but when she pushed, Helen had gotten evasive and insisted on changing the subject.

On top of that troublesome case, when she'd spoken with Dr. Abbott's wife yesterday, she'd been left with more questions than answers. She'd spent the past few days searching the lab's computer system for a reference to the project, but hadn't found anything, which in itself was odd. And now, as discreet as she'd tried to be in her investigation, she was certain she'd gotten someone's attention.

The first strange thing she'd noticed had been a black van parked across the street from her house, then a couple days later, she noticed it following her to work. She'd also noticed a balding man loitering three mornings in a row across from the coffee shop where she frequented. Not knowing what else to do, she'd locked down all her social media settings to private, changed the locks on her house, and started asking for a security escort to her car at night after work. She also started varying her normal routine, leaving for work at different times and taking lunch at her desk where she felt safer. Maybe she was simply being paranoid, but if someone was watching her, she wanted to throw them off. Still, there was only so much she could do to protect herself if her suspicions were true. And she knew that, like Helen, Dr. Abbott, and Olivia, if they wanted to get to her, they would.

Whoever *they* were.

Someone took Gavin's place in the front of the church and began reading a favorite poem of Helen's, but no matter how hard she tried, she couldn't concentrate. There was, of course, a chance that she was completely wrong in her theories. Helen *had* been depressed. She had confessed that herself. She'd said her son had been working too much, and her daughter-in-law was talking divorce and planning to move back east with Helen's grandchildren. With no other family, and her husband having passed away a few years ago, Helen was afraid of being alone. She'd told Caitlyn she couldn't imagine life without her grandchildren.

But had she really been that afraid of living?

Caitlyn couldn't believe that.

Fifteen minutes later, the minister dismissed the guests and she started making her way toward the front of the church to give her condolences to the family. She'd met Helen's son and daughter-in-law, along with their three boys, at a Christmas party last year, and couldn't imagine what they had to be going through right now. No matter how Helen had died, the reality was that she was gone.

Her son was in an intense conversation with someone, so Caitlyn turned her focus to Helen's daughter-in-law, who was standing a couple feet from him, looking lost.

"Anna . . ." Caitlyn reached out to squeeze the woman's hand. Anna's face was pale, emphasized by her stark black dress. "I'm so sorry about Helen."

"You worked with my mother-in-law, right?"

"Yes. I'm Caitlyn Lindsey."

"Of course." Anna fiddled with the metal strap of her purse. "I remember meeting you. We appreciate your coming. She talked about you a lot."

"How are you doing?" Caitlyn asked. "Like you, I'm having a hard time dealing with her death."

*And the fact that she'd killed herself.*

"I'm not sure any of this has sunk in, to be honest," Anna said. "Or how Gavin is going to deal with this."

"Do you really believe she committed suicide?" Caitlyn felt a burst of guilt surface as the words slipped out of her mouth before she had a chance to filter them. But she needed to ask the question.

Anna's brow furrowed. "I . . . I'm not sure what you mean—"

"I'm sorry." As much as she needed answers, she'd just pushed too much. "I'm just having a hard time believing the coroner's conclusion, but I shouldn't be talking about this. Not now."

Anna let out a soft sigh. "I admit I've thought the same thing. It was just so . . . unexpected. But everything the authorities uncovered was true. She'd been depressed ever since her husband died. I tried to be there for her, but obviously I didn't do enough."

Caitlyn shook her head. "I never meant to imply that you were to blame, Anna."

"I know, I just . . ." The woman wiped away a stray tear, then pressed her lips together. "I'm sorry. Will you excuse me. I need to go to the restroom."

Anna vanished out the side door, leaving Caitlyn standing alone in the small crowd of guests. She walked back down the center aisle of the church and into the lobby, the guilt still pulsing through her. She'd never meant to imply to Anna that she or her husband hadn't done enough, but now she'd managed to upset the woman. And all she wanted was answers.

"Caitlyn?"

She turned around at the sound of her supervisor's voice, surprised to see him. "Dr. Kaiser. I didn't think you'd made it. I didn't see you come in earlier."

Mike Kaiser was wearing a pin-striped suit from a decade ago, along with one of his signature bow ties. She'd been trying to speak to him for the past few days but had been told he was going to be out of the office for the week.

"Helen's death is horrible, isn't it?" he said, shoving his hands inside his pockets. "Strange how you can work with someone for so long and miss something like this. You were close to Helen. How are you?"

"She was a good friend," she said, surprised at his unexpected concern. "To be honest, I don't know how I missed the warning signs."

"I suppose you never really know a person, do you?"

Caitlyn shook her head. Except she had known her. Or at least she thought she had.

"I'm sorry, but I have a meeting to get to." The older man started toward the front door.

"Dr. Kaiser, wait . . ." Caitlyn caught up with him. "I was hoping to speak to you this week about Helen. I wanted to ask you about a side project she was working on. A research project called Starlighter."

Dr. Kaiser tugged on the end of his bow tie. "Starlighter?"

She tried to read his reaction. Surprise? Wariness? Or maybe she was just imagining things. "Helen mentioned the project before she died. She seemed . . . upset. Worried about something that was going on."

"I'd have to check into it, but there are usually a few side research projects that I'm not involved in. Projects employees work on before they come to me wanting to move forward. Have you asked anyone else about it?"

"I talked to Susanne, Helen's immediate boss—"

"And her response?"

"She hadn't heard about it either."

Dr. Kaiser's frown deepened. "Just be careful who you talk to about this. I hardly think Helen's death had anything to do with a project from work, and I'd hate to have unsubstantiated rumors circulating."

"Of course not." There was something in the tone of his voice she didn't like. Surely he wasn't threatening her. "You know, forget it. I'm sure it's nothing. Helen just . . . she seemed upset, and I suppose, like all of us, I'm just looking for answers."

She pulled her leather gloves out of her coat pocket and headed out the door behind him. No matter how crazy it sounded, she was still convinced there was a connection between the three deaths and the lab.

The wind whipped around her, sending a shiver down her spine. She glanced out into the parking lot, looking for signs of the black van she'd noticed following her but didn't see it.

Maybe she was losing it.

Or maybe she was going to be next.

Shaking off the morbid thought, she hurried toward the car, her heels clicking against the sidewalk. A minute later, her gloved fingers gripped the steering wheel as she headed home. Thanks to the impending ice storm, schools would probably shut down tomorrow—something she'd been told happened whenever the temperatures started to dip toward freezing. It took an arctic blizzard for schools to close in Albany. She flipped on the turn signal and eased into the left lane, watching the flow of traffic surrounding her. All she wanted was to get home before the brunt of the storm blew in. At least for now, the roads were still dry, just heavy with the evening rush hour.

A truck changed lanes in front of her, forcing her to slam on her brakes. Her seat belt caught and jerked her against the seat. A breath of air shot out of her lungs as the car behind her narrowly missed rear-ending her. Her hands shook, her pulse racing at the near accident.

Caitlyn eased off the gas and let another car pass that was going at least ten miles over the speed limit. Sleet started splashing against her windshield. Beating an impending storm shouldn't be an excuse to speed. She blew out another deep breath, trying to stamp down the growing anxiety that had settled in her chest.

Ten minutes later, she pulled off the highway and headed south. It was almost dark now, and the wind was picking up steam, but at least the traffic had finally thinned. Another twenty minutes and she'd be home. She'd pull out a microwave dinner from the freezer and go over all her personal notes as well as the police records she'd obtained regarding Olivia's murder. There had to be something she missed. Something to prove there was nothing to worry about. If only she could convince herself that was true.

A vehicle bridged the gap behind her when the road went down to two lanes as she headed toward her subdivision. The dark van put on his blinker and started to pass her. A second later, it rammed into the side of her car. There was no time to compensate for the collision. She lost control of her vehicle as it headed off the slick curve and rolled down the embankment into a ditch.

## 2

The impact with the car's air bags felt like a head-on collision with a train. Smoke filled the air. Fine dust settled around her. She couldn't breathe. Couldn't think. The car rolled one more time, then settled upright.

For a long, terrifying moment, the only thing she could hear was her heart pounding. She braced her feet against the floor, then slowly started checking for injuries in the dark. She drew in a couple deep breaths, trying to calm down. Nothing seemed broken. No doubt the rush of adrenaline that could overwhelm pain would fade soon, but at the moment she couldn't discern any injuries.

Suddenly she could hear the cars rushing by on the road above her. She looked up, but the incline was too steep for her to see anything more than the glow of headlights as they passed. A familiar wave of panic engulfed her. Surely someone had seen the accident. Someone would call 911 and report it. But it was dark. What if no one had even seen what had happened?

Or worse yet, what if the driver of the other car was still out there? It had looked a lot like that black van. Hadn't it? What if this had been an attempt on her life? What if they wanted to make sure she didn't walk away from the accident?

She tried to shove aside the growing fear as she attempted to restart the car. Maybe if she could get the engine running and the heater back on, she wouldn't freeze. She tried to start the engine for a fourth time, but the motor wouldn't catch. There was no way to know what kind of damage had been done to the car, which meant it wasn't going anywhere. The morning news had warned about being out here in the weather. How long would it take for hypothermia to set in? Minutes? Hours? It didn't matter really. She wasn't going to be here long enough to find out. She slipped her hand down to unbuckle her seat belt, but the metal clasp was jammed. She pushed the release button again.

Nothing.

*I know you're out there, God. I need a miracle. Please.*

Temperatures were already hovering around freezing. She couldn't get out. Couldn't start the car. Even if she had blankets or water in the car, she wouldn't have been able to get to them. Unless someone had seen the accident, more than likely she wouldn't be found until morning.

And morning might be too late, because they were going to come back. They wanted her dead. She knew that now. Someone had found out she'd been asking questions. And now she was going to die. Just like Olivia and Dr. Abbott. Just like Helen.

She searched the front seat again, this time for her phone. It had been sitting on the console, but the car had flipped. It could be anywhere now.

A shout from the embankment interrupted her search. She could see the light of a flashlight or cell phone as someone hurried down to her car. If someone wanted her dead, would they announce their presence? It didn't seem likely, but did it even matter? Whoever it was would find her, and if it was the same person who'd rammed into her car, there was nowhere for her to run.

Seconds later, a shadow appeared at the driver's-side window. It was an older man, holding a couple of blankets. He tapped on the window.

She glanced at him while she struggled to unlock and open the door.

"Name's James Keller." Cold air whipped into the car as the door swung open. "Are you okay?"

Her hands were shaking and her head hurt, but at least she could move her fingers and toes. "I think more than anything else I'm just cold, but my seat belt's jammed, and I can't get out."

"Just take a deep breath and hang on. My wife's already called 911, but it's better that you don't move."

"I think I'm okay. Really. I can move my hands and my feet."

"Is there anyone else in your vehicle?"

"No . . . just me."

"What's your name?"

Her name. Why did everything seem so fuzzy? "Caitlyn. Caitlyn Lindsey."

"Caitlyn . . . don't worry about the seat belt right now. I want you to put these blankets around you. You need to stay warm."

"Okay." She pulled the thick flannel around her neck and arms and tried to slow her breathing, but she was starting to hyperventilate. No . . . She couldn't panic. She was fine. She just needed to convince herself. "I was driving home and this van . . . it came out of nowhere. Ran into the side of me, and before I knew it, I was here."

"I know. My wife and I saw it happen, and we'll make sure the authorities know."

She let out a huff of air in relief. "Thank you. I wanted to call for help, but I can't find my phone."

Flashes of the crash played through her mind, over and over like a stuck record.

"Caitlyn . . . Do you have anyone you want to call? It might be nice to have someone meet you at the hospital."

"I don't know."

She needed to focus on getting out, but for some reason, even a small decision like that seemed complicated. What would he say if she told him that someone had run her off the road in an attempt to scare her? Or maybe to kill her.

Two men were scrambling down the embankment. She could see the lights from the emergency vehicles flashing above them. Still feel the cold seeping through the blanket he had given her.

"Her name's Caitlyn Lindsey." Her rescuer took a step back from the car. "My wife and I saw the accident. Someone ran her off the road. Her seat belt's stuck, so she can't get out, and she's pretty shook up."

The paramedic took the older man's place. "Ma'am, my name's Clint. We're going to get you out of here in just a few minutes, then take you to a hospital to get checked over."

"I don't need to go to the hospital. Please . . . if you can get me out of here, I just want to go home. I'm fine. Really."

"I understand, but we need to make sure you don't have a head injury or any internal injuries. The first thing I'm going to do is cut you out of your seat belt."

She nodded. She hated feeling so helpless, but cold and fatigue had overcome her, and she was too tired to argue. Besides, there were only two things she could think about. She was certain of it now. One, everything she'd thought might be true was true. And two, someone wanted her dead.

And both terrified her.

The paramedics somehow managed to carry her up the steep embankment. Her body trembled as much from the cold as from fear, as they put her on a backboard and then placed a brace around her neck.

One of the men started checking her vitals. "Can you tell me what happened?"

"I was driving home, and someone ran me off the road."

"Can you tell me today's date?"

"Of course . . . It's . . ." She tried to fight her way out of the fog. "February seventeenth."

"Good. Does anything hurt?"

"I don't think so. I'm just so . . . so cold."

"We'll get you warmed up, but we do need to get you checked out at the hospital."

She nodded this time, deciding not to argue anymore. Fatigue pressed through her, and she couldn't keep her eyes open as the ambulance pulled back onto the main road. At least for the moment she was safe.

Three hours later, Caitlyn picked up her cell phone from the table beside the hospital bed and checked her messages. Even though she had no obvious injuries, the doctor had insisted she stay overnight for observation, but she still hadn't told anyone where she was. She'd been lucky, the doctor had told her after finishing his examination. No broken bones, no internal injuries, just a few bruises. Her only regret now was that she'd been unable to thank her guardian angel for showing up at the scene and calling 911. He'd disappeared into the night after the ambulance came.

But that wasn't what was on the forefront of her mind right now. What worried her was the chance that the accident could make the evening news cycle, which meant whoever had run her off the road might be able to find out that she was alive—assuming that they wanted her dead. Even if they'd just wanted to scare her, they'd done a good job. She glanced out into the hallway where a couple of the nurses were chatting, unable to push away the uneasiness. She wasn't safe here. If they came after her again . . .

The row of machines routinely checking her pulse and oxygen levels hummed in the background. She needed help from someone, but who? She could call her best friend Amber, but she was out of town for the week at her mother's. Besides, even if she were home, there was nothing she could do. Not really. But if not Amber, then who? She could call someone at church, but even that seemed risky. The last thing she wanted to do was put someone else's life in danger.

Josh Solomon's name surfaced, and not for the first time. In fact, she'd considered calling him ever since Helen's death. She pulled her legs up toward her chest and rested her chin on her knees, wondering if it was time to call him. Josh was a police officer, but he was also Olivia's husband and had spent the last year dealing with her death. Calling him would mean asking him to dig into his wife's death again, something he might not want to do. But from everything she knew about him, he was an outstanding detective, and there was no way he was going to be able to pass up new information about his wife.

But was it fair to try to drag him into this when she didn't have any solid proof of what was going on? On the other hand, what more proof did she need? Someone had just run her off the road. She glanced at the door of her room, a plan formulating in her mind. Despite the doctor's concerns, she couldn't stay here. Especially if there was a chance they could find her.

She drew in a deep breath, decision made. She couldn't do this on her own. It was time to make the call, even if Josh Solomon ended up thinking she was crazy. She could arrange to meet him nearby, then tell him what she knew. What happened next would be up to him.

She placed the call, then drummed her fingers against her leg while she waited for someone to answer.

"Houston PD."

"Yes . . . I need to speak with Detective Solomon."

"One moment, please, I can transfer you."

After the first ring, it went straight to his voice mail. Caitlyn paused, debating for a moment if she should leave a message or not.

"Josh Solomon? This is Caitlyn Lindsey. I worked with Olivia at MedTECH Laboratories. I really need to talk to you as soon as possible. It . . . it's about Olivia, about her . . . murder. I need to speak to you in person. It's important. There's a diner three blocks from your precinct that's open late. I'll be there in about an hour and will wait until they close. Please . . . please come if you can." She hung up, realizing how presumptuous she'd just been. She'd assumed he'd listen to the message and come, but there were no guarantees he'd even hear her message tonight. Or if he did listen to it, there was a good chance he'd conclude the message was a hoax and simply delete it. Still . . . what other option did she have? All she could do now was go to an ATM, pull out her savings, and pray that Josh Solomon showed up.

# 3

Josh looked up from his paperwork as his partner sat down on the edge of his desk in the middle of the precinct bullpen.

"I'm beginning to wonder if you ever go home, or if you've started sleeping here," Quinton said.

Josh waved off the comment. "I go home at night."

Which was true. For the most part.

"You know you're working too much. This case will still be here tomorrow. Just like it was here yesterday and the day before that. Burn yourself out, and you won't be able to work at all."

Josh frowned. He'd tried going home early, but his job gave him a purpose for what little life he had left. It was the one thing that made him feel like he was doing some good in the world. The one thing that kept him from thinking about what he'd lost and continued to hold him together when everything else was falling apart. And as long as it did that, he had no desire to change anything.

"Tell that to the crazies out on the streets that won't stop killing each other." He sat back in his chair and caught his partner's gaze. "I want this scumbag put away and going home isn't going to make that happen."

"A good night's sleep in your own bed might clear your mind and make it happen faster. As your partner, I've always appreciated your attention to detail. As your friend, I'm telling you to go home. We'll pick up in the morning." ·

Josh frowned, though he knew his friend was right. Over the past year, Quinton had become more like a father than a partner. Part counselor, part spiritual advisor. And the only real reason he was still on the job.

After Olivia's death, he'd gone along with everyone's advice of not doing anything rash for at least six months. Eventually, he planned to sell the house and find something smaller and closer to his work. Maybe it was time he did that. Took another step forward.

"Don't forget Val is expecting you for dinner Friday night."

He stared at the folder in front of him. "Yeah. I'll be there."

"Josh?"

He looked up. "Sorry. I'm just focused on this report."

"Like I said, you need to go home and get some sleep."

"I'm waiting for a call. As soon as it comes through, I promise I'll be gone."

"Why don't I believe you?"

He checked his messages, hoping his informant had called back. Instead there was a message from a number he didn't recognize. He pushed play and listened to the message.

"Josh Solomon? This is Caitlyn Lindsey . . ."

Josh dropped the phone like it was on fire as he finished listening to the message. Why would Caitlyn Lindsey be calling him about his wife's death? Why would anyone be calling him about Olivia's death?

"Was that your informant?"

Josh stared at the phone, unable to reply.

"Josh? I haven't worked with you for the past three years to not know when you've seen a ghost. Who was that?"

He still didn't answer. Instead he pulled out his keys, fumbled for the smallest one, then unlocked the bottom dented desk drawer and pulled out a thick binder.

Quinton shook his head. "Man, why do you still have that book at your desk? Your wife's case is closed. You know all that's going to do is torture you."

He'd asked himself the same question more than once. Her murder investigation had ended in two arrests followed by convictions. Hanging on to her murder book was nothing more than holding on to his pain.

"Do you remember Caitlyn Lindsey?" Josh asked.

"The name's vaguely familiar."

"She worked in the same lab as Olivia. They were pretty good friends. Same age. A lot of the same interests. They ate lunch together at work a lot. We actually double-dated a couple times when Olivia managed to get her to agree to a blind date. It never went very well though. I don't know if it was the guys Olivia picked or what, because she always seemed really nice."

"Is that who called?"

Josh rubbed the back of his neck. "She wants to talk to me about Olivia's murder."

"Why would she want to talk to you about that?"

"I don't know."

Quinton drummed his fingers on the desk. "If you ask me, you need to just erase the message. The men who killed Olivia are in prison. There's no reason for you to meet with her."

"Tell me why it is that just when I think I'm finally dealing with the fact that she's gone, something brings up that night all over again."

Like her birthday last week. And their anniversary next month.

He shook his head. Maybe that was what was bothering him. He'd almost forgotten the anniversary, a fact that bothered him as much as the fact that he still kept her murder book in his desk drawer. He missed her, but parts of her were starting to slowly fade, and he didn't know how to bring them back.

"I've sat with hundreds of people over the years," he said. "Had to tell them that the person they loved wasn't going to come back. But do you know what happens when you're on the other side? You feel as if you're drowning, and just when you manage to make it to the surface and catch your breath and feel like you're finally headed in the right direction, something happens, and you're pulled under again."

"I think you should erase the message. Nothing she has to say is going to change anything."

Josh considered his partner's advice, but he wasn't sure he could just ignore the call.

"When's the last time you saw Caitlyn?" Quinton asked.

"I don't know. Probably the funeral. She was also the last person Olivia called before she died. She was interviewed at the time by the detectives handling the case."

He flipped open the binder, avoiding the crime scene photos, and instead went straight to the section that held the notes and transcripts from the lead detective's interviews with Olivia's friends and coworkers. He stopped at Caitlyn's interview, though he wasn't really sure why. He'd memorized every haunting detail of his wife's case.

"According to the interview that was collaborated with phone records, Olivia called Caitlyn from our house an hour before she was murdered. But Caitlyn could never answer the one question that has bothered me ever since Olivia's death. Why didn't she call me and tell me she was home? It just . . . it doesn't make sense."

It wasn't the only thing about her death that still bothered him. Her final words implied she'd been hiding something. And he had no idea what.

"What did they talk about?" Quinton asked.

Josh skimmed through the notes. "Olivia wanted to meet for

breakfast the next day and talk about a project she was working on. It was nothing unusual."

"So it was just a normal call between coworkers."

"Yeah."

"Did she mention to Caitlyn that she was home from the conference?"

Josh nodded. "Told her she'd be at work in the morning, and that she'd come home early because she'd decided to skip the afternoon and evening sessions. Which made no sense to me at the time. Olivia told me she was looking forward to the speaker."

Quinton stood back up and folded his arms across his chest. "You've gone over this hundreds of times, and like I said, nothing's going to change. The case is closed."

That was true, but there had been a handful of inconsistencies in the case that had plagued him—besides why she'd come home early and not told him. The only items stolen, a handful of jewelry, had been explained away by the fact that they'd encountered Olivia and panicked. The other robberies in the area had taken place when no one was home. The district attorney said the suspects had gotten careless. In the end, they were able to prove that her murder was connected to the string of robberies. And that Olivia had simply been in the wrong place at the wrong time.

It had taken the DA less than an hour to present his case, and the jury even less time to make their decision. They'd deliberated forty-three minutes then were back in the courtroom with their verdict. Rudolph Beckmann and Larry Nixon had been convicted of capital murder and sentenced to life in prison.

"So you don't think I should call her back?"

"I can't make that decision for you, but I have a feeling you won't be able to let this slide. And I suppose you're right. If she does have information for you, then what can it hurt? If what she has turns out to be nothing, then you haven't lost anything but an hour of your time."

He picked up his phone. Quinton was right. As much as he'd
rather ignore the call, he knew he wouldn't.

"Go see what she has to say, then go home and get some sleep."
Quinton must have known that as well. "We'll finish up the rest
of this paperwork tomorrow. You're not going to be worth anything if you don't get some sleep. In fact, what you really need is
a vacation."

"A vacation? Right."

Everyone kept telling him that he should get away for a week
or two. That he needed to find time to relax. But the thought of
getting away—alone—only meant he'd have more time to think.
And that was something he wasn't ready to do.

A minute later, Josh grabbed his coat off the back of his chair
and headed out into the cold.

———

Josh slid into the booth at the back of the diner and signaled
to the waitress for a cup of coffee. He glanced around the space,
surprised he beat her here. She'd sounded so urgent on the phone.
He was still uncertain he'd made the right decision to show up,
but there was no going back now.

The waitress greeted him with a tired smile and a pot of fresh
coffee. "Cream or sugar?"

"Black's fine. Thanks."

Olivia had managed to talk him into drinking his coffee straight,
instead of the three spoonfuls of sugar he preferred. Somehow,
even after her death, the habit had remained.

Five minutes later, Caitlyn walked into the restaurant, wearing
an army-green jacket and high-top winter boots. She wore her dark
hair down past her shoulders like he remembered it. Dark brown
eyes. A smattering of freckles across her face. But it was the worry
lines across her forehead that caught his attention.

"Caitlyn?"

"Sorry I'm late." She slid into the booth, then set the backpack she was carrying next to her. "It took me longer than I thought to get a taxi."

"That's okay."

She caught his gaze. "I was afraid you wouldn't show up."

"Honestly, I almost didn't."

The redheaded waitress was back at his table. "Can I get you anything?"

"Coffee's fine for me as well."

The waitress grabbed the pot and filled the empty mug.

Josh studied Caitlyn's expression. She was clearly nervous about something. She kept looking at the door, as if she were worried someone was about to find her.

"You sure you don't want anything to eat?" he asked.

"This is fine for now. Thank you." Caitlyn held her coffee mug in both hands and took a sip. "Thank you for meeting me."

"You're welcome, but I'm not sure why I'm here. Your message was cryptic, to say the least. And my wife . . . Olivia . . . her murderers were convicted months ago. I'm not sure what there could be to talk about."

"I know." She pushed a strand of her hair behind her ear before reaching for a packet of sugar, exposing a bruise on her left cheekbone.

Josh leaned forward, his voice barely above a whisper. "Caitlyn . . . what happened?"

Her hand reached up to the spot. "I was in an accident earlier tonight, but I'm all right."

"That doesn't look like you're all right."

She shrugged. "Someone ran me off the road and my car flipped into a gully."

He studied her expression, realizing it wasn't just jittery nerves he saw reflected in her eyes, but fear.

"I'm sorry. Did the police catch whoever did it?"

"No. Thankfully, a Good Samaritan stopped and called 911. But my seat belt was jammed, which means if he hadn't found me, I could have been there all night."

"You went to the hospital, didn't you?"

"Yeah. They checked me over, though I . . . I left before being discharged."

"Caitlyn—"

"I'm fine. Really. There was no need to stay."

"You don't look fine. You've got a bruise on your face, and what if there are other . . . internal injuries."

"Really, I'm fine. They checked me out. I'm just cold. Which seems funny." She shot him a forced smile. "I grew up braving New York winters. This is nothing, but I can't warm up."

"None of this sounds like nothing. What about your car?"

"A tow truck took it away, so it can get looked at by a mechanic, but I'm pretty sure they'll say it's totaled. But that doesn't matter right now." She took another sip of her coffee. "That's not why I'm here."

He tried to remember everything he knew about the woman from the few times he'd been around her during work-related parties and on the double dates. Caitlyn always seemed incredibly focused on her work. She was funny and had never hesitated to talk about her faith and church. But the real reason he was here was because Olivia had always spoken highly of her and liked her. And he couldn't walk away from possible new information on his wife's murder.

Caitlyn ran her thumb back and forth across the top of the mug. "I was at Olivia's funeral, but never really had the chance to tell you how sorry I was. Not personally, anyway. She was a good coworker and friend. I miss her."

"Thank you." He waited for her to continue, unsure of where their conversation was going. "But I'm still not sure why you wanted to see me."

"Like I told you on the phone, I need to talk to you about the night she died." She looked up from her coffee and caught his gaze. "I know this is going to sound crazy, but the men who were convicted of her murder . . . I'm not convinced they were the ones behind it."

He leaned forward. He couldn't have heard her correctly. "I'm sorry . . . What did you say?"

"I believe it's very possible that either the wrong men were arrested and convicted, or if they did kill her, they were hired."

The realization of what she was saying hit him in the gut, totally unexpected. The movements around him seemed to decelerate, to move in slow motion. Just like the night Olivia died.

He shook his head. "That's not possible."

"I know it sounds crazy—"

"Crazy . . . impossible . . ." He paused, trying to rein in the confusion flooding his mind. "I'm not sure why you're coming forward now, saying this. When Olivia died, you were interviewed, and you never implied you had any information contrary to the DA's."

"That's because I didn't know then what I know now. There are some things that have happened that have made me question the jury's decision."

"I still say that's not possible." It didn't matter that he had his own set of doubts he'd kept quiet about all these months. He wasn't sure he wanted to hear what she was saying. That he wanted to relive Olivia's death all over again. It had taken all the energy he had just to move forward with his life. "I was an eyewitness and saw the men exit my house that night. There was evidence found in my home as well that proved it was them."

"True, but the men you saw leaving your house that night . . . they wore hoodies and it was dark. It had to have been hard to make a positive ID. And despite finding both fingerprints and DNA at the crime scene, Beckmann and Nixon always insisted they weren't there that night. All the DA had was circumstantial evidence."

Josh sat back in his chair. The truth was, he couldn't refute what she was saying because he'd already thought all the same things. DNA and fingerprints could be planted.

"What if they didn't kill your wife?" she continued. "What if they *were* the ones robbing the neighborhood but weren't at your house that night? What if they were set up to take the fall for her death?"

"They confessed to robbing nine houses," he said.

"But never to the murder."

"Why come to me now?"

"More coffee?" The waitress stopped in front of their table with a fresh pot.

"We're fine," he said, waving her away. "Thank you."

He stared at his half-empty coffee mug, wishing they were in a more private place.

"Josh . . . Detective Solomon . . . here's the bottom line," Caitlyn said. "I believe that the death of your wife wasn't a random burglary. I think she was murdered by someone who wanted her silenced." Caitlyn leaned forward. "Someone who now wants to silence me."

# 4

She caught Josh's expression and knew she was going to have to find a way to quickly convince him of the truth of what she'd just said, or he would end up walking out on her. Not that she'd blame him. He was probably still searching to find closure with his wife's death, and now she was trying to blow the whole case open again. But her gut still told her she was doing the right thing.

"Please, let me explain."

He hesitated before answering. "I'm listening."

His response surprised her. She wasn't sure she'd have been quite as open to listen if she were in his shoes. Unless he had his own doubts . . . "Nine months after Olivia's murder, her immediate boss—and mine—died of a heart attack."

Josh frowned. "I hadn't heard about that."

"A week ago, another one of our coworkers, Helen Fletcher, died. The medical examiner's report classified her death as a suicide."

"Okay, but I'm still lost. What does any of this have to do with Olivia's death?"

"All three deaths seem like tragic, yet isolated events with no connection. But I believe that all three were working on the same project in the same lab. I believe their deaths are connected." Caitlyn paused a moment to let him catch up. At least he was still sitting across from her.

"Wait a minute." Josh shook his head. "I still don't see a connection. Olivia's murder doesn't exactly fit in with a heart attack or a suicide."

"You weren't involved in the investigation of your wife's murder."

"I wasn't officially assigned to the case, but I did my own investigation on the side. She was my wife, and I was determined that whoever murdered her was going to pay."

"Did you ever have any suspicions during your investigation that the detectives were on the wrong track?"

His frown deepened. "Honestly? I did."

So her instincts had been right. He'd seen his own inconsistencies in the case. Which was going to make it that much easier to get him to listen to what she had to say.

"There were a number of things about that night at your house that were different from the other break-ins, weren't there?" she asked.

He took another sip of his coffee before answering her question. "Normally they made sure the owners were gone by studying their routines and schedules," he said. "They took their time once they were inside. Everything they did was well thought out. But they entered our house even though the bedroom light was on and could be seen from the front yard. They only stole a handful of my wife's jewelry that wasn't even worth a hundred bucks."

Caitlyn nodded. "Exactly. There were also two other instances where the burglars encountered homeowners, but both times they simply bolted, and there was never any evidence they had weapons or had any desire to harm the homeowners. And while I'm sure MOs might shift over time, I believe these inconsistencies are significant. On top of that, Rudolph Beckmann always insisted he had an alibi."

"Go on."

"Not only are Dr. Abbott and Helen dead, someone just tried to kill me. I think it's all related to Olivia's death."

He sat back against the seat. "But why?"

"I think they were killed to cover up something they'd discovered in the lab trials of one of the vaccines they're testing. Then, when I started asking questions, I must have talked to the wrong person, because now I'm convinced someone wants me dead as well."

"That's why you were run off the road? You're saying they were trying to kill you?"

"I don't think it's a coincidence that I was run off the road by a hit-and-run driver. It looked like the same vehicle I've seen following me the past few days."

She could tell he was trying to process her words. If she were in his place, she wouldn't want to believe what she was saying.

"And then there's Helen. We were close friends, which is why, despite the coroner's findings, I don't believe she committed suicide." She leaned forward and caught his gaze. "If I didn't believe what I was telling you right now, I wouldn't have come to you, but I don't have anywhere else to go. Not only were you Olivia's husband, you're a cop. I need your help."

"This is a lot to take in." He reached up and rubbed the back of his neck. "And to be honest, while I saw the inconsistencies in Olivia's case, I just . . . I don't know if I can go down that road again."

"I understand your hesitation. Really I do." She passed a slip of paper across the table. "But I wouldn't be here if I wasn't convinced I was right. Here's my number. I'll give you till noon tomorrow, but if you don't call, I'm going to leave Houston and figure out a way to discover the truth on my own. In the meantime, I'll leave you a file I put together of what I know, but if you want to know what really happened to your wife, I think we need to help each other."

Caitlyn grabbed a file folder out of her backpack, slid it across the table, then headed for the front door of the diner without turning around. She'd tried not to show the depth of her fear when she was sitting at the table, but if she were honest, she was terrified.

She was used to spending her days in a lab, where everything she did was orderly and by the book. Life had settled into a routine over the past two years between work and church activities. Fearing for her life had left her feeling helpless and lost. She had friends and family she could call on for help, but she couldn't put their lives in danger. At least Josh Solomon was already involved.

She'd tried to read his facial expressions, but at this point she had no idea if he'd agree to help her or not. Just like she had no idea where she'd go if he didn't help her.

She'd pulled out all her savings, even though the money wasn't going to last long. She was going to need another income. She could always fall back on waitressing in some small town as far away as she could get, but leaving wasn't going to help her find out the truth. A blast of cold wind whipped around her as she stepped outside. She hoisted the emergency bag she'd kept in the back of her car and walked to a motel a couple blocks away from the diner. Three minutes later, she ducked inside the shady lobby of the motel, thankful for the blast of hot air, and walked up to the man sitting at the reception desk, who was chowing down on a bag of fast food.

"I need a room, please."

"How many nights?"

"Just one."

She glanced around the shabby lobby, suddenly second-guessing her decision. Paint was peeling off the walls, and there were a couple large stains on the carpet. Her main objective was to find a place to spend the night without giving a credit card. But the reviews were way off the mark and she wondered if she should have found something in a better neighborhood.

"Forty-eight dollars."

She handed the man cash.

He studied her, a little too closely. "I'm going to need a credit card for any . . . incidentals."

"Sorry, I don't have one."

He frowned, then shrugged. "Doesn't matter. Just sign here."

She scribbled the name of an old friend from junior high.

"Martha Johnson?"

She forced a smile. She was never going to get used to this.

A minute later, she dumped her bag onto the foot of the yellow bedspread inside her room, trying to settle her escalated fear levels. Maybe she was making a mistake, but going to the police wasn't an option. At least not until she had more solid evidence.

Which left her back at square one, with Josh Solomon.

A knock on the door pulled her out of her thoughts. If she'd been followed, if someone knew she was here . . . She moved to the door, her heart racing as she looked through the peephole. It was the maid with an armful of towels. She pulled open the door an inch, leaving the chain in place.

"I have your towels."

"Thank you." She undid the chain, took the towels, then quickly relocked the door.

She glanced at her phone, but there was still nothing from Josh. Had she been wrong to go to him? Beckmann and Nixon had been convicted by a jury with evidence presented by the DA. And now she was saying all that evidence was wrong, and he needed to listen to her.

She wasn't sure she'd have believed it if she were in his shoes either.

If he didn't help her, all she knew to do was run.

# 5

Josh tightened his fingers around the steering wheel as he headed out of his driveway to work. He hadn't slept more than a couple hours last night, and even a second cup of coffee this morning hadn't managed to clear his mind. After a year of adjusting to his new reality, the nightmares had just started to fade.

And now Caitlyn Lindsey had managed to resurrect them all over again.

He'd spent half the night going through Caitlyn's files as well as Olivia's murder book. During the investigation, he hadn't been allowed to work the case officially, but that hadn't stopped him from assembling the details of her murder into a thick binder. He'd carefully examined and taken personal notes on every crime scene photo, forensic report, case note, witness interview, and suspect profile, ensuring that nothing in the investigation was missed or overlooked.

Six days after he buried his wife, they arrested and charged two men with her murder. Six months later, the trial ended, and the judge gave the men life in prison. Hardly a fair trade-off, as far as he was concerned, for the loss of his wife.

Today, every fiber in his body told him to walk away and forget

47

everything Caitlyn Lindsey had tried to convince him of. A boss with known heart issues, a depressed grandmother, and a robbery gone bad . . . That was his emotional response. Because how could there be a connection between the three cases? Despite all that, over the past few months he'd managed—for the most part—to come to terms with the fact that Olivia was gone. It was something that could never be undone. Something he was going to have to live with the rest of his life. Digging into a closed case wasn't going to change anything.

And while Caitlyn believed someone was after her, that didn't mean her accident was connected to Olivia's death. So someone had run her off the road. How many times had that happened, and not because someone was trying to purposely kill the other driver? No. More than likely she'd simply been in the wrong place at the wrong time.

*The wrong place at the wrong time.*

That's what everyone had told him about Olivia. He'd struggled to believe it then, and nothing had changed. Conflicting arguments continued to circle his thoughts, along with the memories.

He flipped on his blinker to turn onto the main road leading out of his neighborhood, then realized what had been nagging him since he left the house. He'd left the binder with Olivia's case notes in the kitchen. He let out a sharp sigh. If he did decide to meet with Caitlyn, he wanted to have those notes with him.

Irritated at himself for his forgetfulness, he made a U-turn at the next road, then headed back toward his house. His heart wanted to dismiss everything Caitlyn had told him and label it all as nothing other than paranoia. There were dozens of conspiracy theories out there related to scientists and their unexplained deaths or disappearances. But all those theories really did was connect the dots of unexplained events and try to make sense out of them. He and Olivia had laughed over them and never put any stock in them. But the real issue stopping him from calling Caitlyn back was that he had no desire to relive that night. He was the one who had to live with the fact that Olivia was never coming back.

And that he was a cop who hadn't been able to save his own wife.

He turned back onto his street. He could still hear her talking to him as she lay dying.

*I need you to know the truth about what happened . . .*

Josh pressed his fingers against his temples, trying to push away the last words he'd heard from his wife. He'd never told anyone what she'd said. Not even the detectives who'd worked on the case. Partly because he had no idea what she was talking about, and partly because he'd wanted to erase the questions her death had left him with.

But what had she been trying to tell him?

As much as he didn't want to believe it, he'd been plagued with his own doubts surrounding her death. Things that hadn't completely added up, leaving him with one sobering question.

Had they sent the wrong men to prison?

He parked in his driveway, then headed back toward the house again, allowing the questions to resurface. Questions he didn't have answers for.

He'd been searching for closure the past few months. He'd always believed that when they found the killer, he'd be able to start moving on with his life. It had helped—to a degree—but not completely. His coworkers and friends kept telling him it would take time to heal. That it was okay to let himself grieve. And while he couldn't change the past, he could change his future.

He stopped for a moment on the front porch and pulled the paper out of his pocket where Caitlyn had written down her number. The easy thing to do would be to simply walk away and pretend that all his questions had been answered. That the men now sitting in prison had murdered his wife and deserved to be there. Case closed. The last thing he wanted to do was reopen it, but he knew this was his chance to confirm in his own mind if the judge and jury had made a mistake, and to know what Olivia had been involved in. He'd call Caitlyn when he got to work and tell her he'd decided to at least look at what she had.

He shoved the paper back into his pocket, then hurried inside, armed with at least a tentative plan. Hopefully he wouldn't regret the decision. Something creaked as he crossed the wood floor. He paused, then stepped into the darkened space he rarely entered and flipped on the light. He studied the shadows. Nothing was out of place. In fact, nothing had changed since Olivia's death. Not the colorful throw pillows dropped onto the couch, or the knickknacks set on the coffee table, or the books stacked neatly in the wall cabinet. He let out a sharp breath. His imagination was clearly working overtime. There was no one here, only the perpetual ghosts haunting him. He turned off the light and made a mental reminder to call a realtor. It was time to move forward. He'd sell this house and find himself something smaller and closer to his work.

The hairs on the back of his neck bristled again. He stopped, listening for anything out of place. Listening for the sounds of an intruder. Silence greeted him, but the feeling that something was wrong didn't leave.

They came at him with a full-blown tackle to his midsection and a punch to his face. Stars erupted as his head smashed against the wall, but they'd made their mistake by giving him a heads-up that he wasn't alone.

He caught his balance, then managed to slam his fist into the first man's jaw, knocking him to the ground. Pain seared through his knuckles, but at least he was still standing.

Josh spun around and faced the second man just in time to block his punch. He slammed his fist into the man's rib cage, twisted his hips, then swung a second punch at his temple. The man groaned as he went down, his head thumping hard against the wooden floor. A second later, the room was quiet, but not Josh's mind. Anger flared through him. They'd been here before. In this house. Murdering his wife. It might not be the same people, but he had no doubt this was somehow related to Olivia's death.

He grabbed a couple zip ties from the kitchen drawer. "Next time try messing with someone on your own skill level if you want to win."

One of them struggled to get onto his knees, his breath still knocked out of him. Josh stepped up in front of him. "We can always continue if you'd like."

The man dropped back to the floor and groaned.

His phone rang, but he ignored it as he tied up the first man. The other one groaned from across the room, holding his side. He'd probably leave with a broken rib, which was fine with Josh. Maybe it would teach him a lesson.

He finished securing them and propped them up so they sat with their backs against the wall and their hands behind them. Clearly, this was not how they'd expected this to end. He took a step back, then froze. A blue binder lay flipped open on the floor not far from the men's feet. Olivia's murder book. A spike of adrenaline surged through him. This was no random burglary he'd just walked in on. He'd left the notebook on the kitchen table when he left this morning. He was sure of it. Which meant the break-in was somehow connected to Olivia's death. But why?

He picked up his phone and moved in front of them while making a quick call.

"Nothing to say?" he asked once he'd hung up.

Both just stared back at him.

"Fine. I've just called for backup."

He wiped away a trail of blood on his face with his sleeve and frowned. He'd have a shiner, but his hours of defense training had paid off. And he was pretty sure these guys were already regretting their decision to come after him.

He stood over them, arms folded across his chest, legs spread. "They'll take you in and book you, then let you talk. I'm thinking the DA will probably start with three years for the felony assault of a police officer, plus a felony burglary conviction has the potential sentence of twenty years or more." He glanced at his watch. "Or while we wait we could play a game where whoever talks first gets a shot at immunity. If I'm right, this break-in is tied to my wife's murder, which means there's a whole can of worms about to be opened up."

"Murder . . . Wait a minute." The one with the cracked lip spoke up for the first time. "I didn't sign up for nothin' to do with murder."

"Shut up, Mac."

"Why should I? They didn't tell us you were a cop, and I don't know nothin' about a murder."

Josh smiled at the confession. "That's a start, though it might have been smarter to know what you were getting into before you broke into my house, then tried to take me down. So start with this. Who hired you?"

They looked at each other. "Nobody."

"So I'm guessing you're not interested in a deal."

"We don't know his name—"

"I said shut up, Mac."

He studied the two men. Tattoos on their necks and hands, wearing jeans and light jackets. Neither looked like they were a day over twenty. He was pretty sure they weren't here on their own, which meant they'd been hired by someone to do their dirty work. They'd watched him leave for work, then broken in, but why? To steal his case files on Olivia's death? Why would anyone do that? Everything in there was public record. It made sense that this was somehow connected to his talking to Caitlyn last night, but even that left him with a dozen questions.

Everyone knew he'd accepted the jury's verdict and had declared the case closed. Quinton was the only person he'd spoken to about talking with Caitlyn, and he'd bet his life on his partner's loyalty. What he did know was that this was no coincidence. He'd met with Caitlyn only hours ago about a snag in his wife's case, and now this morning someone had broken into his house to steal his case notes.

He just needed to find out why.

He glanced at his watch and switched his thoughts back to questioning these guys. He had all of three, maybe four minutes before backup arrived. And since he was certain he wouldn't be able to question the suspects later, now might very well be his only chance. At least it seemed like he could use them against each other. Mac was clearly interested in saving his own skin.

He grabbed another zip tie and secured Mac's partner-in-crime to the leg of the solid wood cabinet. Olivia had inherited it from her grandparents and the piece weighed at least two hundred pounds. He figured his best chance of getting the information he needed was getting Mac alone. He pulled him just out of hearing distance, but close enough in case the other guy decided to do something stupid like try to escape.

Mac shook in front of him, looking like he was about to either cry or wet his pants. Josh frowned. All he wanted was answers.

"Okay, so someone hired you to break into my house. I want to know why. Why did you have that file?"

"I was just . . ." Mac lowered his voice. "We got paid to break in and grab the file. Cash up front. I didn't ask questions."

"I'm sure you didn't. How did this person contact you?"

"Just a number. My brother"—he jerked his head toward the living room—"he's done odd jobs for him before. This was the first time I've worked for him."

"You know, next time you need some money, you might want to think about applying for a job flipping burgers, not assaulting people. The risk of going to prison for working at a place like that is typically a lot lower than working for some thug."

Mac's jaw quivered as he glanced back toward his brother. "We weren't supposed to run into you. We watched you leave."

"Why the file?"

"I don't know. Didn't ask."

"Do you have your boss's number? Some way to contact him?"

"No. He calls us. So what happens now? I told you what I know."

"You told me that you were hired, but you don't know who hired you or why. You don't seem to know much. Which puts you in a very bad place."

Sirens screamed in the distance as he sat the man back down next to his brother.

His phone rang again, and he picked it up, ignoring the exchange going on between them.

"Josh?" It was Quinton. "I've been trying to call you. Wanted to check in on you."

"Sorry, I'm fine, but I've been a bit . . . occupied."

"What's going on?"

"I just met up with a couple thugs in my house, but everything's under control."

"What? Are you okay?"

"Yeah."

"Where are they now?"

Josh glanced across the room. "Let's just say they've been subdued, and they won't be going anywhere for a while. I've already called for backup."

"Wait a minute . . . another burglary?"

"They were after my notebook on Olivia's case, though I'm still not sure why."

"Because you spoke with Caitlyn Lindsey?"

"Don't you find it odd that someone shows up with evidence that the wrong men might be behind bars for my wife's murder, and less than twelve hours later these guys show up in my own home?"

"I'll meet you at the precinct. And Josh . . . be careful."

He glanced at the file Caitlyn had given him and opened it up again. The notes were precise. No wordiness. Just the facts as she saw them.

He made a decision. He'd take in the evidence he had and talk to his captain. Then he'd call Caitlyn. He'd at least listen to what else she had to say and see if they could come up with a plan. All he wanted was the truth.

# 6

Josh exited the interview room after spending forty-five minutes giving his statement to a fellow detective and headed toward his boss's office. Part of him wondered if he was jumping the gun by going to the captain with Caitlyn's suspicions. In reality, he probably should wait until he had something more concrete, but the break-in at his house had convinced him Caitlyn was right. How much more concrete could he get? Someone was behind this, and they needed to find out who. And getting the captain on board was going to be the quickest way to get to the bottom of it all.

But there were questions that wouldn't stop nagging at him. If Caitlyn's car accident last night was connected to the break-in at his home this morning, who knew he'd met with Caitlyn? The only person he'd told was Quinton, and he trusted his partner with his life. The logical explanation was that someone was following Caitlyn.

But who?

He rubbed his day-old stubble and winced at the bruise just under his eye as he stopped in front of Captain Matt Thomas's office. The man had joined law enforcement after spending a decade in the Army, including time as a drill sergeant. He was tough, but fair, and if anyone could advise Josh what to do, he could.

Josh knocked on the open door. "James told me you wanted to see me."

"I heard about your fight." The captain nodded for him to come in and take a seat across from him. "Your face looks worse for wear, though I heard you won."

Josh wasn't in the mood for small talk. "What do you have on the suspects?"

"They're being questioned right now, but so far it looks like they're nothing more than a couple of bored kids making stupid decisions."

Josh dropped the file Caitlyn had given him onto the desk and sat in the chair across from his boss. "Is that what they're telling you?"

"Do you have another theory?"

"They were after my files on my wife's murder, which makes me believe they were hired to break in. And if that's true, it means there's a connection with her death."

The captain tapped his pen on the desk and frowned. "Detective Masters has shared with me your theory, but according to the arresting officers, they're a part of a gang. Probably looking for something to sell for a quick fix. You just happened to return home, and from the looks of their injuries, they clearly messed with the wrong person."

"So . . . wrong place at the wrong time."

How convenient. How familiar. But he wasn't buying it. "They might not know anything," Josh continued. "But someone hired them. How do you explain the fact that they had my files?"

"They told you they were hired?"

"Actually, yes. The younger one."

"Then either he changed his story or thought that blaming someone else was going to be his way out. I'll have the detectives see if they can get anything else out of them, but a connection to your wife's murder seems like a stretch to me. This is Houston—you of all people know it's possible for crime to strike the same person more than once."

Josh reined in his initial response. Jumping to conclusions wasn't the answer, but neither was sitting back and ignoring the obvious.

"I understand what you're saying," he said, "but here's another thing. What if one of the men convicted in my wife's murder actually had an alibi and someone doesn't want this information coming out?" Josh leaned forward and tapped the folder he'd put on the desk before continuing. "Rudolph Beckmann always claimed that he wasn't at my house that night. He claimed he was out drinking with a friend, but that so-called friend adamantly denied they'd been together."

"Detectives followed up on that, but it was a dead end. But listen. If I was facing as much prison time as those two are, I'd be desperate for an alibi as well." The captain flipped open the folder. "You said you got this information from one of your wife's coworkers."

"Yes. And as much as I want to believe Olivia's killers are behind bars, I have my own questions. I can't help but wonder if some of those questions deserve answers."

"I'm not sure what to say, Detective. And to be honest, when you called, I'd hoped you were planning on taking some long-deserved time off. Instead I discover you trying to dig up details on a case that's been closed for months. None of this seems very credible from my standpoint. And I'm pretty sure the DA isn't going to want to reopen a case simply because you have questions."

Josh eyed his boss sitting across from him. His tone—and that of every officer in the precinct—had always been sympathetic. Crime had affected one of their own, which meant it had affected all of them. He'd received tremendous support he'd appreciated in a time of need.

But for the first time there was something different in his captain's expression. Skepticism? Doubt? He wasn't sure.

"And there's another issue at play here," the captain said.

"What's that?"

The older man leaned forward. "After months of your community being hit with a string of break-ins and then on top of that a brutal murder, how's it going to look if the public suddenly finds out we're not sure if we caught the right men? That whoever was behind it is actually still out there, still on the run?"

Josh's fists tensed in his lap. "Wait a minute. You're telling me that this has somehow become about public relations? Because I don't care how it looks. I want to make sure that the right men are behind bars. That my wife's killers are behind bars."

The captain sat back in his chair and shook his head. "This has everything to do with being careful not to jump to conclusions with no real evidence to back them up. Despite this information you believe you have, I believe the right people are sitting in jail."

Josh stared at a photo of the captain's family and weighed his response. He'd never had any issues with his boss, but something in his gut told him there was more at play here and he needed to be careful.

"Listen, you know that I have no desire to open up my wife's case again, but neither can I rest easy knowing that the wrong men have been convicted. Especially when I was one of the key witnesses in the case. If I was wrong—"

The captain looked at the file on his desk and said, "What do you really know about Caitlyn Lindsey?"

"What do you mean?"

"When I heard from your interview that a former coworker of your wife started playing detective because she believes there's some conspiracy going on, I took the liberty of digging into her background. For starters, did you know that she has a juvenile record?"

Josh kept his expression neutral. More than likely a juvenile record had nothing to do with what was happening right now. But still, he didn't like what he was hearing. Had he been so emotionally caught up in Caitlyn's story that he'd lost his objectivity?

"What does that have to do with this?" he asked. "And since when do we make someone's testimony automatically suspect because of a juvenile record? We both know that there are dozens of innocent explanations that could be behind that."

"You're right, but that's not all. It seems that Caitlyn Lindsey has a habit of stirring up trouble. Six years ago, she came forward with allegations against the company she was working for that connected the lab to clinical fraud. There are many people who believe those allegations were false, yet the company ended up paying for the wrongs she accused them of. Bottom line, I sense a pattern here."

"I don't remember seeing anything about that in the case files."

"It wasn't in the file."

Josh caught the defensiveness in the captain's voice and frowned, but the seed of doubt had been planted. What did he really know about Caitlyn? Was there an ulterior motive? If she had one, what would it be?

His jaw tightened. None of this made sense.

"Here's the thing," the captain said. "You, of all people, should want this behind you. Not reopened. Do you know what a circus it's going to be if this gets out? Unless something substantial comes up, my advice to you is to let it go. It's the only way."

His boss might have just given him an explanation all wrapped up in a neat and tidy box, but he wasn't sure he was ready to totally throw away his theory.

"So because the guys we arrested were a couple of goons with records, we just turn a blind eye? What if the real killers are still out there?"

"I'm not saying we turn a blind eye. What I said was we trust

60

the system that convicted your wife's murderers. I am 100 percent convinced that the right men were convicted. Reopening this case is a mistake, and I think you know that. Listen, the weather's supposed to warm up this week. When's the last time you took a day off? Got out of town, slept in till noon, did a little winter bass fishing, or played golf, or headed to Galveston?"

Josh frowned at the sudden redirection of the conversation. "It's been a while."

So long he couldn't remember, but a vacation was the last thing on his mind right now.

"This is what's going to happen," the captain continued. "You're going to take the next two weeks off. I don't want to see you in this office. I don't want to hear about your digging into any of your cases, especially your wife's. And when you return, come back with your head on straight. Do you understand?"

Josh hesitated at the veiled threat. "I understand." He stood up, wishing he had a comeback or a more compelling argument or more solid evidence, but he didn't.

"And Josh?"

He stopped midstride to the door.

"Despite everything I've just said, I do know this isn't easy for you. If I were to be completely honest with you, I'd have to say I probably would have listened to Caitlyn too. My wife died of cancer seven years ago, and at the time I asked myself all kinds of what-ifs. What if I'd done something different. Said something different. And whenever something reminds me of her today, those same questions aren't far from the surface."

Josh nodded, wishing the captain's words weren't so spot-on.

"All I have to say is, don't go there. The guilt will end up killing you," the older man continued. "There comes a time when you've got to let it go. Trust that you did everything you could, and that's enough. The men who are in prison for your wife's murder are there because they committed a horrendous crime. Anything you do now is only going to make things worse on yourself. Go home. Drive to Galveston or San Antonio. I don't care what you do, but clear your head before you come back."

Josh grabbed the file off the captain's desk and walked out of the office. He'd hoped the captain would have decided to reopen his wife's case, not send him off on some holiday retreat. But whether he liked it or not, there had been some truth in what the captain had said.

He started down the hallway. What if the man was right? After all, what did he really know about Caitlyn? He knew she'd been friends with his wife. She was intelligent, beautiful, charming, and very convincing. She'd voiced the same questions that had nagged at him for months, which was why he'd been willing to listen to her. He had no desire to be a part of convicting men of a crime they didn't commit, but what if his boss was right? What if he was allowing emotion to cloud his common sense? He'd have to look into Caitlyn's background himself so he wasn't going into this blindfolded.

But more than that was bugging him.

"Josh . . ." Quinton caught up with him in the hallway on the way to the bullpen. "What's the update?"

"The suspects are still being questioned, and I've just been ordered by the captain to take off a couple weeks."

Quinton's thick brows rose. "That might do you some good, and you can hardly blame him. You've been working twelve-to-fourteen-hour days. You're exhausted."

"I know, but this whole situation . . . something's off."

"I'll give it to you that you have every right to be upset. Two guys jumped you in your own house. Shoot . . . I'd be ready to come out fighting. But you can't jump to conclusions. Not until there's more evidence."

"I don't know." Josh leaned against the wall. "There was always something wrong about the verdict in Olivia's death."

"I know you've had doubts, but why the second thoughts now? You were one of the witnesses. The evidence was strong against those men."

"It's been easier just to not look back, to try to move on. But what if I was wrong?"

"You think they were set up?"

Josh nodded his head. "Too many things don't add up. If the wrong men are in prison partly because of my testimony . . . I can't let that happen."

Quinton shook his head. "First of all, we don't know that's true, but even if it is, and these guys that broke into your house are somehow a part of it, the truth will come out. Give them time to question these guys. See what they can come up with."

"I don't think we have time. What about Caitlyn?" Josh asked. "Someone's after her. She told me to meet her by noon or she's leaving town."

Quinton glanced at his watch. "Then if you plan to see her, you don't have a lot of time."

He nodded, but there was one thing he needed to do before he left. "I'll catch up with you later."

He continued walking toward the bullpen, paused at his own desk, then slipped in behind the computer monitor and pulled his chair forward. He paused before he typed Caitlyn's name into the database. Her Department of Motor Vehicles information popped up. Her driving record was clean. No outstanding arrest warrants or personal criminal history. Nothing stood out. He switched to a second database.

There was a juvenile record that was sealed.

He tapped his fingers against the desk. Did it really matter? So she'd been in trouble as a teen. Despite whatever it was that she'd done, she'd clearly turned her life around. And it certainly didn't reflect on who she was today.

He did another search, but this time just a Google search. There were a few random photos. An award she'd won for a paper she'd written. One of her at a charity event.

He moved his chair back and grabbed his coat, trying to put together a picture of the woman who'd just ripped open everything he'd worked hard to wrap up. He walked out of the precinct. It was time to dig into the past and find out the truth.

# 7

Caitlyn glanced at the digital red glow of the motel clock as it switched to 11:45. Last night she thought she'd gotten through to Josh. But now it was clear. He wasn't calling. Which had her terrified.

She sat at the end of the bed. Her bag was packed, and she'd pulled out enough cash for at least a week or two. Disappearing might sound simple, but she knew she was fooling herself. Besides, she had no desire to spend the rest of her life running. She'd made a life here, and for the first time in as long as she could remember, she'd finally found a place where she felt like she belonged. She hadn't felt that way since her grandmother had been alive. If she had any choice left in the situation at all, she had no desire to throw all of that away. Or for that matter, put any of her friends' lives at risk.

Which meant she needed Josh's help.

And as far as she was concerned, he needed hers as well.

She fought to push away the panic swirling around her. Josh was a detective. If anyone could be discreet he could. On top of that, she knew enough about Josh to know he was a man of integrity. The few times they'd met, he'd always impressed her.

She'd wait another fifteen minutes. If he didn't call, she'd leave the city but still follow through with her own investigation. She'd checked the bus schedule and decided on three possible routes. All led to small towns, but they were big enough that she should be able to disappear. When someone was on the run, she knew they tended to go somewhere familiar. So that was exactly what she wouldn't do. She'd chosen places where she had no ties. Places where whoever was after her would never think to look. But it also meant she'd be completely on her own.

She pulled back the worn curtain that matched the bedspread just enough to see out into the parking area. A vehicle was pulling in three spaces down from her room.

Her heart pounded. If they'd found her . . .

A man climbed out of the vehicle. Her pulse quickened, then began to calm as he headed away from her room. She dropped the curtain and let out a sharp sigh of relief, then jumped when her phone rang. It was almost noon. It had to be Josh, but why hadn't she asked for his number so she'd be sure?

She took the call but remained silent.

"Caitlyn? . . . Caitlyn?"

"Josh!" She gasped with relief again. "I didn't think you'd call. And I wasn't sure it was you."

He asked for her location so they could meet. She was grateful that, by the time they finished the call, he was only a couple minutes away.

At the knock, she checked the peephole, quickly undid the locks, then opened the door just enough for him to slip inside the room before shutting it behind him. She was acting paranoid, and she knew it. But she had reason to.

She turned around to face him, gasping when she noticed the dark bruise under his eye. "What happened?"

"I had a run-in with a couple guys who broke into my house."

"What were they after?"

"I'm not completely sure, but they had my case notes on Olivia's death."

Her eyes widened. "Why would anyone want to steal your files?"

"That's exactly what I want to find out. Let's assume for a moment that everything you've told me is true. Three people were murdered to cover up something going on in your lab. We're also going to assume there's enough money and motivation in the scenario so that whoever's behind this is in deep and isn't going to simply walk away."

"They're going to take down whoever gets in their way."

"Exactly."

She squeezed her eyes shut for a moment and tried to force back the tears. She'd decided to take a risk and contact Josh because she thought he'd be able to help reopen Olivia's case. But not this. Not someone else getting hurt.

"Are you okay?" he asked.

"Yes, but I never meant for anything like this to happen."

"I don't need an apology. Clearly you were right about all of this."

Caitlyn felt an unexpected wave of relief sweep over her. So he did believe her. Or at least he believed that what she'd told him deserved further investigation. For the moment that was enough.

"I handed over the information that you gave me to my captain," Josh said.

"Okay." That was fine with her. She knew if she could get the authorities on her side, then she might have a chance. "What did he say?"

"He told me to take two weeks off and come back with my head on straight."

"Wait a minute, so he doesn't believe any of this is connected to your wife's case?"

Josh shook his head.

"Then why are you here?"

"Because in the end, I knew I couldn't just walk away. Especially after what happened this morning. Someone clearly doesn't want this case reopened." His gaze shifted momentarily to the floor before he continued. "But before I agree to look into this with you, there are a couple things he brought up that I need to ask you about."

"Of course. Anything."

"Apparently the captain took the time to look you up. He informed me of a couple red flags in your background."

"Red flags?"

"Whistleblower allegations you were involved with at your last job and—"

"My juvenile record." She bit her lip, not liking the shift in the conversation, but she knew she couldn't be defensive. He deserved to know the truth. "How did he get his hands on that information so quickly?"

"I don't know."

"Both were a long time ago, and they have nothing to do with this situation."

"Maybe not, but I need to know the truth."

She sat down on the edge of the bed and glanced at the gray wall behind him, wishing she could escape the place she'd been running from her entire life. Memories pressed in around her, threatening to drag her back. But she wasn't going there. If she'd learned anything from her counseling sessions, it was that she didn't have to let *him* win. He'd tried to make her believe she was crazy, and for years she'd believed it. But not anymore.

*God hasn't given me a spirit of fear, but of power. And of love. And a sound mind.*

That was the truth she was working to convince herself of.

"The allegations against my last employer were actually brought up by six employees—including me—who had evidence of a kickback scheme where federal programs were billed for lab procedures that were unnecessary. In the end the laboratory was forced to pay a settlement that also put four managers in prison. The six of us who brought the allegations forward were, by law, protected, but that didn't mean we didn't pay for speaking up. Six months later, I walked away from my job after prolonged harassment from upper management. And I wasn't the only one. If you want proof, I can get you whatever you want—"

"That's okay. I believe you."

Caitlyn fiddled with the hem of her shirt, feeling the weight of once again having to explain her actions. She'd done it dozens of times, and it always brought unwelcome feelings of shame, even if she wasn't guilty.

He sat down on the chair across from her with a look of interest in what she had to say. She hoped she was reading him right. Because if she couldn't convince him, this was over.

"As for my juvenile record . . . that's true as well." She hated that she was having to explain herself to him, but neither could she blame him. He deserved to hear the truth, whether he chose to believe it or not. "I grew up in an abusive home. My father was drunk most of the time. That is, when he was home, which he usually wasn't. We got pulled over one time by the police. My father was drunk and had made me drive him home, even though I was only fourteen, so I was caught driving without a license, and there were drugs in my pocket that he'd made me put there. He knew if the drugs were found on him, he'd end up doing time, but I'd probably just get a slap on the hand."

She took in a deep breath, trying to find that emotional balance between bringing up her past and the knowledge that it was a past she was free from.

"I'd already run away from home twice, which in South Carolina is against the law because I was under eighteen. I ended up in a secured detention facility for a couple months."

"Wow . . . I'm sorry."

"I don't need you to feel sorry for me. I just need you to understand."

"Okay. Thank you. I know that can't be easy to talk about, but I needed to know. If we start digging, I'm not just putting my career, but possibly my life, on the line. We both would be."

"But if your boss told you to stay away from the case—"

"He can tell me to take a couple weeks off, but he can't tell me what to do with my free time. Anyway, we have another problem."

"What's that?"

"I'm pretty sure someone knew we met last night."

"I turned off my phone's GPS and Wi-Fi—"

"Hopefully that's enough, but someone must have followed you. We're going to have to be extra careful."

A shiver slid through her. She knew it was possible. Whoever hit her car could have waited to see what happened to her, then followed her to the hospital. Had they then followed her to the diner? She thought she'd been careful, but she was no expert at this, and it clearly hadn't been enough.

"So where do you suggest we start?"

"The authorities have never looked at these deaths as being connected, so that's the logical starting point." Josh tapped the file. "In addition to that, I spent a lot of time last night, going over the file you gave me, as well as Olivia's case file, and there are three things I want to look into further. Rudolph Beckmann's alibi—or the lack of it—Helen's suicide, and Dr. Abbott's death."

"I agree."

"You said you spoke with Helen's daughter-in-law. Have you spoken to anyone else in her family to see what they think about the medical examiner's conclusion?"

"Not yet. Her funeral was only yesterday. I've met her son a couple times and know that they were close."

"You said she hinted at problems at work, and that she specifically mentioned the Starlighter project. Maybe she told him something she didn't tell you."

"I think it's worth looking into," she said.

"Agreed. I'd also like to speak with Dr. Abbott's wife. See if she knows anything."

Caitlyn glanced around the room. "What about the motel? I paid cash and didn't give them my real name, but if you think someone is following us . . ."

"I think it might be wise to move to a different motel. If we're going to dig into this, we're going to need to stay off the grid and keep as low a profile as possible."

She nodded, but she was afraid that if she was next on the killer's list, keeping a low profile wasn't going to be enough.

# 8

Josh followed Caitlyn's instructions and pulled into the quiet neighborhood where Helen had lived, trying not to have second thoughts about their plan. His captain's words kept repeating through his mind—his clear warnings of leaving the case alone. But there was no way he could ignore the truth now. A phone call to Helen's son, Gavin, had confirmed that he would be working at his mother's house this afternoon, trying to get it ready to put up for sale.

Caitlyn glanced up from her phone. "The next left is her street. House number 775."

"You've been to her house?"

"A couple times, though typically, we went out somewhere together. Dinner for her birthday. A movie every once in a while."

Josh parked around the block from Helen's one-story home. It had neatly kept flower beds and a front porch with a couple of rocking chairs.

Caitlyn paused before opening the car door. "Do you think someone managed to follow us here?"

"No, but I'm still feeling overly cautious. My boss might have answers for what happened, but I don't want to take any chances."

"I agree."

"And let's not mention I'm a cop unless we have to." They got out and he locked the car with the fob. "We're just a couple of friends, sorry for the death of his mother."

"I could talk to him by myself if you think that would be less intimidating."

"I'll let you do most of the talking since you knew her, but I want to be there."

"Good." She shot him a weak smile. "I was hoping you'd say that."

Gavin was working in the open garage as they walked up the drive toward the house. There was a row of boxes lined up against the wall, with a can of beer on top of one of them. A rush of memories flooded through Josh. Going through Olivia's things after she died. Waking up in an empty house. Coming home to the loud silence at night.

He reined in his thoughts. He'd known that looking into this case again was going to be emotional, but the triggers were coming from places he hadn't expected. He hadn't been prepared for that.

"Gavin Fletcher?" Caitlyn stopped at the edge of the garage. "I'm the one who called you earlier. Caitlyn Lindsey. I worked with your mother at MedTECH Labs."

"Caitlyn . . . My mom mentioned you quite a few times. You were at the funeral, weren't you?"

"Yes."

"She always told me how much she enjoyed working with you."

"The feeling was mutual. I'm still struggling with the fact that she's gone." Caitlyn pressed her lips together for a moment. "This is a friend of mine. Josh Solomon."

"I'm very sorry for your loss." Josh reached out and shook the man's hand, leaving Gavin to make his own assumption as to who he was. "I know this hasn't been easy for you."

"I appreciate that, because honestly, I'm still pretty numb." He waved his hand at the garage. "I'm having someone come by later today to talk about doing an estate sale. I just need to pull any personal things I want to keep, though at this point, I have no idea what."

"My advice would be not to rush," Josh said. "Give yourself time to grieve, and make sure you don't get rid of something you might later want."

"You sound like a man speaking from experience."

Josh nodded. "You could say that."

"Listen . . ." He turned back to Caitlyn. "I don't mean to be rude, but I didn't understand from our phone conversation why you needed to talk to me."

"Your mother and I were good friends, and to be honest, I can't believe that she killed herself. Did that seem possible to you?" Caitlyn glanced at Josh, and she continued. "Your mother . . . she was clearly upset before she died, and she spoke to me a couple times about something she was worried about at work. Something about a project she was working on."

"Wait a minute." It was clear she had his attention now. "You think her job was the reason she took her life?"

"Honestly . . ." Caitlyn glanced at Josh again. "I don't know why Helen felt she had to take her life."

"I don't either, though I suppose it shows you how clueless I was. If someone had told me before she died that she was considering killing herself, I would have thought they were crazy. I mean . . . she was my mom. I never would have imagined her doing something like that. Not in a million years. She was always the rock of our family, and now . . . And now she's gone, and I'm suddenly left with nothing."

"I really am sorry."

"Me too, but nothing's going to bring her back."

"I know you've just started going through her things, but did your mother have any work she brought home? Anything from the lab?"

"A few things, but some men from her work came by earlier this morning. Told me it was some kind of formality. They wanted to make sure she didn't have anything that might have been property of the lab, so I gave them the briefcase she took back and forth to work every day."

"And have you found anything else?"

"Actually, after they left I found a couple of her lab notebooks in her bedroom. I suppose I should hand those in as well, but it's not exactly a priority at this point."

"Did they give you a business card or a way to contact them?" Josh asked.

"Yes . . . one of them did. It's here." Gavin reached into his pocket and handed Josh the card.

"Thomas Knight . . ." He turned to Caitlyn. "Did you work with anyone by that name?"

Caitlyn shook her head. "I don't recognize the name, but that doesn't mean they don't work there."

"We believe they're looking for something," Josh said.

"Wait a minute . . ." Gavin stepped up in front of them. "I need to know why the two of you are here and what's really going on. Clearly you're not here just to give your condolences."

"I'm sorry. You're right." Caitlyn drew in a deep breath. "There are just things that didn't add up for me regarding your mother's death. Questions that I can't find answers to."

"You don't think she killed herself."

She glanced at Josh, then back at Gavin. "Honestly, no, I don't. And I don't think you do either."

"I don't, but wait a minute . . ." He dropped what he'd been holding into one of the boxes. "What's the alternative?"

"We don't have proof of anything. Not yet. But there are some strange things that have been happening."

"Like?"

"Three deaths within our lab in the past few months. Then yesterday someone tried to run me off the road."

Gavin leaned against the stack of boxes. "And you also think all three deaths are related?"

"I do."

"And you, Mr. . . . Solomon," Gavin said. "How do you fit into all of this?"

"Olivia was my wife. The one that was killed in a home invasion a year ago."

Gavin took a step back. "Your wife? Wow . . . I am so sorry to hear that."

Josh nodded.

Gavin shoved his hands into his pockets and frowned. "I'm still trying to put all this together. Ever since the night I got a call from the police, I haven't been able to sleep. If you were to ask me then and again now, I'd still say there's no way she would have killed herself. But what could I do when the coroner's report came out and all the evidence pointed to her suicide? I had to believe what they said. But now . . . If you're right . . ."

"It's what we're trying to find out," Josh said. "But in the meantime, we need you to not tell anyone we were here."

"Why?"

"Because I'm a detective. And the case is officially closed. Everything I'm doing is off the record."

Gavin nodded. "That's fine. I can keep this quiet."

"What can you tell us about the night your mother died?" Caitlyn asked.

"I spoke to her briefly, I think it was around . . . five, maybe five thirty. We were going to have lunch later in the week, something we did about once a month. She always wished we'd meet more often and was looking forward to it."

"What else did you talk about?"

"She asked about the grandkids. Wanted to know if Caleb had a game next week. She always liked to go to the kids' activities, and they loved it too."

"Caitlyn said she'd been upset about issues in your marriage."

"My wife and I have been struggling for a long time, and things came to a head recently. She was threatening to leave and take the boys with her." Gavin's phone rang, and he pulled it out of his pocket, glanced at the caller ID, and silenced the call. "Sorry . . . All I know is that my failing marriage wasn't a motive for my mother to kill herself. She loved my wife and the boys. She wouldn't have done that to them."

"But she did have a prescription for antidepressants," Caitlyn said.

"She'd struggled on and off with depression since my father passed away a few years ago. It's a common prescription. So yes, there were things she was dealing with—even I won't deny that—but she also had things she was looking forward to. She was planning a trip to go see her sister next month. Planning lunch with me and my boys next week. Why would she do all of that when she was going to kill herself?"

"Those are questions we'd like answered."

Gavin's phone rang again. "I'm sorry, but this is the estate agent, so I need to take this. The lab notebooks I found are in the house. I left them on her bed. It's the last door on the left down the hallway. They're all work related, so take whatever you think might help."

"Thank you."

Gavin nodded, then took the call.

Josh followed Caitlyn inside the house, feeling as if he were intruding. The house was homey and tidy, with rows of family photos hanging in the hallway. Caitlyn stepped into Helen's bedroom ahead of him, picked up the first notebook, flipped it open, and started glancing through it.

"What do you think?"

"I'm not sure yet. Looks like notes she was taking on something she was working on, but she's got her own personal shorthand. I should be able to figure it out, but it's going to take some time to go through this. It's several months' worth of notes."

He heard a car engine and went to look out the window. "Caitlyn . . . we might have a problem."

She stood up from the bed. "What's wrong?"

"I can't see them but someone else just showed up."

He could hear raised voices from inside the garage.

"What if he brings them back here?"

"Let's pray he doesn't."

The uneasiness in his gut was back. This was no coincidence. They'd been followed.

"Hey, wait a minute!" Gavin's voice carried from outside. "I didn't say you could go into the house."

Josh grabbed the notebooks, then Caitlyn's hand, at Gavin's clear warning and quickly ran through their options. He signaled for her to be quiet, then pulled open the closet door. He could feel her labored breathing as he pulled her inside and shut the door. Every nerve in his body screamed to walk out and confront the men, but something told him that in this situation, staying hidden was their best option. Captain Thomas wasn't going to appreciate hearing about an altercation that included him and this case.

"Where are they?" one of the men asked.

"Who?"

"Your visitors."

He could hear them rummaging through the house. Opening doors and slamming them in their search.

"They left," Gavin said. "They just came by to give their condolences."

They were in Helen's room now and coming toward the closet. He pulled Caitlyn against him behind some long coats, as one of the men swung open the door.

"If you're lying to us . . ."

He pressed closer to her, wondering why he suddenly felt such a strong urge to protect her.

The closet door slammed shut.

"Why would I lie?"

Caitlyn let out a sharp breath as the footsteps left the room.

A minute later, he heard the car drive away.

Josh stepped back out into the room, Caitlyn right behind him.

Gavin stood in the doorway.

"Are you okay?" Josh asked.

"No. You said you had questions you wanted answered. Well, so do I. Who are those men, and why did they come here asking questions about my mother and forcing their way into her house? They're the same men who took Mom's briefcase this morning."

He looked at Caitlyn. "They were looking for you, by the way. Wanted to know if someone with your description had stopped by asking questions."

"What did you tell them?"

"That I'd had a lot of people stop by to offer their condolences over the past couple days. They told me if I found anything else that belonged to the lab, I needed to let them know. I told them I'd already given them everything I had, but that I would call if I found anything else. Which I definitely won't do now."

"Good," Josh said. "I don't know what they're looking for, but they're not up to anything good. What about a description?"

"I'd put them both in their mid-to-late forties. One had a beard, short brown hair, and was probably five ten or eleven. The other one was taller but a little heavier, with glasses and a receding hairline."

"Thank you," Josh said.

"Sure, but what happens now?"

"We're going to keep searching for the truth. Don't talk to anyone about our coming here. At this point we don't know who's involved, so as far as you're concerned, your mother had been depressed and took the only way out she could."

"Okay. As long as you can promise me one thing. Find out the truth about what happened to my mother."

# 9

Caitlyn started flipping through the pages of Helen's lab files as they headed out of the neighborhood. The encounter at Helen's house had left her unsettled, but at least with Helen's notes, they were one step closer to figuring out what had upset her. And more importantly, what was behind her death.

"Anything stand out in her notes?" Josh asked.

"Nothing so far, but I found out something else that's interesting. I just looked up the name on the business card Gavin gave us on my phone. There's no record of a Thomas Knight in our company. And I know I've never heard of him."

"So it's a fake."

"Exactly. This is our company's official logo, but I'm guessing it wouldn't be hard to come up with a fake business card." Caitlyn turned over the card.

"I'll still pass the information on to Quinton and see if he can find out anything else, though more than likely, if it is a fake name, you're right. In the meantime, I'd like to look into Rudolph Beckmann's alibi."

From the very beginning, the two men convicted of Olivia's murder, Rudolph Beckmann and Larry Nixon, were adamant they were innocent. Beckmann claimed he had an alibi, but when the police checked it out, they said that there was no merit to the claim.

"Who was the alibi?" she asked. "It wasn't in the case transcripts I read."

"Patrick Lindstrom."

"What do you know about him?"

"Not a lot," Josh said. "I know he has a wife—Sharon, I think—and three young children. He works odd jobs, usually picking up day work in construction. According to the detective's report, he was questioned at his home, but didn't back up Beckmann's claims that they were together at the time of the murder, so that line of the investigation was dropped."

"They didn't dig a bit, or try to offer him a deal to get him to talk?"

"From what I read, no. We need to try to talk to him. See if we can get anything out of him off the record."

"Sounds like he isn't going to want to talk to us."

"That's always a risk, but I think it's worth a try." Josh pulled onto the main road back toward Houston. "Do you mind if we grab something to eat first? I don't know about you, but I missed breakfast and lunch."

"I don't mind." She glanced at her watch. It was almost half past two, and the yogurt she'd had for breakfast had been hours ago. "I probably should eat something."

Josh flipped on his blinker, then turned into the drive-thru at a burger joint. Five minutes later, she was biting into a fry while Josh pulled his car into an empty parking spot behind the restaurant. She glanced at the side-view mirror, willing her heart to stop racing. She kept telling herself that there was nothing to worry about. The problem was, she knew that was a lie.

An hour later, they'd finished lunch and were parked in front of a run-down apartment building and headed toward number 17, at the end of one of the breezeways. Josh knocked on the door, then took a step back. A moment later, when no one answered, he knocked a second time.

Finally, a woman opened the door a couple inches, the chain still in place.

"My name's Josh Solomon and this is Caitlyn Lindsey. We're looking for Patrick Lindstrom. We need to talk to him."

"I'm sorry, but he's not here." She started to shut the door.

"Wait a minute, ma'am." Caitlyn pressed her fingers against the door. "Can we just ask you a couple questions? I promise it won't take long. It's important."

The woman glanced back into the apartment. "Please . . . I'm sorry . . . I really can't talk—"

"It's Sharon, right? Sharon Lindstrom? My name's Caitlyn. Your husband's not in trouble. We're just looking for information. It will only take a moment. I promise. Do you know where your husband is?"

"He's working."

"Can you tell me where we could find him?"

The woman hesitated again before answering. "He's a day laborer. Gets odd jobs, so I never know where he is."

"Do you know when he might be back? It's very important that we talk to him."

"He typically gets off about five, but then usually spends a couple of hours at a bar after work."

Josh's phone rang. He hesitated, then turned and stepped to the other side of the breezeway.

Caitlyn turned back to her. "A woman was murdered. We need your husband's help to find out who killed her."

Sharon shut the door, then reopened it, this time without the chain engaged, but Caitlyn caught the fear in her eyes, along with the telltale purple marks on her neck. Bruises hidden with makeup and clothing. A look all too familiar to her.

"Do you know a man named Rudolph Beckmann?" Caitlyn asked.

"Yeah . . . he's a friend of my husband. Or was. I understand he's in prison. The police came here asking Patrick about him last year, but I'm sorry. Like I said, I can't help you. I don't know anything."

"Please . . . I'm not with the police. I'm trying to understand a personal matter about my coworker. She was killed a few days ago. We're not here to get you or your husband in trouble. We just need to talk to him."

"I'm sorry. Really, I am, but like I said, I don't know anything."

Sharon started to step back into the apartment again, but Caitlyn wasn't finished trying. They needed information, and her gut told her the woman knew more than she was saying. "He hits you, doesn't he? Your husband."

"No. I . . . I fell. Please, I really need you to leave."

"I know what you're going through. You're scared. And while I know it's not my business, I know what it's like."

"It doesn't matter—"

"It matters. You matter. I know it's not easy, but for your sake, there are options."

"You're wrong." Her gaze dropped, but she still hadn't moved back inside.

"You have children?" Caitlyn asked.

The woman paused. "They just got home from school. They're watching TV."

"Don't let your children live through this. And you . . . you don't deserve this either."

Sharon's gaze shifted as something seemed to click in her eyes. Whatever was going on behind this door had her terrified, but there was also a look of determination.

"My children. . ." She shut the door behind her, then stepped out on the small front patio, her arms crossed tightly against her chest. "What am I supposed to do?"

"There are shelters and safe houses for you and your children. Counseling . . ."

Sharon moved one hand to the door handle. Caitlyn was pushing too hard. She knew it. And she wasn't even sure why. This woman didn't know her. There was no reason for her to listen to anything she said.

"Wait. I know you're scared and feel like you don't have a choice, but there are people who can help you. With finding a job, with food and rent. You don't have to do this alone. I know there's a shelter not far from here. It's called House of Hope."

"I've heard of it, but—"

"They can help you."

Her gaze darted toward the street as a car drove past. "Maybe, but he would kill me if he knew I was even talking to you."

"He's hurt you before. Do you think talking to me will change anything?"

Sharon glanced down at the bruise on her arm. "That woman who was murdered. What was her name?"

"Olivia Solomon. She was killed a year ago."

"I remember hearing about it on the news. I thought she was killed by someone who broke into her house."

"That's what the jury decided, but we're not sure the right men are in prison."

"And my husband? He wasn't involved in her murder—"

"No. But if it's true he was with Rudolph that night, if there was a reason he lied . . ."

"The police came by a few days after her murder. They asked Patrick questions about that night. Something about an alibi."

"Rudolph Beckmann said he was with your husband that night, but your husband denies that. We just want to make sure the right people are in prison."

"He won't tell you anything, but I know he was at Casey's Bar with Rudolph, the night that woman was killed."

"Are you sure?"

"I know there was some sort of brawl my husband was involved in at the bar. He came home with a black eye and a fat lip."

"Do you know what time?"

The woman shook her head. "Sorry, but no."

"Did you ever tell the police any of this?"

"No one ever asked me." Her gaze dropped. "I've already said too much. I need to go."

"Promise me you'll go talk with someone. Don't let your children lose their mother. I . . . I know what that's like."

Sharon glanced back at the door and hesitated. "And that woman who was killed . . . Olivia . . ."

Caitlyn nodded.

"I hope you find out who killed her."

"Me too."

Josh was waiting for her at the end of the sidewalk when she finished talking to Sharon. She wished she could do more. But she knew Sharon was the one who was going to have to take that next difficult step. A number of people had tried to help her mother get out of her abusive marriage. In the end, her mother had believed the cost of leaving had been too great.

"What did you find out?" Josh asked once they were back in the car.

"She confirmed that her husband was at the bar that night, and came home with a black eye, but she couldn't give me a time."

He started the engine, then pulled away from the curb. "Do you think she'd testify if it came to that?"

"I doubt it. She's terrified of her husband. But what we do know at this point is that it's possible Beckmann was telling the truth. What I don't understand is why Lindstrom would have lied, and why someone didn't get this information during the trial. Finding it out wasn't that hard."

"Which means someone didn't want that information out and

buried it." He gripped the steering wheel. "We still need to talk with Patrick Lindstrom."

"Do you think he'll actually talk to us?"

"Probably not. We need to be careful how we approach him." Josh pulled out onto the street. "He beats her."

"You noticed."

"The bruises . . . the makeup . . . yeah. I saw it far too often when I was working the streets. No wonder she's scared."

"She needs help, but leaving a situation like that is a huge step."

"I know there are always multiple factors involved, but if she'd just walk out—"

"It's not that simple. You told me she was a stay-at-home mom. She's probably never had a job. She has three kids to take care of. He might have threatened to take the kids away. She probably feels as if she doesn't have a choice."

"This sounds . . . personal."

Caitlyn pushed away the comment. "It's nothing."

"You said Lindstrom came home with some kind of black eye. Like he'd been in a fight?"

"That's what she said."

"Wait a minute." Josh flipped on his blinker and made a sharp turn into an empty parking lot in front of a restaurant with a For Sale sign in the window.

"What are you thinking?"

Josh shifted the car into park and kept the motor running. He grabbed a thick binder from the back seat. "I might know why Patrick Lindstrom refused to give Rudolph an alibi."

"I'm not following."

"If I remember correctly, Lindstrom had a rap sheet." He started flipping through the book.

"And that's important why?"

"Here it is." He tapped his finger on Lindstrom's police record. "Patrick Lindstrom had been arrested twice and convicted of two felonies. Once for aggravated assault, and a second time for a DUI."

"Okay."

"Give me a second. I need to call my partner." He speed-dialed the number, then put the phone on speaker. "Quinton . . . I need a quick favor."

"What do you need?"

"Were there any incidents filed at a Casey's Bar with the police the night Olivia was killed?"

"Give me a second . . ."

"Why is that important?" Caitlyn asked.

"It could be why Lindstrom refused to give Rudolph an alibi for that night. If he was involved in an intoxication assault, that's a third-degree felony. Three strikes, you're out."

Quinton came back on the line. "There was a 911 call that night about an assault. Someone got drunk and things got out of hand."

"Was anyone arrested?"

"No. Whoever was involved left before the police got there."

"So no video footage?"

"The place has cameras, but according to the report, they weren't on."

"And no one remembered Lindstrom being there that night?"

"The detectives were unable to find anyone who could back up Rudolph's claims," Quinton said. "Anything else?"

"Not at the moment, but I'll call if I need something."

Josh hung up and turned to Caitlyn. "If I'm right, and that was Lindstrom who was involved in the fight, he knew if he confessed to being there that night, he could go back to prison."

"That would explain why he didn't come forward."

"Exactly. And the police were so certain they had their man that they believed Patrick's story and didn't question him further."

"There is one problem," Caitlyn said.

"What's that?"

"If he wouldn't talk to the police, why would he talk to us?"

"I've been thinking about that. We need leverage."

"Except we don't have any."

"Maybe not, but he doesn't have to know that." Josh turned to face her. "We know the bar doesn't have video of that night, but he probably doesn't know that."

"Everyone has cell phones these days. We make him think we have actual video of him beating up another customer."

"Right. We give him just enough information to make him believe we know the truth."

"We still have to find him," she said.

"That shouldn't be a problem. We need to go get settled into a new motel, then are you up for a stakeout?"

# 10

Josh drummed his fingers against the steering wheel. After an hour of waiting in the semidarkness, there was still no sign of Patrick. He glanced at Caitlyn, who was reading through Helen's notebooks with a penlight. He breathed in the subtle scent of her perfume. It had been a long time since he'd been this close to a woman, which is why he expected to feel uneasy. But there was something different about her. Something that impressed him. She'd come to him, clearly terrified over what was going on, but not once had she succumbed to that fear. And even though he was a cop, he understood fear.

The light from the street lamp a dozen yards in front of them managed to catch the intensity of her expression and the subtle curve of her lips. Something he really shouldn't notice. But *not* noticing her was proving to be harder than he'd imagined.

"I watched how you talked with Sharon," he said, breaking the silence between them. "How you listened to her like you truly knew what she was feeling."

Caitlyn shifted away from him toward the passenger window as if he'd managed to say the wrong thing.

"I'm sorry," he said. "If I'm stepping where I shouldn't—"

"It's fine. I just . . . I didn't tell you everything about my family."

He wanted to know what she was thinking, but he didn't want to push her into an uncomfortable spot. "You don't have to."

"Sometimes I feel like just when I think I'm okay, and I've dealt with everything, it still manages to all come rushing over me." She glanced up at him and frowned. "The same way I imagine you're feeling about Olivia right now."

"Yeah. But I meant what I said," he said. "You don't need to tell me anything that makes you uncomfortable."

"Funny—I used to go to huge lengths to hide my past. At school, at church . . . and now . . . I guess I've come to terms with not only the reality that I can't change the past, but also that it's a part of who I am."

He appreciated her perceptiveness. And her ability to look beyond herself. Over the last couple of months, he'd begun to see the same thing. To finally feel as if he'd begun to slowly heal. But it wasn't something that could be nicely folded up and stuffed inside a drawer. And like Caitlyn said, no matter what happened to him in the future, Olivia would always be a part of who he was. That would never change.

He glanced across the street and waited for her to continue on her own terms. Darkness had settled in around them. He could feel the music from the bar pumping into the night air, even though the windows on his car were up.

"My father abused my mother for as long as I can remember," she began. "Physically . . . emotionally . . . any way he could find to hurt her. Most of the time while she was trying to protect me. And I . . . I never knew how to stop him. How to keep her safe."

"It wasn't your fault, Caitlyn. You were a child."

"Maybe not. But that doesn't really change anything. It didn't save my mother."

"What happened to her?"

"Not too long after that time in the car when the police caught

me with his drugs, he . . . he killed her. Over a burnt pot roast."
She looked up at him, this time catching his gaze. "In reality it was
much more than that, but the pot roast was his excuse."

"Wow. I am so sorry."

"He was drunk that night. He didn't even wait for an explanation when she brought it from the kitchen. Just got up from the
table, pulled out his gun, and shot her." She drew in a deep breath.
"I was put back into juvenile detention, then into foster care, and
for a time I lived with my grandmother, who I loved, but she was in
poor health. Eventually I was sent to live with my mother's older
sister in another state. She loved me but didn't have the time or
the energy to parent a troubled teen. Her kids were grown, and I
think she resented having to deal with me. To her credit, she tried
not to show it and she did care for me. In her own way."

"What happened to your father?"

"He died in prison three years ago. I never saw him after the
trial, and he never tried to contact me. I always said it was for the
better, but as crazy as it seemed, a part of me still loved him, because I knew he wasn't always that way. My parents had once been
in love, planned to start a family, bought a house together, dreamed
of a future . . . There were good times in all the bad times."

"What changed?"

"My mom said he was always moody. But when he lost his job,
he never really got back on his feet. Worked a bunch of odd jobs.
Moved us from place to place, and then started drinking. The
abuse kept getting worse and worse until he stopped trying. Her
family begged her to leave him, but she was scared of so many
things. Scared of losing me. Of his threats . . ."

Josh studied her face. He'd seen his share of domestic abuse
during his years on the force. "What changed for you?" he asked.

"I made friends with a girl at my new school. I started going
to church with her family, hanging out with them on holidays and
weekends. For the first time in my life, I realized things didn't have

to be the way they were. They lived their faith and helped me realize I didn't have to live my life as a victim. I ended up graduating top of my high school class while working twenty hours a week, which got me a presidential scholarship for college. It's hard to believe how many years ago that was. Anyway." She shook her head. "Enough about me. Now that you know everything about my dysfunctional family, what about yours? I'm hoping they were a bit more . . . normal."

"My family?" He couldn't help but chuckle at her comment. Normal, it seemed, was relative. "I had a pretty good childhood. Dad worked long hours, and Mom stayed home with the three of us kids. She gardened, made the best chicken fried steak, mashed potatoes, and coconut cream pie, kept three boys in line, plus managed a hundred other little things every day. My aunt and uncle and cousins lived nearby, and we went to church together on Sunday with family dinner afterward. My mother passed away almost three years ago, but my dad still lives in Kansas where I grew up, not far from my brothers and their families."

"I bet you miss your mom."

"Every day."

She turned to him with that empathetic look in her eyes he'd noticed more than once. "I'm going to guess that you come from a long line of cops?"

"Not even close. The majority of my family—except Uncle Bob—were farmers."

"Really. For some reason that surprises me. What kind?"

"My dad owns a farm that's been in the family for almost a hundred years. Primarily grass-fed beef, plus organic wheat and soybeans."

"Sounds like a great way to grow up."

"It was." He caught her wistful expression and couldn't help but wonder if she ever grieved for the childhood she'd lost.

"What was Uncle Bob?" she asked.

"He was the town's mortician. His wife, my aunt Clarice, ran the local hair salon. She was a trained desairologist—a mortuary cosmetologist."

"Of course." She let out a low laugh. "I think I need to meet this family of yours one day. They sound . . . so normal."

"Normal if you like family reunions with matching T-shirts, ugly Christmas sweater contests, and my aunt Beulah's homemade fruitcake that weighs as much as a brick. Of course, we never turn down a piece. That would be rude."

"Somehow I think I'd like that."

He tried to shake the ridiculous idea of bringing her home to his family and introducing her to his dad and brothers. It was far too soon after Olivia's death to even think about something like that. A few weeks ago, his father had come to him while he was back home for Christmas, initiating a father-son conversation. He reminded him how he understood what it felt like to lose a spouse, but that it was okay to move on. How Olivia would have wanted him to be happy. And how it was okay to be happy.

And his words weren't empty. Six months ago, his father had met a woman at church, and they were planning to get married in the spring. But that didn't mean Josh was ready to open up his heart again.

At the time, he'd filed away the conversation as something to think about much farther down the road. Sometime when Olivia didn't haunt his dreams at night. When he met someone who would do more than make him forget; someone who would make him want to live again.

Caitlyn broke open the bag of caramel popcorn she'd bought at the gas station and popped a kernel into her mouth. "So, what compelled you to leave the family business and join law enforcement?"

"I had a mentor who ended up saving me from getting into trouble."

"So, you were another juvenile delinquent like me?"

"In full disclosure, I was nine."

"Wait a minute." She let out a soft giggle. "You were nine and already heading down the wrong path?"

"Actually, I was smitten with Susie Baker who lived down the street from me and was in my class at school. She dared me to steal a watermelon out of my neighbor's field."

"And you told her that wouldn't be a good idea."

"That's what I should have done."

"Instead you fell for her womanly wiles?"

"Ha! I snuck into the garden that night and emerged with the biggest and what I was sure was the juiciest watermelon I could find. But as I was heading back across the field, someone shone their flashlight on me, and I realized I was caught. And, being the street-smart nine-year-old that I was, I knew if I got caught, I was going to spend the rest of my life in prison. So I started running as fast as I could while our neighbor shot his BB gun into the air above me. Scared me so bad, I tripped and landed smack dab on top of that melon."

Caitlyn started giggling. "And . . ."

"You laugh now, but I wasn't laughing. It burst open, and all of a sudden, I was covered in sticky fruit with a crazed farmer bearing down on me, about to get shot—I was sure—for stealing some of his produce. At that moment I wasn't sure which was going to be worse. Prison or death."

"So what happened?" She was still giggling.

"First of all, you have to understand that Gregory Parker used to raise huge melons and pumpkins and enter them into the Kansas State Fair every year."

"How big?"

"He won first prize one year for a melon that was almost two hundred and fifty pounds."

"Seriously? You're pulling my leg."

"I kid you not. He had a pumpkin weigh in at over six hundred pounds one year."

"Now I know you're pulling my leg."

"Go ahead and google it, because I'm not kidding. You can imagine just how seriously he took his melons. Having one stolen off the vine when it was still growing was blasphemy to him. Anyway, he caught up with me, grabbed me by the back of my pants, hauled me to his yard, and hosed me down. Once I was melon free, he escorted me back home in his truck. On the way, I received the lecture of my life. He told me I had a choice. I could continue with my life of crime, or I could come clean and be a man and maybe . . . just maybe . . . avoid a prison term."

"All over a melon." Caitlyn was still laughing.

"He had me terrified."

"Looks like you took his warning seriously, though I'm still enjoying picturing you covered in sticky prize watermelon."

"My parents didn't think it was that funny. They promptly grounded me for the rest of the summer. No outings with friends, no money for the ice cream truck, and certainly no interaction with Susie Baker. Though somehow I have a feeling they laughed about it behind their closed bedroom door."

Caitlyn was laughing harder now, and her laugh was contagious. She grabbed a tissue to wipe the tears that were streaming down her face.

"It's been a long time since I've laughed till I cried," she said.

"Me too." In fact, he couldn't even remember the last time something had made him laugh. "Honestly, I haven't done much laughing at all recently."

"Are stakeouts always this . . . entertaining?"

"Stakeouts with Quinton require a bag of kale chips and protein drinks his wife sends, topped off with a box of chocolate donuts he buys, and endless talk radio."

He smiled, then looked across the street at the bar. A couple came out, engaged in a conversation, but still no sign of Patrick. He needed to focus on why they were there and not on the charming woman sitting next to him. Though maybe this was a lost cause. He'd give the guy another hour, then suggest they leave. The only way he was going to be able to go back to his boss and be allowed to reopen the case was to go to him with a stack of evidence. Like proving Rudolph Beckmann really had an alibi for that night.

But convincing Patrick to provide it wasn't going to be easy.

"Do you see your family often?" she asked.

"At a minimum, the Fourth of July and Christmas. And then every few years we have a reunion with the extended family."

"I always missed having family. Someone that, if you ever needed them, would help you no matter what. I think that's why even though part of me wants to run from all of this, the other part just wants to find out the truth and stay."

"What makes you want to stay here?"

"I've made friends. Found a church home where I feel involved, and I've started to volunteer with a couple community service projects. Truth is, I don't want to start over again."

He grabbed her hand and squeezed her fingers. "You're not going to have to start over. We're going to figure this out."

"And if we can't come up with proof of what happened? Evidence that your boss will listen to? Then what?"

"Let's not go there. Not yet."

"You're right. I guess I'm just frustrated. Helen's death, the accident. Part of me keeps thinking I'm simply going to wake up and all of this will be over. Of course, if it were over, we wouldn't be here talking about fruitcake and stealing prize-winning watermelons."

He smiled, liking the way she was able to laugh in a tense situation. He liked *her*. Maybe his father was right—it was time to move on. He knew he was lonely. And Caitlyn made him want to smile again. It was something he hadn't done for a long time.

---

"I'll make you a deal," he said.

"What's that?"

"We figure all this out and make it out of here alive, and I'll take you to the Kansas State Fair later this year. I'll show you what a prize-winning melon looks like. We'll ride the Ferris wheel and the sky ride, then eat enough pronto pups, funnel cakes, and barbecue to make you so full you won't want to eat for a week."

"I'd like that."

He caught her smile and felt his heart thud as she turned back to Helen's notes. The purpose of tonight's stakeout might end up being a washout, but he wouldn't complain about the company.

"Wait a minute . . . Of course." Caitlyn tapped on the paperwork she'd been reading. "Jarred Carmichael."

"Who?"

"Sorry, but something just hit me."

"What's that?"

"I found a mention to Starlighter in Helen's notes. She writes that a 'JC' was overseeing it. That has to be Jarred Carmichael. He's a technical manager at the lab, pretty brilliant. We all work under him."

"Jarred Carmichael?"

"Do you know him?" she asked.

"I've heard his name before."

Josh stared at the bar across the street, wanting to ignore the unwanted memory. And wanting to ignore the place he feared this investigation was going to take him.

# 11

Caitlyn leaned her head back against the passenger seat of Josh's car, unsure if she should press him over what just happened. Josh's tone had changed suddenly, and she had no idea why, although it seemed to be Jarred Carmichael's name that had subdued him.

"Did you know him?" she finally asked. "Jarred Carmichael?"

"Not personally. His name just . . . it brought back an unexpected memory."

"Not a good one, I'm assuming."

"What did Helen say about him?" he asked.

"Looks like he was head of this project—Starlighter—where they were struggling to verify the results." She flipped through a few pages and gave him a rough translation of Helen's notes. "Questions about JC. Not sure what to think. Project on schedule, but results seem off. Something going on? JC wants to verify with further testing. Pathogen not reacting as expected. Need to look into results further."

"What does that mean? 'Pathogen not reacting as expected'?"

"It means the immune system is not reacting to the virus the way they thought it would."

"So something was bothering her."

98

But what? What had been going on in the lab that had been worth murdering someone?

"And the only time you ever heard about this project was once from Olivia, and more recently from Helen?" he asked.

She nodded her head. "Helen mentioned it a few days before she died. We were having lunch together, and I knew something was wrong. At first I thought it had something to do with her son, but then she mentioned this project."

"Starlighter."

Caitlyn nodded. "When I pushed, Helen closed off. Now I can't help but wonder what would have happened if I would have pressed harder. Maybe I could have somehow saved her."

"You don't know that."

"I know, but if I'd asked questions, maybe I'd have something that could help us now."

She replayed the conversation she'd had with Helen . . .

*"What do you know about Starlighter?" Helen had asked her.*

*"What do you mean?"*

*"It's a . . . special funded project at the lab." She shook her head. "Never mind. Forget I said anything."*

*"Helen, if something's bothering you, you know you can talk to me—"*

*"Really, just forget it. It's nothing."*

Helen's response had bothered her, because it clearly wasn't nothing. She'd never seen Helen so rattled. And she'd been right. Three days later her friend was dead.

Josh took a sip of his coffee. "I need to ask you a question. It's a little off topic, but something I need to know."

"Of course."

"Did you ever see Carmichael and Olivia together?"

"Together?" Caitlyn shifted in her seat, uncomfortable with the question. "Are you asking if something was going on between the two of them?"

Josh frowned at the question, but nodded. "I'll be blunt. I have reason to believe they were having an affair."

She managed to hold back her shock. She might have worked with the man, but she didn't really know him well. Olivia, though, she had known. And while no marriage was perfect, it was hard to imagine her having an affair. Especially with someone like Carmichael.

"I doubt it. Jarred Carmichael is . . . I don't know if you've met him but . . . let's say he's not exactly what you'd call a catch. He's smart, very smart, but also pretty brash and unpolished. And he's married, though I never met his wife." She shook her head. "So, Carmichael and Olivia? Honestly, that's hard to imagine."

She studied his expression in the dim light, wondering if she should press the issue or let the question drop. She finally decided to ask. "Why do you think she was having an affair?"

"I don't really have any proof, but after she died I found emails and text messages they'd exchanged. Nothing I read hinted at anything romantic or sexual, but when I first read them, I just thought they were being discreet."

"She worked with him," Caitlyn said. "Isn't there a chance the messages were simply work related?"

"Maybe, but at a minimum I'd say they had to have met three or four times outside work."

She looked at him and wondered what else she'd missed. "She never hinted that the two of you were having problems. Not that she probably would have shared something like that with me, but still . . ."

"No. I didn't think so, but I can't . . . it's hard not to wonder."

She could hear the tug of war of emotions in his voice. Olivia was dead, and he was faced with picking up the pieces of what remained, without the chance of ever getting any of the answers he needed.

"I'm surprised you're not married," he said.

His abrupt change of topic was unexpected. Not that she could blame him. Sharing marital problems with someone he barely knew couldn't be easy.

She watched a couple of young people hurry into the bar while laughing about something. But still there was no sign of Patrick.

"I was engaged once," she said, thankful that the sting of the breakup had faded years ago. "He was my college sweetheart. We met my junior year and it was love at first sight. At least it was for me."

"What happened?"

"Our last semester he came to me and told me he'd found someone else. Told me he didn't love me anymore. I was devastated, shocked . . . I suppose I should have seen it coming, but I didn't. Or at least I didn't want to."

"Maybe we're blind to those we love the most. And you've never found anyone else?"

"No. Not that my friends don't try to set me up with eligible men. Like Olivia always tried to do." She let out a soft laugh. "But it's never clicked for me again." She turned the conversation back to Olivia and Carmichael. "What if they weren't having an affair? What if this all has to do with what was going on at the lab?"

"I want to believe that's true, but there's just been a lot of things that don't add up. About the night she died . . ."

She waited silently for him to continue. He looked away, as if he feared resurrecting that moment. Not that she blamed him. How many times had it replayed in his mind, over and over like a broken record? She could guess, because she knew what loss felt like. When only time and distance could begin to heal that brokenness.

"The night Olivia was shot . . . all I could do was hold her while she died."

"I'm so sorry."

"That's what she said to me that night. That she was sorry, that she needed to talk to me. That I needed to know the truth."

"What truth?"

"I don't know. None of it made sense at the time." His jaw tensed. "I told her not to talk. Promised her that she was going to be fine. Which I knew wasn't true. But at the time, all I could think about was that she was dying, and I had to save her. It was later when I started to wonder if she'd been trying to tell me she'd been having an affair. It fit with what she said. I wondered if she could have been talking about Jarred, but maybe she was talking about something else. She died before she could tell me. I never told anyone. It wasn't something I wanted to see hitting the news cycles. It seemed too . . ."

"Personal."

"Exactly."

"And it was. But now . . ." He hesitated before continuing. "I guess it's just hard not to wonder if I'd been a better husband, or worked fewer hours, but I always thought she understood. That she supported me. I don't know."

"From what I saw—as well as things Olivia told me—she was crazy about you, Josh. You remember when she showed up at work on your birthday?"

He shifted in his seat. "I remember I'd been working extra hours on a case and felt like I was never home."

"She never complained to me about your long hours. All she ever said was that she missed spending more time with you."

Josh let out a slow breath. "She called me from the parking lot. Told me she was waiting to take me out to lunch whenever I could take a break. I'd almost forgotten. It turned out to be one of the best birthdays I can remember."

Caitlyn smiled. "She planned that day for weeks. And if you ask me, that sounds like a woman in love."

"But here's what I don't understand," Josh said. "If she knew something was going on at the lab, if she felt that her life was in danger, why didn't she simply come to me? I think she must have been in over her head, but then I feel guilty because I can't imagine why she wouldn't have come to me."

"There could be other explanations," Caitlyn said.

"Like?"

"I don't know. Blackmail . . . coercion. Or maybe she found out something someone didn't want her to know about."

"Maybe." Josh drew in a deep breath. "Do you remember the car wreck she was in a few days before she died?"

"Of course. You think that had something to do with all of this?"

He shrugged. "I never thought of it that way, but in light of what we know now, it could have."

At the time, Olivia had blown it off as nothing. A truck had slid across the median and slammed into her car. Miraculously, she was fine, besides a few bumps and bruises. They'd never thought it was anything but an accident. But what if it hadn't been? What if someone had tried to scare Olivia—like they had her? And then, when that didn't work, they'd killed her?

A man matching the description of Patrick was heading down the sidewalk, drawing her out of their conversation.

"Josh . . . that's got to be him." She grabbed the door handle. "He's walking toward the bar from the west."

"I think you're right."

Bingo. They'd found him.

"He'll react better to me than a cop charging at him." She opened the car door and started to get out.

He pressed his hand against her arm. "I know that the plan was for you to approach him first, but I'm having second thoughts."

"We can't lose him, and if he realizes you're a cop and runs . . ."

He frowned, but she could tell he knew she was right. If he went tearing after him, the man would bolt.

"He's not going to do anything," she said.

"You don't know that."

"Josh."

"Fine. Go, but I'm right behind you."

She took off across the street at an even pace, knowing she needed to find the right approach. She hadn't sat in the car for two hours to not get the answers they needed. And they needed to talk to him now, because they might not get another chance.

Live music sounded from inside the bar. Ahead of her and to her right, two couples walked up to the front door laughing, oblivious to what she was trying to do. Patrick was now twenty-five feet from the door. She lengthened her steps as she crossed the street, ready to meet him on the sidewalk before he got to the front door.

"Patrick Lindstrom?"

The man slowed down. She swallowed hard. His wife's description didn't do him justice. He was easily six three or four and at least two hundred and fifty pounds. A day-old beard covered his face and tats covered his knuckles. A wave of anger went through her at the thought that this man beat his wife and more than likely terrorized his kids. But no one was all bad. If she could find a way to appeal to the man's humanity, maybe he would help them. She'd much rather avoid plan B and Josh taking him down. They'd end up at the precinct in his captain's office.

*God . . . we need him to listen to us. Need him to verify Rudolph's alibi.*

"Patrick . . . I need to talk to you for a moment."

He stopped half a dozen feet in front of her. "Who are you?"

"My name's Caitlyn Lindsey. I was wondering if I could talk with you about Rudolph Beckmann. I understand the two of you are friends."

"Don't know what that has to do with anything. Rudolph Beckmann is in prison for murder."

"I believe he's innocent."

"Who told you that?" He rested his fists on his hips. "I don't know what you want, but everybody in prison claims they're innocent. Doesn't matter to me."

He started past her toward the bar.

"Wait, please."

He stopped again, then noticed Josh.

Caitlyn held up her hand. "He's with me. He's just a friend."

"He's a cop, ain't he?"

"We just want to ask you a couple questions," she said. "That's it."

Patrick hesitated for a split second before pulling out a knife, grabbing her, and pressing the blade against her neck.

# 12

Josh took a step back and held up his hands, trying to take up a position that would help de-escalate the situation. Taking Lindstrom down was possible, but he had a feeling he might not fare as well as he had against the two punks who'd tried to jump him at his house. The man was a two-time felon who beat his wife. The odds of him simply walking away without a fight were unlikely. The list of nightmarish outcomes raced through his mind.

"You don't need to do this, Patrick," Josh said. "We just want to talk—"

"All I'm doing is trying to defend myself. Move another step toward me, and I will hurt her."

"She meant what she told you," he said. "We just need to talk to you."

"Why should I? You're a cop."

"I'm not here as a cop. I'm only here because I need information about something personal. Information I think you have."

"And you expect me to just give you whatever you want? Why should I?"

"Just listen to me. Please," he said, studying Caitlyn's gaze. She was clearly scared, but there was also a spark of determination in her eyes. "A year ago, my wife was murdered. Her name was Olivia Solomon. Rudolph Beckmann and another man were convicted for her murder."

"I had nothing to do with that murder."

"I know. But I have evidence that you gave a false statement about Rudolph's alibi."

Patrick's gaze narrowed. "What kind of evidence?"

"Evidence that you were, in fact, here at this bar with Rudolph the night of the murder. I know that someone convinced you not to talk about him. Someone who told you not to give him an alibi. Maybe they bribed you, maybe they blackmailed you . . . I don't know. All I need to know is who that was."

"You're lying. You don't know anything."

Josh might not know all the facts, but one thing was clear. The man was definitely scared. Using their leverage was a risk, and one he'd have preferred to avoid, but if it got him to talk . . .

"I wouldn't bet on that," Josh said, holding his gaze.

"Why should I believe you?"

Josh prepared to tighten the screws. "I know about the brawl that night. Two of you got into a fight and the other guy was sent to the hospital. If you'd come forward and said you were there that night, you would have been arrested for assault and ended up back in prison."

"You can't prove any of that."

"I told you. I have evidence."

Patrick's expression sobered, and he moved the knife an inch from Caitlyn's throat. Josh finally had his attention.

"What kind of evidence?" Patrick asked.

"Evidence that the district attorney will pay attention to when I show it to him."

Patrick put the knife back into his pocket and pushed Caitlyn toward him. "What do you want from me? Because it sounds to me that you want more than just information."

Before he answered, Josh grabbed Caitlyn's hand and steered her behind him. At least the man wasn't running.

Josh worked to rein in his temper. The man didn't deserve his mercy, but there had to be at least a sliver of good in him. He just needed to find it. "I want you to confirm you were with Beckmann that night at this bar."

"I could walk away right now."

"And I could arrange a warrant for your arrest for assaulting this woman."

Josh tried to draw up a measure of pity for the man. But Lindstrom was trapped, and he knew it.

"I meant what I said. I'm not here to take you in. I've got bigger fish to fry, and I need to know the truth about where Rudolph was that night."

"Why do you need to know the truth?"

"If Rudolph didn't kill my wife, then someone else out there did. Which means for you, if at any time the people who bought you off think that your lie isn't working anymore, they won't hesitate to eliminate you. They've killed three people. So far. I don't think they'll worry about one more."

"And if I still deny everything you just said?"

Josh held up a flash drive. "I can make sure this evidence comes to light."

"You're lying. There was no footage."

"Really? Are you willing to take that chance and end up back in prison? How many people were in the bar that night? Twenty . . . thirty . . . forty? How many of them had cell phones? It was just a matter of time before footage showed up."

"Why not just take what you've got to the police?"

"Because I'm not interested in what you did. I'm interested in who told you to lie."

Josh could tell Lindstrom was still weighing his options. Trying to figure out his best move. One that would get him in the least amount of trouble. If he felt backed into a corner, he was exactly where Josh wanted him.

"He never gave me his full name. He just showed up at the bar. Said I could call him Jigsaw, but someone else called him Shawn. Said he'd pay me good if I would lie about that night. Tell the police I wasn't here."

"And did he pay you?"

"Two thousand that day, three thousand a few days later."

"What did he look like?"

"I don't know. It's been a long time."

"I'd hate to have to shake your memory by taking you down to the station."

Patrick frowned. "Fine. Early forties, glasses, balding in the front, a couple inches shorter than I am—"

"Any distinguishing marks?"

"No . . . Wait a minute . . . He wore a gold ring. I noticed it because it was unique. It was the head of a lion."

"Did you ever talk to the police?"

"They called me in and asked me to tell them what happened. I told them I hadn't been there, and they told me I could go. That was it."

"There was no follow-up?"

"Not with me." Patrick's gaze shifted to the flash drive. "What about the footage? I want it. I need that, and a guarantee that you're not going to share it."

"Sure." Josh tossed the drive to him. "Think twice before you lie to the police again. I promise it will come back to bite you."

Josh took Caitlyn's hand as they walked back to the car, then waited until she'd slid into the passenger seat. "You okay?"

"Yes."

"You're sure?"

"Yes." She looked up, catching his gaze. "Though two adrenaline-laced incidents in barely twenty-four hours is my limit. I'm a girl who likes to watch action on the big screen with a bowl of popcorn, not be a part of it."

"Well, you've still got your sense of humor. That's impressive."

Her smile disappeared. "He deserves to be in jail."

"I agree, but at the moment, there's nothing we can do about it. If I were to bring him in, it would tip off whoever is behind this to what we're doing. We can't take that chance. Now we know we're on the right track and not on some wild-goose chase."

He hurried to the other side of the car and quickly pulled out from the curb before Patrick had a change of heart and came after them.

"That description sounds a lot like one of the men who showed up at Helen's house today," Caitlyn said.

"I thought the exact same thing."

Josh put in a call to his partner.

"Quinton . . ." he said, once he'd picked up. "I need to ask for another favor."

"Of course. What's up? You two okay?"

"For now, yes. I need you to see if the name Jigsaw pops up somewhere. Early forties, glasses, balding in the front. Just over six feet. He wears a gold lion-head ring. We were told by Patrick Lindstrom that this Jigsaw paid him off to lie about his alibi. We also think there's a good chance that he was the same guy who showed up at Helen Fletcher's house."

"How in the world did you get Patrick to talk?"

"Besides the fact that we were actually there to dig up the truth, unlike whoever interviewed him last year? Caitlyn and I came up with a bit of leverage and it worked."

"So you've just managed to prove that Rudolph didn't kill your wife. Considering what's happened, you know this information could get you both into trouble."

"We're already in trouble," Josh said. "We could go to the captain with what we've found. It's definitely enough to reopen the case."

There was a long pause on the line before Quinton responded. "I agree, but I think you should hold off."

"Why?"

Quinton lowered his voice. "Because I don't know who to trust anymore."

Josh glanced at Caitlyn. "Wait a minute . . . what are you saying?"

"If what you've told me is true, there has to be someone out there that's higher up, pulling the strings. And if you go to the wrong person—"

"I'll rocket to the top of their hit list."

"Exactly."

"But we can't just sit on this."

"I agree. Just hold off for a couple more days. Let me keep digging and asking questions."

Josh hesitated. He knew his partner was right, but he still didn't like the fact that there were so many unanswered questions. "You need to be careful. If they find out you're working with me, it's going to be your neck on the line as well."

"Trust me, I know. Just keep your heads down for the moment. We don't need any of this coming back on you any worse than it already is. We can meet in the morning and go over what we've got."

Caitlyn's frown deepened as Josh turned onto the main street that led to their motel. "So where does this leave us now? If we can't turn in the information we have, how are we going to sort this out?"

"We will. But like Quinton said, we need to make sure we take down everyone involved."

"And in the meantime? I can't just sit and wait for answers."

"I can't either. I thought we could stop by the store on the way to our motel. I'd like to get a large poster board and markers."

"What are you thinking? A makeshift crime board?"

"Exactly. I'm impressed."

Caitlyn laughed. "Don't be too impressed. Every crime show has its own version of that board."

Josh smiled. He liked the sound of her laugh. And her ability to find something to laugh about in the middle of a tense situation. "That's because it works. Always helps me to lay out a case and find the connections. I think I'll also pick up one of those mini photo printers while we're there."

An hour later, Josh put their purchases in the back seat of the car and started the engine. Caitlyn had seemed fine in the store, but there was a growing look of fatigue in her eyes. "Are you doing okay? Being held by knifepoint, no matter how it turns out, is terrifying."

"I will be." She let out a soft sigh. "It's strange, but for some reason, I never got the impression that he wanted to hurt me. It was like when my father came to my mother after a fight with flowers and apologized. It's not an excuse, but it was as if he couldn't control the anger, no matter how much he wanted to."

"Dr. Jekyll and Mr. Hyde."

"Exactly."

Josh's phone rang, and he pushed a button on the steering wheel to answer the call.

"Detective Solomon?"

"Yes, who's this?"

"This is Gavin Fletcher. I'm sorry to bother you, but I just found something you need to see. I think you were right about my mother. She didn't commit suicide. She was murdered."

# 13

Caitlyn felt her breath catch at the sound of Gavin's voice. She'd believed all along that Helen had been murdered, but hearing it from someone else seemed to only further legitimize her theory. And that terrified her.

"What did you find?" Josh asked him.

"Something I believe is related to my mother's death," Gavin said. "We need to meet."

"Of course. Just tell us where."

He gave them the location of a Walmart a couple miles from his mother's house. "I'm locking up her place now, and I can be there in about twenty minutes. I'm probably being paranoid, but make sure you're not followed."

"Meet us in the parking lot," Josh said. "I'll be driving the same car we were in this afternoon."

"I'll find you."

The call went dead.

Caitlyn gripped the edge of the seat as they pulled out of the parking lot of the office supply store, while the knot in her stomach tightened. After the recent encounter with Patrick and being held at knifepoint, on top of the realization that someone had murdered her friends, her heart was refusing to stop pounding and her hands felt clammy.

"I don't know about you, but something feels off in all of this," she said.

"What do you mean?" Josh asked.

"Gavin sounded . . . anxious. Distracted."

"Can you blame him? He was told that his mother committed suicide this week, and now we've just managed to convince him she was murdered. That's enough to make anyone feel unhinged."

"True." She hesitated before continuing. "But what if it's more than that?"

His brow furrowed. "What do you mean?"

"Maybe I'm just borrowing trouble, but if those suits who showed up at his house . . . if they wanted to get to us, he would be their perfect opportunity. All they'd have to do is get him to call us and set up a meeting. They know we'll come. I just don't want to walk into a situation we're not prepared for."

"Like Patrick. I underestimated him, but I'm not going to let that happen again." Josh gripped the steering wheel. "I think we need to meet with Gavin, but make sure we don't let our guard down. Are you okay with that?"

She nodded. "Yeah . . . I agree."

But she hadn't missed the concern in Josh's voice. What had happened with Patrick might have shaken her, but it had clearly shaken Josh as well. In agreeing to help her figure out what was going on, he'd also taken on the role of protector, one she could tell he took extremely seriously.

"That said, I tend to believe Gavin." Josh made a left turn and headed toward Walmart. "He doesn't trust those men. He proved that when we were at Helen's house. He could have told them we were there. Could have given them Helen's notes, instead of giving them to us."

"You're right, I'm probably just being paranoid, the same way Gavin is feeling."

She stared out the window, still feeling distracted and on edge despite his reassurances. It felt like all the things she'd been certain about in life had suddenly come crashing down around her and had left her questioning everything. People's loyalties. The truth . . .

Fifteen minutes later, Josh pulled into the parking lot and found an empty spot on the far left side. She glanced out across the lot. Even at this time of night, the place was busy with shoppers and a few loiterers. She watched Josh check out a couple high school kids, then apparently decide they weren't a threat.

Caitlyn studied their surroundings as well, while trying to shake off her dark thoughts. A mom was heading toward her car with a couple of toddlers and a cart. A minivan pulled into an empty parking space a few spaces down from them. On the surface it seemed like another busy night with a parking lot full of shoppers. But that didn't mean they hadn't somehow been followed.

She could sense Josh's pinpointed awareness of what was going on around them. Jaw tense, fists clenched in his lap as he studied the scene. Coming to him had been the right thing. She was impressed with both his insight and his focus, despite his personal connection to the case.

She glanced at the time on the dash. "He's late."

"He'll be here."

Josh was right. Thirty seconds later, Gavin's black pickup pulled in three spots down from them. He got out and headed toward their car—alone—then slipped into the back seat.

Gavin quickly shut the door, then scooted toward the middle, sounding out of breath. "Thanks for meeting me."

Apparently, he wasn't the only one with nerves on edge.

"Of course." She eyed his backpack. "What did you find?"

"I was going through a closet in my mom's house and found a box hidden in the back." He went straight to the reason for his visit and pulled a thick file folder out of his backpack. "This was inside, pages of lab reports from over the past year. I've skimmed through it, but to be honest, I don't understand most of it. That's why I wanted to bring it to you. There are handwritten notes all through it, and that's what got my attention. Because while I don't understand most of it, like I said, what I did get out of it is that something was going on at the lab. Something questionable, and from what I can tell, possibly illegal. Whatever it was made my mother start asking questions."

Caitlyn felt a shiver sweep through her. Something that had got her murdered.

She took the pile of notes from him and skimmed through them. The lab reports themselves were nothing out of the ordinary. They were something they all worked with on a daily basis—detailed notes on trials, results, methods, and conclusions. What stood out was Helen's handwritten notes in the margins that were punctuated with exclamation and question marks.

"I started highlighting things that stood out," Gavin said. "You can see the notes in the margins where she calls into question techniques being used in the lab."

Caitlyn flipped through a few more pages, stopping to read the comments. "It's going to take me some time to go through them, but from what I'm seeing so far, I would agree. She definitely had concerns about this project."

Gavin's fingers gripped the seat back. "Ever since you stopped by, I've been plagued with my own questions. I know there are people who commit suicide and leave family and friends behind grieving over how it could have ever happened. But my mother . . . I just can't believe she'd do that." He drew in a shaky breath. "But to be honest, what almost terrifies me more is the thought that someone else took her life. Why would anyone want to do that?"

"That's what we're going to figure out," Caitlyn said. "And what you just gave us is going to help find out the truth."

Gavin glanced out toward the parking lot. "So what do I do if those men come back again? I've already lost my mother. I can't let something happen to my wife and boys as well."

"Can you leave town for a few days?" Josh asked.

"I can send Anna and the boys back east to her mom's. My father-in-law's not doing well. She'd be happy to go and wouldn't question my sending her there."

"What about you?" Caitlyn asked.

"I don't see how I can leave town. I've got too much to take care of in connection to my mother's death, but as long as my family's safe—"

"And as long as you're not asking questions," Josh said. "You need to keep quiet about this, and your wife as well, if she has any idea what's going on."

A ripple of guilt shot through Caitlyn. "I spoke to Anna briefly at the funeral. I said some things . . . asked her if she really thought Helen had committed suicide. It was insensitive, I know, but I also know your mother and couldn't imagine her taking her life. I was just . . . desperate for answers."

"Don't worry about it." Gavin shook his head. "Like I've already said, we're all struggling over my mom's death and the fact that suicide seemed impossible to believe. I know Anna and I have talked about the very same things, and now it looks like we were right. That's why I decided to come to you."

"I really am sorry," Caitlyn said. "I still can't believe she's gone, but I know this has been even harder on your family."

"What about the police?" Gavin asked. "What's their involvement in all of this at this point?"

"Our plan is to pull this evidence together, then go talk to my captain," Josh said.

*And hope he listens.*

Gavin nodded. "I need to go. I told Anna I was running out to fill up the car, so I can't be gone that long. Just promise me one thing. Please. Please find out who killed my mother."

Caitlyn leaned back against the headrest and let out a deep breath as Gavin headed back to his car. It would take time to go through all of Helen's notes, but what she'd discovered so far was enough to support her theory that she'd discovered something shady, if not illegal, that was going on in the lab. Now they needed to figure out exactly what that was.

"What are you thinking?" Josh asked.

"I think Gavin might be right."

"Have you figured out her notes?"

"I'm starting to. She seems to have been concerned about a virulent virus."

"Meaning?"

"Most vaccines we work with utilize viruses to transport genes into the body." She looked up from the open file. "Most of the time when changes in the genetic makeup are made, the viruses become less virulent, so they're not an issue."

"But . . ."

"The odds are small, but there's always the potential that a virus could become lethal or be harder to immunize against, which is the exact opposite of the result we want. It looks like that could be what happened here."

Josh leaned forward. "So what would be your normal response to something like that?"

"We would go in a different direction."

"But in this case, they didn't."

She shook her head. "It looks like whoever is behind this decided to continue testing."

"So how does that discovery end up leading to murder?"

Caitlyn pressed her lips together, trying to formulate her words. She didn't want to jump to conclusions, but clearly something had gone horribly wrong in this project. And now someone was trying to cover up the evidence.

"I'm not saying at this point that this is what's happening, but in a worst-case scenario, it would be possible, for example, to create a vaccine that attacks cells containing a genetic flag for a specific disease."

"Meaning?"

Caitlyn hesitated. "You would have the building blocks that could—potentially—create a weapon."

"Wait a minute." Josh caught her gaze. "So they're working on a vaccine and in the process, things go wrong, and they discover that they've created a . . . a—"

"A virulent strain. It's one of several possibilities of what could happen."

"And then someone takes that strain with the intent of weaponizing it?"

"It wouldn't be an easy process, but in this case, if someone was able to genetically manipulate that strain so the body's immune system didn't recognize a hostile virus, the results could be devastating."

"Okay." Josh let out a low whistle. "How much would something like this be worth?"

"I'm guessing millions."

"So if you're right, we're talking about a biological weapon?"

She nodded. "It's possible. I remember reading about a case where researchers in Australia accidently produced a killer virus—a modified mousepox that was related to smallpox. Their virus didn't affect humans, but it's the same technology that could be used in biowarfare. Our lab does research for new vaccines. Ninety-nine times out of a hundred, the process makes the virus weaker, which is what we're aiming for. But if you have one that actually makes the virus more virulent, and that virus gets into the wrong hands, the results could be devastating."

"So, what if this really is about biological warfare? What if they created a virus that has the potential of killing thousands?"

Her stomach roiled at the thought. "Then it would be very

possible that Olivia and the others were killed for what they found out."

Silence filled the car as they both sat lost in their thoughts. Mishandling scientific research and unethical conduct wasn't a new issue in her field, but murder . . . how had someone let it go there?

"We need to know who's behind this," Josh said, breaking the silence between them. "That's still the biggest question. But how would something like that work?"

She let out a sharp breath of air. "They'd have had to manipulate the virus so it evolved to the point it could escape detection in the body. Plus, they would have had to find a buyer, which wouldn't be easy."

*What did you get involved in, Helen?*

Caitlyn started flipping through the pages again. "Let's assume Olivia starts asking questions. She digs around and discovers something's off on the project she's working on."

"Who does she go to?"

"I'd assume she'd go to Dr. Kaiser first. And if he doesn't know anything, she'd go higher up. And in the process, someone found out she was asking questions. Wait a minute . . . Here's something interesting."

"What's that?"

"Helen scribbled a meeting with Dr. Abbott." She checked the date. "This was just a few days before he died."

"You said you asked his wife if she'd heard about the project?"

"Yes, but she said she hadn't." Caitlyn nodded her head. "But the three of them worked together, so it would make sense that he was involved in this as well."

"And his death?"

A chill ran down her spine as she caught Josh's gaze. "Just like Olivia's and Helen's deaths were staged, I don't think he died of a heart attack."

# 14

At ten o'clock the next morning Josh drove into the entrance of a parking garage in downtown Houston that was located a couple blocks from the bank where Melanie Abbott worked. Caitlyn had called her this morning, asking if they could meet with her, and thankfully the woman had agreed.

Two minutes later, he pulled into an empty parking space, then quickly swallowed the last of his espresso, hoping the extra shot of caffeine would keep him going today. He'd had a restless night in the new motel he'd insisted Caitlyn switch to and could have used another couple hours of sleep. At least staying in the room next to her had allowed him to keep an eye on her.

"I hate parking garages," Caitlyn said as she climbed out of the passenger seat.

"And why is that?"

Her boots clicked against the cement as they headed toward the street. "For starters, they usually leave me lost and driving in circles."

"So you're one of those directionally challenged individuals?"

"Why does that sound so . . . politically correct and yet so wrong?" She let out a low laugh as she stepped in beside him. "I'd like to say the only place I get lost is driving around parking

121

garages, but I'm afraid the problem goes a bit deeper. It's more of a left versus right challenge."

"Ah . . . Remind me not to let you give me directions the next time we go somewhere."

"Funny." She flinched as someone's car alarm went off a few cars down, the obnoxious sound echoing inside the garage. "And, of course, there's the fact that I always feel like I'm being stalked."

He nudged her with his shoulder. "Well, today you have your own personal bodyguard, so there's no need to worry."

She shot him a smile, but he knew not worrying wasn't going to come easy. For either of them.

Inside the bank lobby, they headed for the receptionist's desk where Mrs. Abbott had told them to go. He took in the large lobby, with its shiny tiled floor, dark wood furniture, and a row of tellers along the back wall, conscious as always of what was going on around him. Especially today. There were eight customers, including a young couple standing at the counter talking to one of the tellers and a businessman in a leather jacket filling out something.

"We have an appointment to see Melanie Abbott," Caitlyn said to the receptionist. "My name is Caitlyn Lindsey."

"Of course." The woman glanced down at her computer. "She's expecting you now. I'll give her a call, and she'll meet you near the row of offices to the left."

Josh pressed his hand against her elbow as they started walking. "Just in case you get lost."

"Very funny."

"I thought so."

Mrs. Abbott was younger than he'd expected, though he wasn't sure why he'd pegged her as middle aged. She looked to be in her late forties, but there was a tiredness in her eyes as if she hadn't been sleeping well. He understood all too well the feeling.

"Caitlyn, it's good to see you again." She shook Caitlyn's hand, then turned to him. "You must be Josh Solomon."

"I am. Thank you so much for agreeing to see us, Mrs. Abbott."

"Please . . . call me Melanie. I'm sure we met before at one of MedTECH's Christmas parties. Olivia was such a sweet woman. I couldn't believe it when I heard she'd died. I'm so sorry for your loss."

"Thank you. And I'm sorry about your husband's passing as well."

"I appreciate that." Melanie motioned toward the hallway behind them. "I thought we could go back and speak in my office. It will be more private there."

"Of course," Caitlyn said.

They followed her down the row of offices, each with a glass door and a nameplate next to it. "I've learned you never know what life is going to throw at you."

"Unfortunately, that's true," he said.

She waited for them to go into the last office ahead of her, then shut the door behind her. "I should have asked if you'd like some coffee. It's not the greatest, but it's hot and someone brought Danishes this morning."

Caitlyn waved off the offer. "I'm fine."

"Me too. Thanks."

The office was neat, but sparsely furnished with a desk, chairs, and a bookshelf, along with a few well-chosen pieces of art on the wall.

Josh stopped in front of a row of three black-and-white photos. "These are fascinating pictures."

"Walter and I both had a thing for architecture. We loved visiting old buildings and churches. He bought me these photographs for our anniversary a couple years ago. These three were all taken right here in Houston over a century ago. City Hall . . . the Rice Hotel . . . and the Harris County Courthouse."

"What a wonderful piece of history," Caitlyn said.

"I've always loved them." Melanie motioned for them to sit

123

down, then scooted in behind her desk. "I have to say I was surprised you called again, Caitlyn, though to be honest, I'm glad you did."

Caitlyn's brow rose slightly. "I hope I didn't upset you."

"When you called the first time, I was . . . rattled. But not because of what you said." She picked up a small orange cube off her desk and started rolling it between her fingers. "I've just found it so hard to focus after Walter's death."

"I've had to deal with the same thing," Josh said.

"Does it get any easier?" she asked. "Because quite frankly, even after three months, I'm at a loss. I come to work because it gives me something to do, but beyond that . . . I usually end up going home and crying over a frozen dinner."

Josh hesitated at his response. Putting his emotions to words had never been his strong suit. "I'm not sure it gets easier as much as the grief gets more familiar. You learn to let those feelings be a part of your day-to-day life instead of them ruling your emotions."

"That makes sense." Melanie shrugged. "At least I have my job. I've worked in this business for almost twenty-five years. Walter and I never had children, but I always loved my job and most of the time it was enough. I guess I'm still searching for a new normal."

"I have to confess that even a year later, I'm doing the same thing."

"But you're not here to listen to me complain." She shook her head. "Your questions about Walter, Caitlyn . . . let's just say they brought back some memories I'm trying every day to forget."

"I'm sorry—"

"It's fine. Really." Melanie dropped the cube back onto the desk. "I'm just going to come out and say what I can't stop thinking. You don't think his death was from natural causes, do you?"

Caitlyn cleared her throat. "There have been questions that have surfaced in connection to one of the projects he was working on. I'm just trying—we're trying—to find out the truth."

"About the project you mentioned? Starlighter?"

Caitlyn nodded.

Melanie moved to the window. "The project name isn't familiar, like I told you, but that doesn't surprise me. Walter didn't talk to me much about the specifics with his job." She turned around to face them. "But here's what I didn't tell you. Walter was upset about something the weeks leading up to his death, but he wouldn't tell me what was wrong. He'd became paranoid. He was always worried someone was following him. He added extra security to the house, and always had to double-check to make sure the doors and windows were locked. I've never seen him like that, and he wouldn't tell me what was going on. All he would ever tell me was not to worry."

"You said that was out of character for him?" Josh asked.

She leaned against the edge of the desk and nodded. "He was always fairly laid-back and wasn't one to spend a lot of time worrying. After he died, I tried to put it all behind me. And in the end, he was gone, so what did it matter. But when you spoke with me a couple days ago, it all came back. I decided to go through his office—something I've been putting off since his death."

"Did you find something?" Caitlyn asked.

"I did, but I have no idea what it means, other than the fact that before my husband died, he hired a private investigator." Melanie turned to Josh. "But you're not going to like what was in the photos."

"I'm sorry . . ." Josh leaned forward in his seat, not understanding. "What do you mean?"

Melanie blew out a sharp breath, then pulled a manila envelope out of the top drawer of her desk and handed it to Josh. "I found an envelope of surveillance photos, presumably taken by the private investigator Walter hired. There are photos of your wife in here."

Josh felt as if he'd been punched in the gut. "Wait a minute . . . my wife? Why would your husband have surveillance photos of Olivia?"

"I don't know. But there are two other sets of photos in there as well. Two men meeting at a café, and then other photos of one of those men with another woman. Your wife is the only one I recognized."

Josh's gut churned while he went through the photos one by one. The first half-dozen pictures were of Olivia sitting across the table from another man at a restaurant, talking intently about something. He kept flipping through the photos. There were several more of the two of them meeting. At a coffee shop . . . at a park . . .

"Do you know who she's with?" Josh handed one of the photos to Caitlyn.

He caught the hesitation in her voice before she answered.

"Jarred Carmichael."

J. C. The supervisor Helen had mentioned in her notes. The man who had been meeting with Olivia without Josh's prior knowledge.

He flipped through the rest of the photos, trying not to jump to any false conclusions about the photos of his wife with another man. "This man . . . this is the assistant district attorney. Nigel Hayward."

"There are photos of him talking with another man, and some with another woman." Melanie said. "Do you know either of them?"

"Not personally," Josh said.

"I wish I could tell you more," Melanie said, "but I can't. Because I have no idea why Walter would hire an investigator or why there are photos of your wife in there."

Josh didn't know either, but none of the reasons he could come up with were good. He turned the envelope over. "There's a phone number scrawled here."

"I tried calling it," Melanie said, "but never got ahold of anyone."

Josh pulled out his phone, then punched in the number on the back of the envelope.

After a minute, he shook his head. "No answer and no voice mail set up. I'll have my partner try to trace it and find out who it belonged to."

Melanie's fingers gripped the edge of the desk. "I heard some-one else from the lab died recently."

Caitlyn nodded. "Helen Fletcher."

"I've met her as well. Is her death related to all of this?"

"We believe so."

"And this Starlighter project? Is that the connection?"

"From everything we know, yes," Caitlyn said. "Did you find any-thing else in his office that might have been related to the project?"

"I didn't find anything connected to his work. Just the photos." Melanie brow furrowed. "Maybe this is a dumb question, but do you think my life's in danger? If he was murdered . . ."

"To be honest," Josh said, "it's possible. Have you noticed anyone following you? Anything out of the ordinary since Walter's death."

"No, but I've probably been too distracted to even notice." Melanie smoothed out her skirt. "But now that you mention it, there was something I almost forgot about until now. A few days before Walter died, someone broke into our house."

Josh sat forward in his chair. "Did you file a police report?"

"We did, but the only thing that was stolen was some of my jewelry, and oddly enough some of Walter's pain medicine he had left over from surgery on his shoulder."

"That's actually not surprising," Josh said. "The black market for prescription drugs is huge and thieves know that."

She picked up the orange cube again. "I have some vacation time saved. Maybe I should go visit my sister till all this blows over."

"I was going to suggest you do exactly that. Just until we have some more answers." While he didn't want to scare the woman, he also didn't want to water down the reality. "Can we ask you one more thing, Melanie?"

"Of course."

"I know this is personal, but what can you tell us about Walter's death? Was there anything that stood out at the time? Anything that seemed . . . off?"

"According to the report, my husband died of a heart attack, which I suppose didn't surprise anyone. He'd been taking heart medication for years."

"So there was no autopsy?" he asked.

"No."

"Had he been taking any other medicine?" Caitlyn asked.

"He had a handful of prescriptions to regulate his blood pressure and cholesterol. Plus he'd been taking antibiotics for bronchitis."

"Do you remember the name of the antibiotic?"

"I think it was . . . amoxicillin. I could check, though. Walter was at high risk for arrhythmia, so his doctor had to be careful about what drugs he prescribed."

"If you'd check, that would be great. And in the meantime . . ." Caitlyn looked at Josh before standing up. "Go to your sister's, and we'll be in touch."

"Of course. Because if there's even the slightest chance that you're right—and I can't believe I'm even saying this—and someone murdered Walter, I need to know the truth."

Caitlyn dropped the envelope of photos into her purse before they headed toward the door. "And that's what we're going to find out."

They walked in silence through the lobby until they stepped out into the cold and headed back toward the garage where they'd parked.

"What are you thinking?" she asked.

"I didn't want to say anything in front of Melanie, but the man in the photograph . . . the balding man that was with the assistant DA in some of those photos . . . he was in the bank lobby when we arrived."

"The bank lobby?" she asked. "Are you sure?"

"Positive. The balding man in the sports coat was in the east corner of the lobby when we walked in. The second one was filling out a form in the center of the room."

LISA HARRIS

"I noticed that he matches the description of the man who showed up at Gavin's house, but they couldn't have been following us then. Not if they were at the bank before us."

"I think you're right, but I believe they were following Melanie."

"Okay, then what if—like with Olivia—the break-in at the Abbotts' home wasn't just a random one."

He shoved his hands into his pockets. "I'm listening."

"Drug interaction is a complex issue all doctors have to deal with every day, because if you combine certain medications, the results can be devastating."

"Like heart medicine and antibiotics?" he asked.

"Exactly. Especially with someone at high risk for arrhythmia. There are certain antibiotics that they've linked to an increase in arrhythmia-related cardiovascular deaths."

"His doctor would have known that." His mind raced through the possibilities. "But you're not thinking the doctor made a mistake. You're thinking someone switched his antibiotic."

She nodded. "A break-in a couple days before he died seems way too convenient. They might have noticed the pain meds missing but probably wouldn't have thought to look for something being switched. I want to look something up quickly."

She ducked inside an alcove where they were out of the wind, then pulled out her phone, while he studied the mostly empty streets with just a few cars going by. Nothing stood out. Nothing seemed out of place. But neither could he let his guard down. Another piece of the puzzle was falling into place, and he didn't like the picture that was emerging.

"Look at this," she said a minute later. "Unless you were paying attention, this generic pill for amoxicillin looks very similar to a seven hundred and fifty milligram of another antibiotic that has a proven risk factor of disrupting the heart's electrical activity."

"Meaning murder was possible."

"Yes, though unfortunately, without an autopsy, I don't know if it could be proven. But is it possible? Definitely." They started walking again toward the parking garage. "I know that's not what you're thinking about right now. These photos don't prove they were having an affair, Josh. They look more like business meetings."

He wanted to forget the photos he'd just seen, but he knew Caitlyn was right. Olivia loved him, but she had been hiding something.

"It proves they were involved in something outside work and that there was something she needed to tell me," he said as they crossed the street. "Something she was trying to apologize to me for. Something she should have told me about. Why didn't she just tell me?"

She paused on the sidewalk and looked at him. "What do we do now?"

"Besides identifying the man in the pictures with the assistant DA, I could really eat a burger and fries."

"A burger?" Her eyes widened.

"You're probably starting to notice a trend here . . . I tend to eat when I'm stressed."

"And I'm the opposite. When I'm stressed, I can hardly look at food." Her arm brushed against his. "I'm sorry. This is scary for me, but I haven't forgotten how personal this is for you."

"Maybe this is what needed to happen. I've always suspected there was more to Olivia's death than what the DA presented in the trial. It's just that now I know my gut was right." He wanted to push away the emotions but knew that ignoring them wasn't going to make them disappear. "Maybe in the end, this is going to be the final closure I've been looking for, so I can move on with my life."

"So do you know of any good burger joints around here?" she asked as they approached the entrance to the garage.

"I do, actually. What do you know about Houston's underground tunnel system?"

"A tunnel system?" She shook her head. "I didn't know there was one."

"Then I think it's time you discovered one of Houston's best-kept secrets." He slowed down, then opened one of the glass doors and waited for her to slip inside. "The original tunnel was built sometime back in the early 1900s and was constructed to link two movie theaters. Throughout the following decades, as more buildings were put in above ground, they continued adding the tunnels below ground as well. There are over six miles of tunnels, linking dozens of office buildings and businesses. They're all climate-controlled, which is why they are so popular with employees working in the office towers and stores above ground, especially as an escape from the weather."

He steered her into the tunnel, glad he'd suggested this. They both needed a distraction from everything that was going on, and a historical tour combined with an early lunch sounded like the perfect combination as far as he was concerned. And the company wasn't bad either.

He glanced back as they turned onto another corridor and felt any feelings of a reprieve vanish.

"Caitlyn . . ." Josh's fingers squeezed her elbow. Two men, walking fast, were behind them, and this wasn't the first time he'd seen them. This wasn't just another coincidence.

She looked up at him. "What is it?"

"They found us. We're being followed."

# 15

*We're being followed?*

Caitlyn felt the hairs prickle on the back of her neck as she glanced behind them where a couple dozen people were rushing through the long, narrow tunnel like a bunch of worker ants.

"Which one?" she asked.

"There are two of them." He grabbed her hand, forcing her to pick up her pace. "One's in a sport coat and the other one—the same one that's in the photos we have now—is wearing a leather jacket."

She glanced back and quickly picked them out of the crowd. She hadn't been surprised at his precision recall, but she was impressed.

"We need to find out not only who they are, but what they're after," he said.

Her fingers tightened around her purse strap. "Do you think they're after the photos?"

"The photos . . . Helen's notes . . . more than likely both."

She looked up at him, catching his dark expression, and realized not for the first time how personal this was for him. She wished she could do something to fix the situation. Wished just as much that she could fix his heart. She'd heard the hurt in his voice when he'd looked at the surveillance photos of his wife. She knew what betrayal felt like. Knew what it felt like to lose someone you loved. And she hated being the one who had stirred up the hornet's nest.

Right now, though, wasn't the time to think about that. The dots were starting to connect, and she didn't like the picture that was beginning to emerge. Helen found out something and started asking questions. Questions that had gotten her murdered. Just like Olivia and Dr. Abbott. And if they weren't careful . . .

"They broke in and tried to take your case file notes," she said as they passed a barbershop with an older man in a suit and tie getting his hair cut. "They were clearly looking for what Helen might have known or left behind, and now they've targeted Dr. Abbott's wife in order to find out what she might know."

"Exactly."

They were circling in, ready to take down any loose ends.

"What are we supposed to do?" she asked.

"I've got my Glock, but no doubt they're armed too, which means confronting them will be a risk. Especially with people around."

"You know how I said I hated parking garages . . . Now I think I'll add tunnels to that as well."

They kept hurrying through the long maze of corridors, until most of the people who'd been behind them had ducked into a couple elevators, which left the hallway quiet except for the sound of footsteps behind them.

She glanced at a color-coded map of the sprawling underground labyrinth on the wall. The tunnels—reminding her of an airport with its overhead lights and shops—enabled people to commute to work, but how were they supposed to evade someone with deadly intentions?

"What are you thinking?" she asked.

"That I'm not going to get my burger after all, though I know that's not what you were asking." His hand tightened around her fingers. "To be honest, I've lost my appetite."

"Any ideas then?"

"I want to know who they are, but if we're going to have a confrontation, it needs to be on our terms. We need as many witnesses as possible, but I also don't want to risk anyone else's life. The last thing we want right now is an active shooter situation."

She knew he was right, but a confrontation terrified her. Whoever was following them was armed and involved in a situation where the stakes were big enough that people had lost their lives.

They hurried past a group of tourists who'd decided to book a walking tour and explore Houston's underground.

"Are they still back there?" she asked.

"Fifty . . . maybe seventy-five feet."

"So what do we do?"

"Sometimes the best way is the most direct way."

They rounded another bend in the tunnel. There was a food court ahead of them with tables and chairs set out for the growing lunch crowd.

"I'm going to talk with them."

"Okay . . . What can I do?"

"Do you have your phone with you?"

"Yes." She pulled it out of her purse.

"We're going to need photos of the men, so Quinton can try and identify them."

"I can do that."

"But I want you out of the way." He slowed his steps. "There's a shop ahead of us with glass walls and quite a few customers. Take the photos from inside, but if anything goes wrong, I want you to call 911, find the nearest exit, and get out of here."

"I'm not going to leave you—"

He looked down at her. "Promise me, Caitlyn."

She hesitated, then nodded, knowing he wasn't going to argue with her. "I will, but you need to be careful too. Please."

"I will."

A moment later, she slipped inside a shop filled with knick-knacks and home décor and picked a spot near the entrance, partially hidden by a display. One that kept her out of sight and yet gave her a good angle to zoom in on the men's faces.

Josh turned around and started walking toward them. She waited for the camera to come into focus, then snapped a string of photos. By the looks on the men's faces, it was clear they'd been taken aback by Josh's approach. The location he'd chosen meant the men following them couldn't do anything without causing a scene, and while she had no idea what their agenda was, her gut told her that was the last thing they wanted.

She snapped a couple more photos, hoping they would be sharp enough for Quinton to be able to identify them. She took a step back as one of the men looked beyond Josh to where she stood. She snapped another photo, unsure if he'd discovered where she was. A blur of people passed between her and the men. She shifted her gaze away from the phone. The group of tourists they'd passed in the tunnel earlier had arrived, laughing and joking loudly as they scouted out the different places to eat.

She scanned the growing crowd, panicked when she realized she'd lost Josh and the other two men. Where were they?

She shoved her phone into her back pocket and rushed out of the shop. Her anxiety mushroomed. There were two armed men tracking them down, who'd been involved with at least three deaths, and now she couldn't find them. She tried to stuff down her panic. They knew she was here. Might already know that she had the photos Melanie had given them . . .

Her fingers pressed tighter around the strap of her purse as she started turning in a slow half circle, searching for Josh. The noise of the lunch crowd surrounded her. Someone shouted out a lunch order. Her own heart pounded. She understood his need to keep his investigation quiet and they did have Quinton, but they shouldn't be doing this alone anymore. They had enough to convince the captain to reopen the case. They might not have all the answers, but they definitely had enough to link the three deaths at the lab and open up a new investigation.

She finally caught sight of Josh's suit jacket as he slipped out of the crowd and hurried toward her.

She let out a sharp sigh of relief at finding him. "Where are they?"

"They ducked into the crowd and I lost them. They clearly weren't looking for a confrontation."

Because they wanted what Melanie had given them. She was sure about that. But while the men might have forfeited this round, she also knew this wasn't over.

He gripped her elbow as they started walking. "We need to get out of here too."

"Agreed."

They started back toward the parking garage in silence, leaving the crowded section behind so only their footsteps echoed in the quiet hall. Josh's body language was both on edge and alert. And he wasn't alone. A sense of uneasiness had settled in her gut. An unnerving feeling that there was nowhere they would be safe. At least meeting with Melanie had been worth it. They now had both the photos from her as well as the surveillance photos Caitlyn had just taken with her phone.

"I have the closeup photos of their faces," she said.

"Good," he said as they exited the tunnels and hurried toward the car. "We'll send them to Quinton as soon as we get out of here and hope he can identify them."

The figure came at them out of nowhere, slamming into Caitlyn's side and knocking her onto the pavement. She reached for her purse, which had slid out of her hands, but it was too late. The attacker had already grabbed the bag and was running.

"Caitlyn—"

"I'm fine. Go."

Josh took off after the man, shouting for him to stop. A car squealed around the corner, and the man jumped into the passenger side of the car before slamming the door shut behind him. A second later they were gone.

"He grabbed my purse. He got the photos."

"Forget about it. None of that matters as long as you're safe."

A woman wearing a suit and tennis shoes ran up to them. "I saw what happened from a few cars down. Are you okay?"

Caitlyn nodded, trying to catch her breath. "I think so. Or at least I will be."

Once her heart stopped racing and her legs stopped shaking.

Josh helped her to her feet, then wrapped his arm around her waist to help walk her to the car. "You're sure you're not hurt?"

She shook her head. Her pants had torn at the knee when she'd fallen, and she was sure there was going to be a bruise there, but besides that, nothing else seemed to hurt.

"I got their license plate number and just called 911." The woman followed them to the car. "The cops should be here any minute now."

"We appreciate your help." Josh had her sit down on the edge of the passenger seat, then turned back to the woman. "Could I have that license plate number?"

"Of course . . . I just can't understand why someone would do that."

Josh grabbed a pen and pad from the car console, then wrote down the number. "Again, I appreciate everything you've done, but I'm going to go ahead and take her home now—"

"Don't you think you should stay until the police arrive?"

"The thieves are long gone. I'd rather just get her out of here."

Caitlyn leaned her head back against the seat and tried to slow down her breathing while Josh slid into the driver's seat and started up the engine. She looked over at Josh. "She wasn't going to give up, was she?"

"No she wasn't. Are you sure you're okay?"

"Just shaken." She grabbed her phone from her pocket, surprised it wasn't cracked. "At least we have my phone and the photos I took of those men, but we needed those pictures."

"I've got the PI's number on my phone. We should be able to get copies from him. What about your purse?"

"There wasn't anything of value in there except a little cash. I left my credit cards and driver's license back at the motel in the safe. Now I'm glad I did."

"Me too."

"Agreed."

"Josh . . ." She struggled to put into words what she was thinking. Not sure what his reaction would be. "I'm not sure what you're going to think about this."

"What is it?"

"I think we need to go to your captain. Surely we have enough to convince him to reopen the case."

"Actually, I think you're right."

"You do?" His answer caught her off guard, but also relieved her.

"Yes, though first I think we should go back to the motel and spend the rest of the day organizing what we have so far," he said. "That would give you more time to go through Helen's notes, and I want to track down the PI who took those photos of Olivia. We can see if we can get copies, and if Quinton can trace this license plate number."

"Okay."

"Oh, and there is one other thing," he said, flipping on his turn signal.

"What's that?"

"I never did get my burger and fries."

# 16

At half past seven the next morning, Josh pulled into the motel parking lot with a box of donuts and coffee, hoping the combination of sugar and caffeine would be enough to counteract the lack of sleep from last night. More than likely he wasn't the only one feeling sleep-deprived today. He and Caitlyn worked past midnight, trying to put the information they had into some kind of logical order before they took it to the captain.

He stepped out of the car as Quinton's gray Ford pulled in beside him.

"I was hoping you'd have coffee." Quinton met him on the sidewalk and held his hands out for the donuts. "From what you told me on the phone, it sounds as if Caitlyn Lindsey's getting under your skin."

Josh dismissed the comment with a frown. "I'm worried about her, but that's it. And the captain did tell me to get away for a while."

Quinton laughed as they headed for room 29. "Somehow I don't think working on a closed case in a sleazy motel on the outskirts of the city is what he had in mind."

"This isn't sleazy," Josh countered. "It's got . . . character."

"If you say so." Quinton stopped to face him. "But seriously, when I told you it might be worth finding out what she wanted, this wasn't what I was thinking of."

"Trust me, I never imagined I'd be relooking into Olivia's murder either. But so far we've been able to verify everything she came to me with."

"I've got a few of my own updates to share. Does Caitlyn know I'm coming?" Quinton asked before knocking on the door to her room.

"Yeah, she knows. Though don't be surprised if she seems a bit cautious. The last couple days have shaken her up quite a bit."

"Frankly, I don't blame her. I'd be spooked if I were her."

Caitlin answered the door wearing a pair of sweatpants and a T-shirt, with her hair mussed and a sleepy expression on her face.

"I didn't wake you up, did I?"

She shot him a smile as she ushered them in. "If that's a nice way of asking me if I just crawled out of bed, you'd be right."

She double-locked the door once they were inside, then turned to Quinton.

"It's nice to meet you, Detective."

"You both had a long night, I heard," Quinton said, shaking her hand.

"And even after Josh left, I struggled to go to sleep."

"Looks like you've been doing more work," Josh said, glancing at their board covered with sticky notes, photos, and a timeline.

"I kept working through Helen's journal and notes. There's a lot to go through."

"I have a feeling you're going to need this." Josh handed her one of the coffees. "Did you sleep at all?"

"I feel like I heard every creak of this old motel, but I also had some pretty vivid dreams, so I know I slept some."

Just not enough probably. Or at least that was how he was feeling.

Josh grabbed a maple donut from the box, then pulled the chair from the desk. "Hungry?"

"Not really, though I can definitely use the caffeine. Thank you."

Quinton stopped in front of their board. "For someone who's supposed to be on vacation, you've been busy."

"True, but there's a lot to go through here," Josh said.

Quinton turned back to them. "Were you able to confirm that the men who attacked you in the parking garage yesterday were the same men that showed up at Helen's house?"

"We were. We sent a couple of the photos we sent you from the tunnels to Helen's son, and he confirmed they were the same men who came to his house claiming to be from the lab."

"I've got a couple things for you, though you're not going to like some of what I found out."

Josh shrugged. "I haven't liked anything about the past thirty-six hours. What have you got?"

"For starters, it looks like the car in the parking garage driven by the guys who followed you was stolen. And in fact, I almost didn't catch it because it was a cloned vehicle."

Caitlyn shook her head. "What does that mean?"

"It's a common practice by organized theft rings where they use the VIN number of a legally registered car in order to cover up a theft," Josh said. "It makes it easier for the car thieves to sell stolen vehicles and get away with it."

"Almost like stealing the car's identity?"

"Exactly," Quinton said. "Which means, so far I haven't been able to identify who was in it, though I have widened my search to include security cameras. On the positive side, I was able to trace that number you gave me from the envelope the photos were in."

"And . . . ?" Josh asked.

"The number belonged to a Samuel Johnston." Quinton grabbed a donut and sat down. "I spoke to him briefly on the phone. He's a private detective here in Houston who works mainly on divorce

cases but also does a lot of surveillance and tracking down missing people."

"What did he say?"

"He told me that Dr. Abbott hired him. He was paid to follow
two men, Jarred Carmichael from the lab and the assistant DA,
Nigel Hayward. Then a couple weeks before he died, the doctor
sent him a check and told him he didn't need his services anymore.
Johnston never tried to ID the man with the assistant DA."

"That's strange."

"Agreed."

"Did you tell him that the photos were stolen?" Josh asked.

"I did, and he sent me copies I can email you, but so far I haven't
been able to ID the man."

"I hope you warned him to watch his back," Caitlyn said. "They
have his number now as well."

"He knows that, but we all need to watch our backs." Quinton
took a sip of his coffee. "Because there is something else. There's
definitely something going on at the precinct."

Josh frowned, not sure he was ready for another bombshell.
"What do you mean?"

His partner shook his head. "I was called in by a couple detectives to answer some questions, then told that I needed to keep our
conversation to myself or there could be consequences."

Josh reached up and rubbed the back of his neck, feeling the
beginnings of a tension headache coming on. "What did they want
to know?"

"Lots of personal things about you and Olivia and how you
got along."

Josh set his coffee down on the desk behind him, his stomach
knotting as he struggled to digest what Quinton was telling him.

He rubbed the back of his neck again. "If I stay here and try
to run my own investigation—especially against the captain's
orders—we both could lose our jobs, Quinton. I need to go in and

try to set the record straight. Answer whatever questions they're asking. They're going to call me in anyway, and now that we have proof that Beckmann's alibi was good, we have the evidence we need, even if it's just circumstantial, to look somewhere else for her killer. At least it's enough to show them—"

"I still don't think that would be wise."

Josh stopped in front of Quinton. "Why not?"

"Because we don't even know who's behind this. Just give me another forty-eight hours until I can figure out who's pushing this agenda. And in the meantime, my advice is for you to lay low. Act like you really are on vacation. You could use one."

Josh sat back down, his frustration mounting. What he could use was answers. "Do you think you can find out more without getting yourself caught up in this?"

"That's my plan. The truth will come out, Josh."

"And in the meantime?" Josh walked back across the worn carpet toward the window, his restlessness winning out. "Because no matter how discreet we try to be, we can't get information without asking questions."

"There are a few more things we can do from here," Caitlyn said. "I still need to finish going through Helen's notebooks and the lab reports we got from Gavin. We also need to ID both the men who followed us in the tunnels and the surveillance photos from the private investigator. If they don't have records, we could try a google image search and see if something pops up."

"Agreed," Quinton said. "But you both need to keep your heads down, because someone's out there pulling the strings, and until I find out who it is, we have to be careful."

"What about you?" Josh asked, facing his partner. "If they find out you're helping me—"

"Don't worry. I'm being careful."

Josh hesitated. Careful might not be enough. Quinton had a wife and two daughters. He wasn't going to risk his partner's life.

They needed someone on the outside who could help them. Someone who couldn't be connected to him. And someone who had access to what they might need.

A name surfaced that might work. Josh grabbed a second donut, wondering if he was making a mistake. But there weren't a lot of options open at this point.

"You keep up with what's going on at the precinct," he said, "but I have someone who might be able to help with some of the legwork."

"Are you sure we want someone else involved?" Caitlyn asked.

"There are questions Quinton can't ask without drawing attention to himself. I have an old friend who worked as one of my informants. His name's Eddie Macklin. He has connections and is the kind of person that if you need information, he can get it for you. I never gave up his name in all my years of working on the force, so no one should be able to connect him to me."

"So he's safe," Caitlyn said.

Josh nodded. As safe as anyone could be in a situation like this.

"And you think he'd agree to help us?" she asked.

"I think it's worth contacting him and finding out."

"What could he do?"

"He could ID the man in these photos, for starters."

Quinton shook his head. "I don't know if I like that idea. If we bring someone else in, we risk things going south."

"And if we do nothing? What happens then?" Josh asked.

"I can do the legwork."

Josh shook his head. "You shouldn't be digging into this. The captain needs to see you following protocol."

"What about your job?" Quinton asked Caitlyn. "What's going to happen if you don't show up? Will that raise any red flags?"

"I called my supervisor after the wreck. Asked him if I could take off a few days to recover."

"And he agreed?"

"I sent him a photo of the car. He couldn't exactly argue with me."

"Good. At least you don't have that to worry about."

She took a sip of her coffee. "But I have been wondering if I need to go back to the lab."

"What do you mean?" Josh asked.

"Whatever's going on happened there."

"Maybe, but I'm not sure that's where you need to be right now."

"There's got to be a computer trail," she said. "Helen's lab reports are telling, but there are still a few blanks I'm working to fill in before I have the complete picture of what was going on."

"And if whoever's behind this discovers what you're doing?"

Caitlyn looked up and caught his gaze. "If we're going to discover what's really going on, it's a risk we're going to have to take."

# 17

The front windows of Eddie Macklin's pawn shop on Fifth Avenue reminded Caitlyn of the place her father used to take her when he'd run out of money after drinking too much before payday. He'd grab a piece of her mother's jewelry or something else he thought might sell and try to convince whoever was behind the counter that it was actually worth something. Usually all he got from the venture was enough to keep him drunk another night or two. On the days he wasn't drunk and was feeling generous, he'd let her buy a soda from the vending machine that sat next to the cluttered cash register. His good mood never lasted, but sometimes she'd forget for just a moment that he hit her mother when he got mad. For that moment she was just a girl happy to have her father's approval.

But those days had been few and far between.

Josh paused before getting out of the car. "You okay?"

She brushed the memory away. "Just nervous. Are you sure you trust this guy?"

"I do. He's a good guy. He served in the Marines for almost a decade, until he was injured. Then he set up his own security firm. He's got connections all over, is IT savvy, and if he doesn't know someone, he knows someone who knows someone. He's always come through for me in the past. And he's got the resources we need right now."

"How much is this going to cost?"

"Don't worry about that. He owes me." He reached out and squeezed her hand. "We're going to figure this out. I promise."

She frowned, because not worrying didn't really seem like an option at the moment. She got out of the car and prayed he was right.

A bell jangled as they walked inside. The place was as cluttered as the window, with case after case of weapons and ammunitions, knives, jewelry, and electronics, surrounded by piles of sports equipment. A customer was talking to an employee in his early twenties at one of the counters.

Caitlyn took it all in. "If I ever decide to arm myself, I'll know where to come."

Josh started walking toward a man who came from the back of the store. "Eddie."

"Josh Solomon?"

Eddie looked exactly like what she'd imagined after Josh's brief description. Clearly ex-military, by the way he carried himself, along with his short haircut, tattoos, and hardened physique. Definitely not someone she'd want to meet in a dark alley, but someone she hoped would be able to give them the contacts they needed.

Eddie gave Josh a bear hug. She hadn't expected that either.

"Well, I have to say, you're the last person I imagined walking into my shop today. It's been a long time. Probably since your wife's death." The man's smile faded. "How are you?"

"It's been a rough year."

"I'm really sorry she's gone."

"Me too."

Eddie glanced around the store. "I suppose you're not looking for a good deal on a used stereo system or smartphone?"

Josh laughed. "Actually, I was wondering if we could talk about something in private."

"Of course. Andrew . . ." He signaled to his employee. "I'll be back in a few minutes."

"No problem, boss."

They followed Eddie through a door in the back, then waited while he shut the door behind them. The room was set up like a small apartment. There was a tiny kitchen with a fridge, hot plate, and microwave on one side, a couch and flat-screen TV on the other, and a desk piled with receipts and office work.

Eddie shoved a pile of clothes off the couch and into a laundry basket. "Sorry about the mess. I've been sleeping here the last few nights, working late on inventory."

"How is Jeanette?" Josh asked.

"Jeanette's doing great, but her mother's in town, and while I love my wife . . ." He let out a low chuckle.

"You prefer working on your inventory," Josh said.

"Exactly. It's good to see you, Solomon." He glanced at Caitlyn. "And I'm being rude. Who's this?"

"Caitlyn Lindsey," Josh said. "She worked with Olivia."

"It's nice to meet you, despite the difficult circumstances. Why don't you both sit down and tell me what's going on."

She sat on the edge of the cracked leather couch next to Josh, then pulled a pair of socks from under her and tossed them into the basket. At least they looked clean.

"Sorry. Can I get you a drink?" Eddie asked. "I've probably got a couple of Cokes in my fridge."

"I'm fine. Thanks," she said.

"Me too. Listen." Josh leaned forward. "You've got a shop to run, so I'll get right to the point. We need your help."

Eddie sat down on the coffee table in front of them. "And you know I'm always happy to serve my local police force."

"This time the situation is both sensitive and . . . personal. I'm going to have to lay low for a while, but I also need some answers."

"You're in trouble?"

Josh glanced at Caitlyn. "In a manner of speaking, yes."

"You came to the right place. So what are you looking at? If you need to disappear—"

"We're not there yet. For now, we just need information."

"Okay." Eddie pressed his hands against his thighs. "You know me. I have my sources, and I can be discreet with whatever it is you need."

Josh hesitated. "Olivia's death is involved in this. The two men who were arrested for her murder . . . I don't believe they killed her."

Eddie let out a low whistle. "Okay . . . that is personal."

"It is, but there's more. Two of her coworkers are dead, all within the last few months."

"And you think there's a connection?"

Josh nodded. "We know there's a connection."

Eddie turned to Caitlyn. "Do you have any idea what Olivia and the others were working on?"

Caitlyn nodded. "We have lab notes from a project called Starlighter that both Olivia and another coworker, Helen Fletcher, had concerns about. Helen died of an apparent suicide a few days ago, according to the ME."

"But I'm sensing you don't believe it was suicide."

The reminder stung. "Definitely not."

"I have to ask the obvious question, Solomon," Eddie said. "You're a cop. Why not just go to your boss with all this?"

"My partner wants me to hold off. We're both getting . . . resistance. We don't know who might be involved, if you get my drift."

"So you need to stay sidelined for now."

Josh nodded. "That's one way to put it."

"Then I'd say it's time we find some answers. What exactly do you need from me?"

"I'd like you to do a background check for a man who goes by the name of Jigsaw," Josh said. "We believe his first name is Shawn. We also need some surveillance photos identified." Josh nodded at Caitlyn, who handed Eddie the file they'd put together. "This is everything we have so far."

"Anything else you need from me?" Eddie asked.

"We also need to know everything you can come up with about MedTECH Laboratories," Josh said. "Its backers, and anything shady that might be going on there. But I can't have any of this traced back to either of us, and I need it yesterday."

"I'd forgotten you're such a demanding client." Eddie chuckled. "Anything else?"

"One last name." Josh flipped open the file. "Jarred Carmichael's a lab employee we believe is involved in whatever's going on there."

Eddie turned to Caitlyn. "What kind of access do you have to the lab?"

"I'm still an employee, with access to most departments and files. Why?"

"If you want to find out what's going on in that lab, their computer files seem like the logical place to start. All the test data and research should be in the system. It's very possible that the information is coded or hidden, but I'm guessing it's there. To find out exactly what they're working on, I'm going to need access to their mainframe. And to be honest, I'd prefer not hacking into their system or using any other illegal methods."

"I agree," Caitlyn said. "The only problem is that the lab has a state-of-the-art security system in place to ensure their intellectual property isn't stolen. I'm no IT expert, but we're talking firewalls, intrusion prevention systems, and web security procedures. It's all going to depend on how secure the information we need is, but if I can get evidence of what Helen wrote about, in addition to her notes, we'll have what we need to go to the authorities."

"What exactly is Starlighter?" Eddie asked.

"It's an experimental vaccine project they were working on. On the surface, everything about the reports appears normal, but there seem to be some discrepancies with the results."

"What exactly are you saying?" Eddie asked.

Caitlyn glanced at Josh, who nodded. "There's a chance that the virus in question could potentially be used as a weapon."

Eddie let out a low whistle. "Do you have any concrete proof?"

"I have Helen's notes that point to it, but that's why I need to get into the lab."

"I can run profiles on the names in question like you want, but from what I'm hearing from you right now, I have to agree. We're also going to need to get into those computers."

"How would I get the information?"

"You should be able to transfer the files onto an external drive."

"And how long will it take?" she asked.

"It depends on how big the files are and on the download speed of the connection. Hopefully, it will only take a few minutes. All you have to do is get into the building, go to a computer terminal, and download the files. We can sort through them later."

She let out a sharp breath of air. All without getting caught. Simple.

"What if they've erased the files?"

"From what I've heard from you so far, that's possible, but even if they have, there's still a good chance that they'd be recoverable. I can give you a flash drive with a file recovery program. It will run a self-contained search without leaving an electronic trail." He turned to Josh. "And in the meantime, I'll see what I can come up with on your suspects. Do you have a safe place to stay?"

Josh nodded. "We're checked into a motel about twenty minutes from here. No names, and they take cash."

"I'd suggest changing motels every couple days."

"We will."

"I'd also suggest you don't come back by the store." Eddie

crossed the room, then pulled something out of his desk. "Here are a couple of clean phones. My number's already programmed into the contacts. You can get ahold of me with them."

"Wow." Josh's brow rose. "You're prepared."

"You're not the first person to ask me for this kind of help. I try to be ready." Eddie turned to Caitlyn. "And there's something else you're going to need."

He pulled out a second item from his desk. "This is a wireless earpiece that will allow you to communicate with Josh while you're inside the lab."

"How does it work?" she asked.

"You can connect it to your mobile phone's Bluetooth. With you both wearing one, Josh will be able to hear your voice and what's going on around you. And you'll be able to hear him, and no one will have a clue." Eddie grabbed a flash drive from another drawer. "I'll show you quickly how to recover the files."

"I appreciate your help," Josh said.

"Forget it. What are friends for. And besides . . . I owe you."

A minute later, they headed for the car in silence, her mind distracted as she worked through the plan Eddie had laid out for her. And as she contemplated, not for the first time, the severity of the consequences if anything went wrong.

"I like him," Caitlyn said, as soon as they were both settled into the front seat of his car.

"Like I told you, he's a good guy."

"You never told me why he owes you."

"He got himself into some trouble a few years back. A client blamed him for a breach of security and tried to kill him."

"You saved his life?"

"Nothing official, but he ended up with a bullet in his leg and spent six weeks in the hospital."

He pulled back onto the street heading west through traffic.

"You okay?" she asked after a few minutes of silence.

"Just trying to work through all of this. I know we need to, but I'm not sure I like the idea of you going into the lab."

"I'll be fine. I promise."

"You sound like me now. Making promises you can't keep. Whoever's behind this is working in that lab. I think we can be sure of that. Which is calling it a bit too close." He took the ramp onto the freeway. "We need to come up with a solid plan. What time of day is best. The layout of the building. Contingency plans if something goes wrong. And anything else we can think of that will make sure nothing does go wrong."

"Okay." She started working through his questions. "I think the best time is late afternoon. There'll be fewer people for one, and Carmichael comes in early every day and is usually gone by three."

Josh turned off the freeway and made a right turn, the opposite direction of the motel.

"Where are we going?"

He pressed on the accelerator, then made a sharp left-hand turn. "We've got another tail."

# 18

Josh took another turn, then glanced in the rearview mirror. The other car made the same turn. They were keeping their distance, but they were definitely tailing them.

"You're sure they're following us?" Caitlyn asked.

Josh caught the panic in her voice. He couldn't blame her. It was a repeat of the tunnels all over again. This was no coincidence.

"The black sedan two cars back. They've been behind us for the past mile or two and have followed us on every turn."

Caitlyn studied her side-view mirror. "I see them, but how did they find us? It's definitely not the same car from the garage yesterday."

"No, it's not."

But if it wasn't them, then who?

"Do you think they knew we were at the pawn shop?" Caitlyn asked.

"I'm not sure exactly where they picked up our trail, but I don't think so. I was pretty thorough ensuring no one followed us there, or when we left." He glanced in his rearview mirror again. "I'm going to try and slow down. If we can get them to pass us, we might be able to get the license plate number to run."

He took his foot off the accelerator and dropped his speed five, then ten miles an hour. The cars between them passed until the sedan was only a couple car lengths behind them.

"They're slowing down as well, but I got it." She grabbed a pen from the console and wrote the number down.

"Good girl." Josh put in a call to his partner, who picked up on the second ring. "Quinton, we've got a tail. I need you to run a license plate for us."

Caitlyn read the plate number out loud.

"Give me a minute," Quinton said.

Josh kept his speed steady while they waited for the information. The other car had to know they'd been made but were making no moves to back off.

"Okay," Quinton said, coming back on the line. "I've got it, but you're not going to like this. Your tail is someone from the department."

"The department?" The answer startled him. He looked again into the rearview mirror, but the other car was still too far back for him to identify the driver and passenger. "Why would someone from the department be following us? If they have questions, they could just call and talk to me."

"I wish I knew, but I can't answer that."

Whatever was going on, he didn't like it, because he wasn't the only one involved in this. He had to think about Caitlyn's safety as well.

The black sedan flashed their police strobe lights and signaled for them to pull over.

"Quinton . . . I'm going to need to call you back."

He hung up the call and flipped on his blinker.

Caitlyn turned around again. "Do you think we should stop?"

"I'm not sure we have a choice, and on top of that, I want to know what they want."

Josh pulled into the parking lot of a strip mall and parked in an empty spot, trying to work through the next step. He'd never been one to be rash. Never one to jump to conclusions, but everything about this felt wrong. And his gut told him that there was going to be no walking away from this unscathed.

He brushed his hand across Caitlyn's arm. "I want you to stay in the car."

"Josh—"

"Please?"

She nodded as he pushed record on his phone, dropped it into his pocket, then slid out of the driver's seat.

He recognized the two detectives who got out. Mike Sanchez had a wife and two little girls and a reputation for making even the most hardened criminal confess. Brent Adams was a divorcé who spent more time working than Josh did, if that were possible. What they were doing out following him, he had no idea.

"Detectives . . ." Josh stopped in front of them. "When did you start patrolling the streets?"

"We were out following up a lead on a case and recognized your car," Adams said. "Wanted to see how you were doing."

"You could have called."

Sanchez shoved his hands into his pockets and caught Josh's gaze. "I guess you heard they reopened your wife's case. That has to be upsetting."

Josh fought to keep his reaction neutral, but the information hit him in the gut like a sucker punch. Two days ago, he'd sat in his boss's office, begging him to reopen his wife's murder. And now the captain had done it without even telling him.

"I'm sorry . . ." Adams glanced at his partner. "We assumed you knew."

"Captain Thomas must have come across some new information since I spoke to him last," Josh said.

"I'd assume the same thing, though we were just as surprised as you are." Adams shook his head. "All this time we've all believed that Olivia's murderers were safe behind bars."

"Do you know what they've found?" Josh asked. He wasn't going to pass up an opportunity to get information about what might be going on at the precinct.

"All we really know is that there have been rumors going around the precinct," Adams said. "Rumors that there were problems between you and your wife. Rumors that the captain is looking closer to home for a new suspect."

*Closer to home?*

Josh studied their expressions, trying to determine the motivation behind the conversation, but the implications weren't lost to him. "He thinks I was involved in her death."

Saying it out loud left a sick feeling in the pit of his stomach.

"It's a theory that's come up, though we find that hard to believe," Sanchez said. "And I know for you to have her case resurrected like this has to be disturbing."

The reality of Sanchez's answer sliced through him. While the man's spoken empathy seemed genuine, he had to be wrong. Why would the captain think he was involved? He was the one who'd come to him with new information. The one who had begged him to reopen the case. Why would he have done that if he was guilty?

"Who's the woman in the car with you?" Adams asked.

"Just a friend."

He kept his tone nonchalant. He wasn't ready to buy in to their concern over him and the situation, and on top of that, while he didn't have anything to hide, he had no intentions of getting Caitlyn involved any more than he had to.

Adams took a step backward. "Just . . . be careful."

A warning or a threat? At this point, he didn't know anymore.

He turned around and headed back to his car. The only advantage he had at the moment was that the people working inside this precinct knew him. And knew he always worked with integrity. That had to count for something. They'd known Olivia from

Fourth of July picnics and Christmas parties. They'd seen him interact with his wife. Had to know they'd had a solid marriage.

Or had they known? Every couple had secrets. Every person had secrets. Did they assume he had some of his own?

"What's going on?" she asked as soon as he'd slid back into the driver's seat.

"Let's just say they didn't stop us to wish us a good day. They were fishing for information. And I think they wanted to see my reaction. Olivia's case is being reopened."

"What?"

He shook his head. "That's all I really know. That and I'm pretty sure they're looking at me as a suspect."

"You can't be serious."

If only he wasn't.

"Why would they think you're involved?" Caitlyn caught his gaze. "It doesn't make sense. You're the one who went to the captain, asking him to reopen the case. Why would you do that if you'd killed her?"

"I don't know."

"Did they threaten you?"

"No."

"Then what did they want?"

"All I can come up with is that the same people who set up Beckmann have realized everything is about to fall through."

"So someone needs another scapegoat and is trying to pin this on you," she said.

His chest muscles tightened. "I think that's very possible, and the husband's always the number one suspect."

"But how can they prove something that never happened?"

"They managed to squelch a man's alibi in a murder trial. It wouldn't be that hard to plant evidence." Another thought shot to the surface. "What if they weren't breaking into my house to steal something—"

"But to plant information."

He heard the fear in her voice, but there was no use sugarcoating the situation. And at least he wasn't the only one thinking that.

"Can I ask you a question?" he asked.

"Of course."

"You're putting a lot on the line here." His jaw tensed. "Why do you seem so convinced I didn't kill Olivia?"

"Because just like I know Olivia loved you, I see that same love in your eyes that you had for her. There's just no way I could believe she was having an affair or that you murdered her."

He felt his muscles relax slightly at her answer. He hadn't realized how important it was to have her believe him. "You know that things are going to get far worse before they get better."

"I realize that."

"If they do put out a warrant for my arrest, and I turn myself in—if this is a setup—this isn't going to end well."

The panic refused to lessen. Who was he kidding. At least three people were already dead. This case would never make it to trial. Not if the goal was to eliminate him without any questions being asked. He'd be dead long before the trial.

"I was looking at running," she said. "At least until I had enough irrefutable proof."

He caught her gaze, surprised at her response. "Do you know what happens when the law goes after a fugitive?"

"Honestly, no, and I really don't think I want to find out."

"I hope you never have to. Because they'll be given a search warrant to get into your house, your computer, and your phone. Cyberanalysts will go over everything they find. They'll go through your online profiles, find out who your circle of trust is and who you'll contact, and learn everything they can about you. They'll go through your bank data, which means you can't withdraw a dime without them knowing what you're doing. And on top of that, they'll learn everything there is to know from your subscriber, so they can track your phone. Every police department across the country is going to have your photo, and every officer within a two-hundred-mile radius of this point will be on the lookout. There will be nowhere to run."

He was scaring her. He could see it in her eyes. But what if he couldn't save her. That's what scared him. He wasn't going to be responsible for something happening to her.

Not again.

"You feel guilty for Olivia's death, don't you?" she said. "Guilty over the fact you couldn't save her?"

He stopped short at her question and felt the familiar sense of guilt seep through him.

She lowered her head. "I'm sorry. I shouldn't have said that."

Silence hung like a heavy curtain between them. Familiar waves of panic engulfed him.

*I can't do this, God. Not this. Being accused of murdering my wife? How do I end this?*

The only thing left driving him now was his need to find out the truth, and his desire to keep Caitlyn safe.

"She was my wife," he finally said. "And I couldn't save her."

"Josh—"

"If I had been there that night, if I had communicated better with her, and found out what was going on with her and especially what was bothering her, none of this might have happened—"

"It's not your fault. It never was. And I don't think anything you did would have stopped this."

"But I'm a cop and I couldn't save my wife. Sounds pretty weak to me."

His phone rang again, and he glanced at the caller ID. It was Quinton.

"What's up?" Josh asked. "I was just about to call you."

"I just found out something you need to know. The captain made the decision to reopen your wife's murder investigation."

Josh let out a sharp breath. "I know."

"How?"

"I was pulled over by my tail, and they seemed pretty happy to give me the latest update."

"What exactly did they want?"

"Honestly, I'm not sure. Which is why I think I need to go in and talk to the captain," he said. "Make him listen to reason—"

"Not yet. I still want you to give me a little more time to find out what's going on from the inside. Besides, if they had anything on you at all, they would have already brought you in. Them letting you go proves they have nothing at this point."

"Maybe."

Josh hung up the phone a minute later, unable to shake the sudden paranoia that had taken hold of him. If he didn't know who to trust in the department, he had no idea who he could go to. He glanced at the clock on the dashboard, wondering what their next move should be. He could go home and search his house, but he was certain someone would be there watching. And if he did find something, they could in turn accuse him of hiding it. If this continued, they would find a way to bring him in. He was certain of that.

"If we can find out who we're up against, then we have a chance of stopping this." Caitlyn's voice broke into his thoughts. "If we put everything that we have together, they'll have to see the truth. But we need that information from the lab."

He had to admit she was right about one thing. The only way they were going to be able to put an end to this was to find out who was behind it.

"I know the layout of the building," she said, "and the schedules of most of the employees on that floor. If we go at the end of the day, there will be fewer people to deal with."

"Which will also make you more obvious." He shifted his thinking to her plan. "Any guards during the day?"

"A couple security guards and a receptionist. They won't think twice about me being there. Trust me."

He hesitated. He heard the wisdom in her words, and yet at the same time he was concerned about her involvement. So many things could go wrong. If they were caught, it would only add to the guilt he was carrying.

She reached out and squeezed his hand. "I don't expect you to tell me everything's going to be fine. But we need to do this."

"I know."

"You're sure?"

"Are you trying to talk me out of it now?"

She shot him a smile. "No."

He studied her face and caught the determination in her eyes. He'd never met anyone so focused and determined. And stubborn, for that matter. The woman had managed to wear him down with her insistence on doing this with him. He wasn't sure if he wanted to bawl her out . . . or kiss her.

Josh shoved away the second thought. A fresh wave of apprehension swept through him. Their main objective might be hunting down who was behind this, but keeping Caitlyn safe had suddenly become his priority.

# 19

Caitlyn worked to calm her nerves as Josh pulled into the parking lot of the MedTECH Laboratories the next afternoon. They'd worked on a plan, with her drawing up schematics of the lab, names of employees who worked on the floor, and where security required access badges in order to gain entry. Josh had been insistent they didn't just have a plan A but backup plans in case something went wrong.

"Second thoughts?" she asked as he turned off the engine.

"Second thoughts? I'm way beyond that. I think this is by far one of the riskiest things I've ever done. This is crazy, you know. Breaking in to your lab."

"I'm not breaking in. I work there."

"You know as well as I do that your boss wouldn't approve of what you're about to do. As much as we need to find those files, I'm more worried about your going in there by yourself and getting caught."

"It's the only way. Besides, they'd never let me bring a friend with me inside, let alone a police officer."

"I could come with you as a techie."

"With your snazzy sports jacket?" She looked at him and frowned.

Even paired with a button-down shirt and jeans, he looked too over-dressed for her workplace. And way too good-looking. She shoved back the random thought. "I don't think so."

"Caitlyn, I'm serious."

"Trust me, I'm taking this very seriously."

"Fine. You've got your earpiece in?"

"Everything's ready. I'm good to go."

He squeezed her hand. She hesitated, then pulled away from his touch. She shouldn't feel anything toward him. Just because he'd agreed to work with her didn't mean her heart had to respond. He wasn't looking for love, and for that matter, she wasn't either.

"Just promise me you'll be careful," he said. "Don't take any risks, and if for any reason you feel that your life is in danger, get out. I'll be here waiting."

"I know, and I'll be fine. Stop worrying."

She slipped out of the car, knowing that nothing she said was going to stop him from worrying. And if she were honest, she was just as nervous about their plan. She might have access to the lab as a part of her job, but what she was about to do definitely broke the rules. And if the people who'd run her off the road—the people who'd killed Olivia and Helen—were inside that building and caught her . . . What would they do if they found out she was not only in the lab but planned to download files they didn't want to get out?

Despite her concerns, her resolve hadn't wavered, and in turn she'd appreciated his input. He'd insisted on being familiar with exit points as well as the level of security. The only way into the section of the building where she worked was via access-card systems using an embedded RFID microchip that worked like an electronic key. For those working in increased levels of security, those labs included biometric access, but they wouldn't have to worry about that. Her other concern had been the security cameras. All lab entrances had security cameras and were monitored by security personnel.

They'd eaten an early dinner at a busy mom-and-pop restaurant famous for their hamburgers, where they'd managed a bit of small talk, and he'd convinced her to eat a few bites. On the drive over he'd said even less, making her wonder if he was apprehensive about her getting caught, or if he was mad at her for roping him in to all of this. Either way she couldn't help but wonder if he already regretted the decision.

She headed up the brick sidewalk toward the front of the four-story building. No. Nothing was going to go wrong. All she had to do was walk into the lab, go to her desk and download the files, and get out of the building.

If her downloading the files triggered some security protocol, it wouldn't take long for them to track down who was behind it. The lab she worked in didn't deal with hazardous materials, so security was minimal. But even with that thought in mind, she was going to have to get in and out as fast as possible, while having as little contact with other employees as possible.

"Caitlyn." Josh's voice came through her wireless earpiece.

"This might take a bit of getting used to. I feel like I have a voice in my head."

"Don't you normally?"

"Funny. What do you want? I'm not even through the front doors yet."

"Just testing out the system. Making sure it works."

She let out a low laugh, wondering what people were going to think if they caught her talking to herself. "It works. Relax. I'll be in and out before you know it."

"I'm counting on it."

She walked through the building's glass doors that led to a large lobby. Whoever had designed the space had veered away from the typical sterile feel of a laboratory. Instead, brick walls, tile floors, and a handful of comfy chairs with turquoise accents framed the receptionist's desk where Marjorie sat, directing calls and dealing with customer service.

Caitlyn waved at her, then headed straight toward the elevators, avoiding any chance of a conversation. This was no social visit. The fewer people who saw her and spoke to her, the better.

The elevator beeped and a second later the doors swooshed open. Caitlyn stepped inside and pushed the button for the third floor.

"I'm in the elevator."

Another employee hurried into the elevator right before the doors closed, but he had his eyes glued to his phone, not even acknowledging she was there. Maybe staying invisible was going to be easier than she thought.

On the third floor she headed down the narrow hallway toward the restricted access area. She stopped in front of the lab door and slid her card across the keypad. Nothing.

She swiped her card a second time, but once again, the light stayed red.

Caitlyn tried to ignore the wave of panic and let out a sharp huff of air. What if they'd shut down her access to the building? What if they somehow knew she was here? She tried to shove down the panic, but it only multiplied.

"What's going on, Caitlyn?" Josh asked.

"My card won't work."

"Has that ever happened before?"

She hesitated at her answer. "No."

"You need to leave. If they're on to you—"

"We don't know any of that. Not yet. Just give me a minute."

"Something wrong, Caitlyn?"

She jumped at the sound of her name. One of the security guards was heading down the hall toward her.

"Bruce . . . hey . . . I don't know. My card's not working."

She swiped it a third time. This couldn't be happening.

"I've never had issues before, but I can't open the door." She tried to keep her tone even, but her laugh sounded higher-pitched than normal. Bruce didn't seem to notice.

"Believe me, you're not the first. I've been bugging management to upgrade the system."

"That must be the problem." Caitlyn shrugged.

She was okay. Security would have been given a heads-up if they'd deactivated her card.

He stopped in front of her. "I heard you were out sick."

"I was, but I'm much better." She wiped her sweaty hands on her pants. "Just coming in for a little while today. You know how it is. I'm gone a day, and already the work is piling up."

"I can imagine," Bruce said.

"Caitlyn." Josh's voice came through her earpiece again. "Forget the file. You need to get out of there. If they've deactivated your pass, then they're looking for you."

She ignored Josh's warning and smiled at Bruce instead. "I'll try one more time, but you don't mind using your pass key to get me in if it doesn't work, do you? I can have IT fix mine later, but I really need to check on a few things."

"Sure. No problem."

"Caitlyn." Josh's warning voice came through again.

"Thanks. I really appreciate it."

She swiped again. The pad turned green and she was in.

She rested her hand against the open door. "Guess it was just a glitch after all. Thanks anyway."

"See you around."

She worked to steady her breathing as she walked down the narrow hallway toward her desk, praying she didn't run into anyone. All she needed to do was get in, make a copy of the files, and get out. She could do this.

Bruce would definitely remember she'd been here, but there

was no way to avoid it. She glanced at Helen's station. Her things had already been taken out, reminding her once again what was at stake. She'd been right about the time of day. The lab was fairly empty. The few employees there were working on different stages of research, depending on their specific job assignment. The lab itself felt much more sterile than the welcoming lobby. And unlike most office jobs, there were no private spaces.

She logged in with her username and password, then pushed enter.

Bingo.

"I'm in."

"Good girl. Don't stay a second longer than needed."

"Trust me, I won't."

She could feel her heart pounding in her throat as she typed in the search parameters like they'd gone over and waited for the results. Nothing. Maybe they had erased everything. She typed in another search, trying not to panic. If anyone found out what she was doing, not only would she be fired, she'd probably be arrested, but it was a little late to think about that now. Like the last time she'd searched, she wasn't finding what she needed.

"I'm not finding anything related to Starlighter," she said, trying to keep the frustration out of her voice.

"Go ahead and try the recovery program," Josh said.

She glanced at the clock on the wall, her pulse racing. It was 5:16, and she was already four minutes in. She needed to get this done and get out of here. She connected the flash drive to the side of the computer and waited for the program to pop up.

Ten seconds later she found it. A folder titled Starlighter. She clicked through prompts to start the recovery process, making sure the files were downloaded onto the external flash drive.

Seven minutes remaining.

She glanced around the lab. So far no one in the room seemed interested in what she was doing, but even that didn't help the knot in her stomach. She drummed her fingers against the desk, willing the files to hurry.

Two and a half minutes . . .

*Hurry . . . hurry . . . hurry . . .*

How had she gotten to this point? Stealing files from her employer? She pushed back the thoughts. There were times when breaking the rules was the right thing to do. Like when you had to find out the truth. Right?

"How much time?" Josh asked.

"Two minutes."

She knew he wouldn't relax until she was back out in the car with him. And neither would she.

"Caitlyn . . . hey . . . I hadn't expected to see you here." Patricia Cox was walking toward her. "I heard you were in a car accident."

Clearly, news spread fast.

"Yeah. I was, but I'm fine. Just a bit shaken up."

"That's so scary."

"It was." She forced a smile. "But thankfully, I just got a few bumps and bruises. I'm just supposed to take it easy the next day or two."

Patricia leaned against the side of the desk. "It's crazy out there, isn't it? Had some insane driver almost run me off the road a couple weeks ago. Don't think he even knew I was there. Never looked. Makes you think about how fragile life is. How it can be over in an instant. Like Helen."

"I know." Caitlyn shifted so her friend couldn't see the computer screen. "It's going to take me a long time to get over her death."

The files finished downloading. Caitlyn grabbed the drive, shoved it into her pocket, and stood up. "I'm not staying. Just stopped by to get an update on one of my projects."

"Glad you're okay."

She walked out of the lab into the hallway, trying to look as if she had every right to be there.

Three men in suits stepped out of the elevator at the other end of the hallway.

Caitlyn made a quick one-eighty and started down the opposite direction.

"I might have trouble," she whispered.

"What do you see?"

"Three suits coming down the hallway. Not sure who they are, but they're heading in the direction of the lab."

Her heart rate picked up. It could be nothing. HR dressed more like executives, but what were they doing here at the end of the workday when most people had already left? Unless they knew she was here and were looking for her . . .

"Did they see you?" Josh asked.

She turned another corner and picked up her pace. "I don't know. And I'm not hanging around to find out."

"You need to get out of there. Now."

"There's a stairwell at the end of this hallway. I'm going to take it."

"As long as you can get out of there without getting caught, you should be fine. They shouldn't be able to trace the download to you."

"Then what do they want?"

She pulled open the heavy fire door and started down the stairs, her heart beating too fast.

Someone opened the stairwell door two flights above her.

"I don't think they're with HR. They're following me."

"You need some kind of distraction."

Her mind raced for an answer.

*The fire alarm.*

Things were quickly spiraling out of control, but what option did she have? She pushed through the heavy metal door to the second floor, rushed down the hallway, broke the glass, and pulled the alarm.

"What's going on?" Josh asked.

"I just found a way out of here."

She ran to the other end of the hallway where there was a second stairwell. People weren't supposed to use the elevators during a fire, but a couple of employees stood waiting for the next one heading down. She had no idea if management or security knew who had been searching the computers, but she certainly didn't want to find out. She needed to get out of the building and off the property, and the sooner the better.

Her chest was heaving by the time she got to the ground floor. The lobby was already filled with a dozen people trying to figure out if this was a real emergency or a false alarm. In another few minutes police and firemen would be here.

"I need everyone to file out of the building." Someone had taken charge and was treating this like a real threat. Maybe this hadn't been such a good idea after all. She went through her options. There was a side door she could go through.

"Go around to the west side and meet me there," she said.

She couldn't worry about security cameras. She had to focus on getting out of the building with the flash drive without getting caught.

# 20

Josh pulled the car around to the west side of the building, his heart pounding as he waited for Caitlyn to emerge from the side door. Everything he'd feared going wrong had. And more. All because of a foolish decision he'd made. He slammed his hand against the steering wheel. Why had he agreed to do this?

"Caitlyn? Where are you?"

"Almost there."

He could hear her heavy breathing as she ran through the building. He hated the helpless feeling raging inside him, but there was nothing he could do but wait until she got out.

He finally saw her emerge from the side door, and he leaned over to open her door. Seconds later he was racing toward the parking lot exit, unsure of where to go next.

"Are you okay?"

She blew out a sharp breath. "I will be, once my heart stops pounding."

He agreed, but at the moment he didn't care. He never should have let her do this. He knew all too well what these people were capable of doing. And now if they didn't find a way out of here, they were going to be the next victims.

There were several other employees that were heading to their cars and leaving the property. That meant they'd have a better chance of getting out without being stopped. In the distance he could hear the sound of sirens as the fire department answered the call. He hoped there wasn't a camera that had caught her pulling the alarm, but being accused of setting off a fire alarm seemed minuscule compared to what they were facing.

"I don't know what happened." Her chest heaved as she tried to catch her breath. "Bruce must have said something. That's the only thing that makes sense."

"Well, we're not sticking around to find out." He took a left and merged onto the four-lane road running parallel to the lab, ready to get as far away from there as possible.

"I have the downloaded files." She opened up her clenched fist, revealing the drive. "I just . . . I just hope what we need is on it."

He caught the doubt mixed with fear in her voice. Not that he blamed her. His heart was still racing after the close call. He stopped at a red light, then turned to her. "You're still shaking."

"What just happened was way too close," she said. "I know it was a risk, and I know I chose to go in there, but if I'd gotten caught, if they figure out what I did . . ."

He looked closely at her. Her hands were trembling against her knees. He was glad she'd been able to download the files, but all he wanted to do at this point was to keep her safe. She'd reminded him, though, that keeping people he loved safe wasn't always possible. And he still had no idea what to do to make sure nothing happened to her. He'd spent his entire career focused on keeping people safe. He'd failed Olivia. He couldn't fail Caitlyn.

"Right now, I just want to get as far away from here as possible," he said. "And hope we weren't caught on camera. All we need now is the police looking for us."

"Despite my juvenile record, my adult record is spotless. Not even a parking ticket." She let out a soft chuckle. "So what is the penalty for stealing company files and setting off a fire alarm?"

"Let's just say it wouldn't look good on either of our records."
He couldn't help but smile. At least she hadn't completely lost
her sense of humor. "Were you ever able to get a good look at
the men?"

"No, but it wouldn't surprise me at all if we're looking at the
same men who showed up at Helen's house, and then again in
the tunnels."

He glanced over at her and felt his heart surge. A part of him
wanted to stop the car so he could pull her into his arms and tell
her everything was going to be okay. He'd been impressed with
how she'd handled the situation. Impressed she hadn't let fear
stop her.

"Josh . . . I think we're being followed again. The silver BMW
three cars back. It's got to be the same men from the lab."

Josh checked the rearview mirror. "I see it."

His fingers gripped the steering wheel tighter. Funny how two
days ago, he'd wanted to dismiss Caitlyn's ideas as the work of
an overactive imagination.

He glanced into the rearview mirror again. Traffic was light
this far out of the city, and the other car was now two car lengths
behind them. Whoever it was didn't seem to be keeping their presence a secret. But why not?

"Josh . . . It looks like a roadblock ahead of us."

"I see it."

Two unmarked vehicles sat at the bottom of the long stretch
of road, blocking the four lanes. Josh ran through the obvious
solutions, immediately taking out the option of stopping. He
had no idea who had set up the roadblock—whether it was an
official police blockade, or if someone else was behind it. He
wasn't going to risk finding out. The other two options were to
barrel through the barricade, or find a way around it. And since
ramming through two cars head on didn't seem viable, he was
down to one option.

"What are you going to do?"

"Just trust me."

He pumped on the brakes, praying he'd be able to reduce his speed quickly enough. He glanced at the speedometer. He needed to get his speed down as much as possible before he made the U-turn. He was still going way too fast.

"Hang on . . ."

He eased completely off the gas, spun the wheel, and the car skidded a full one hundred eighty degrees, barely missing the two cars blocking the road in the process. Once the car had made the U-turn, he pressed on the accelerator, giving it all the gas he could, then took off back up the road.

"They're still behind us," Caitlyn said. "At least two of them are following us."

He took a sharp left off the main road, trying to put as much distance as possible between them.

The first shot shattered the left rear window. He pressed harder on the accelerator.

"Caitlyn . . . you okay?"

"Yeah . . . just get us out of here."

"Stay down."

More shots sounded, and a second bullet hit the rear window, but he'd managed to widen the gap between them. He had no idea where to go. He knew the majority of the officers in his precinct were clean, but all it would take was one or two involved in this. Or there was always the possibility they were being fed the wrong information. Which meant he couldn't go in. And he needed options. He wound his way through a couple of neighborhoods, turning every few blocks and praying that he was throwing off whoever was after them, but he could still see them behind him.

Up ahead, the lights of a train crossing had started flashing. His mind grabbed onto another option. If he timed it right, he might have just found his way out of this.

"Hang on," he said again.

He gunned the engine, trying once again to broaden the gap between them and the car following him.

He took a sharp right, across the tracks, as the train sped toward them. The crossing gate dropped down behind them. Seconds later, the train roared past, leaving their tail trapped on the other side of the tracks.

Caitlyn let out a sharp breath of air.

"You okay?" he asked.

"We're alive. I guess at this point that's all that matters."

Neither of them said anything else as he kept driving, winding through the maze of neighborhoods, then hitting the highway north and putting as much distance as he could between them and their pursuers.

When he finally felt as if there was no way they could be found, he slowed down, found a quiet street, and parked next to the curb. He flipped on the overhead dome light, needing to assess what kind of damage had been done. The side and back windows had been blown out and the car had taken at least one other hit.

Caitlyn sat still beside him, staring straight ahead into the darkness. Her chest heaved with each breath, her lips pressed together, and her face had paled. He couldn't blame her. The rush of adrenaline had yet to settle down in his own chest. They'd both come very close to losing this time around.

"Don't move." He pulled a shard of glass out of her hair and then checked her over, needing to make sure she wasn't hurt worse than just a few scrapes where the glass had shattered.

"What are we supposed to do?" she asked. "They have to know what I did. And they're not going to stop until they find me."

"Let's worry about that in a few minutes." His frown deepened as he ran his hand down her left arm, looking for more glass. "You're bleeding."

She winced and pulled away. "I'm fine."

"You're not fine. You need to take off your jacket. I need to see how serious this is."

"Josh . . ."

He helped her pull off her jacket. He wasn't sure what had happened, but they were looking at more than just a cut.

"Ouch."

"Just a minute . . ."

"What is it?"

Realization shook him. "Caitlyn . . . you've been shot."

"What?" She twisted her head so she could see the injury.

"It looks like the bullet grazed the soft tissue of your upper arm before embedding into the dashboard."

She stared at the wound in disbelief. "If it had struck another few inches to the right . . ."

"Don't even go there. I don't believe in luck, but I do believe in miracles, and this was a miracle, Caitlyn."

She winced again as he wiped blood from her arm, still trying to assess the damage the bullet had done. He grabbed a first-aid kit from the back seat. He needed to get her to a doctor, but first he needed to clean the wound, then get the bleeding stopped. He carefully used an alcohol pad from the kit, making sure there wasn't any glass in the wound, then covered it with a piece of gauze.

"Ouch!" She pulled away from him again.

"I know it hurts, but I need you to be still. I'm going to try and get the bleeding to stop, then we'll get you to a hospital. You're going to need antibiotics and probably stitches."

"How deep is it?"

"Not very."

She caught his gaze. "Do you think it's safe? The hospital will have to report what happened."

"It's going to have to be."

"So does this mean when people ask for an interesting fact about me, I can tell them I've been shot?"

He grinned at her. "You'll be the life of the party."

A big tear slid down her cheek and he reached out and wiped it away. "Hey . . . do you trust me?"

She nodded. "I'm just so scared. Of what could have happened. Of what is going to happen . . ."

"We got out of there. We're both alive and okay. And we're going to put an end to this. I promise."

"I don't think you can promise that. They shot at us. Someone wants us dead . . . I've never been so scared in my life. They found us once. They'll find us again."

"I won't let that happen." He leaned into her as he held the gauze against her arm. Close enough for him to realize that his heart rate wasn't accelerated just because of what they'd been through. He pulled her against him and let her lay her head on his chest. "I'm sorry. So sorry about all of this."

"It's not your fault. None of this is your fault. If anything, it's my fault. I'm the one who convinced you to get involved. I just don't know how to make this stop. When is it going to end?"

Her hair brushed against his face. He could feel her heart pounding next to his. He didn't want to get anyone else involved, but without help he wasn't sure they were going to be able to get out of this alive. He didn't have any answers. Which scared him. Finding the truth was what he was good at. Evaluating a situation, then making a plan that went along with it. It wasn't personal, it was his job. Why, then, did his heart feel so drawn to her?

He pulled back, then replaced the soaked gauze with a new one. "Can you hold this for a sec while I secure it?"

She nodded.

He grabbed the tape from the first-aid kit, then worked to secure the gauze. "Try to keep pressure on it. I know where a hospital is not too far from here. We'll get you treated, then see what we can find on that drive."

He put the supplies away, then started the engine. As much as he would prefer to simply disappear, she needed to see a doctor. "Things are going to look better in the morning," he said as he pulled away from the curb.

"Is that your way of cheering me up? I've just been shot, which means I'm not really seeing the silver lining in all of this."

"I know you're scared. To be honest, I am too."

"If we go to the hospital, the cops will get involved," she said.

"Better the cops than the men who just tried to shoot you."

Josh's phone rang, and he pulled it out of his pocket. It was the burn phone Eddie had given him, which meant it was either him or Quinton.

He answered the call and put it on speaker. It was Quinton. "What have you got?"

"Sorry I took so long to get back to you. Where are you?"

Josh caught the concern in his partner's voice. "Headed to the hospital. We were just ambushed outside the lab. Caitlyn was shot. The bullet just grazed her arm, but I'm taking her to the hospital to get cleaned up."

"Wait a minute . . . she was shot? Is she okay?"

"I'll be fine." Caitlyn said. "It hurts, but Josh cleaned me up."

"Do you need stitches?"

Caitlyn looked at Josh.

"I'm not sure, which is why we're heading to the hospital."

"That's not your best move right now."

Josh switched lanes. "What do you mean?"

"Unfortunately, we've got another problem." There was a long pause on the line. "New evidence just came through the precinct. Evidence that would exonerate Rudolph Beckmann and Larry Nixon of your wife's murder . . . and implicate you."

Josh's head felt as if it were about to burst. "What are you telling me, Quinton?"

There was another long pause on the line. "The DA has just requested a warrant for your arrest."

# 21

Waves of fear rippled through Caitlyn as she listened to Quinton's raspy voice. This couldn't be happening. What they'd feared was no longer just an unsubstantiated concern they were working to prove. If the DA's office was involved, someone had managed to infiltrate the arm of the law. And that's what scared her.

"What kind of evidence did they find?" Josh asked.

"They got a search warrant for your house and found the murder weapon that killed your wife in the attic," Quinton said. "On top of that, there's now a sworn confession from Patrick Lindstrom that he lied about Rudolph's alibi."

She couldn't believe what she was hearing. The case against Rudolph had just unraveled like they'd hoped, but the outcome they were looking at was far from what she'd imagined.

How had this happened?

"So our assumptions on the break-in at Josh's house were correct," Caitlyn said. "They weren't just there to steal a file on Olivia's case, they were there to plant evidence."

"I agree," Quinton said. "But so far the two they arrested are denying that they know anything about Olivia's murder. They were just there to grab a few valuables to fence."

"What about the fact that one of them told me he was paid to break in and steal that file?" Josh asked.

"He claims that whatever he said to you, he said out of duress. And to be fair, you do have quite a left hook," Quinton said. "I saw the kid's shiner."

"Funny." Josh let out a low laugh. "But I'm still convinced he was telling me the truth."

"It sounds more to me like somebody got to him," Caitlyn said.

"Yes," Josh said. "But the bottom line is that no matter how you look at it, the gun in my house is simply circumstantial evidence. The DA has to realize that anyone could have planted it."

"Circumstantial or not, it's enough for them to reopen the case and turn their attention to you. On top of that, I just got called into the captain's office. He started asking me questions again about Olivia's case and your marriage. Asked me if I knew you were planning to ask her for a divorce."

"A divorce? What are you talking about, Quinton?"

There was a long pause on the other end. "They found divorce papers, signed by you, in the back of her desk."

"More lies," Josh said, the anger evident in his voice. "I didn't want a divorce, and I didn't kill her."

"I know that, but someone's determined to make it look like you did, and she resisted, and so you killed her. And you have to admit, what the captain's looking at is compelling."

"But there's still something I don't understand. Why are they trying to frame you?" Caitlyn asked. "Why not just search for the truth? If it wasn't Rudolph, then the killer's still out there. Why not find him?"

"Because someone doesn't want the truth known." With Quinton still on the line, Josh headed back down the road toward the freeway. "Probably because they want to protect whoever did kill her, and as the husband, I make the perfect scapegoat."

All three fell silent.

Caitlyn pressed her hand against the gauze, soaking up the blood on her arm, and tried to ignore the throbbing pain shooting down it. Funny how she hadn't felt the pain until Josh found the wound. Funny how over the past few days, things had at first seemed surreal. But not anymore. Now it was all too real. Planted evidence, false testimonies, and now forged divorce papers . . . someone was putting a lot of effort into ensuring he went down.

Josh flipped off the overhead dome light as darkness began to settle in around them. The last thing they needed was to give any pursuers a target.

"This has gone way too far," he said. "I need to talk to the captain. He'll listen to me—"

"I don't think you understand, Josh," Quinton said. "You were right about being a scapegoat. Someone's behind this and determined to take you out, but the problem is that I don't know who it is. That's why I'm doing everything to find out, but in the meantime, I even told the captain up front that I had my own suspicions about you. I need him to trust me, so I can stay in the loop and figure out who's behind this."

Josh let out a sharp sigh. "Did he believe you?"

"Far as I could tell, he bought it, but he made it clear I'm not going to be in on the case as things progress. My advice is to stay under the radar. Let me try to handle things from here until I can figure out exactly what's going on."

"You suspect him?" Josh asked.

"No, but neither can I take any chances at this point."

"Okay. We can try and stay under the radar, but they're going to be looking for me. And while I have no idea how they did it, Adams and Sanchez found me once. If they find me again, they're not going to let me go with nothing more than a veiled threat. They'll arrest me," Josh said. "We can keep switching motels, but once we hit the nightly news, someone's going to see us and talk."

"I've been working on that. Have you got cash?"

"Enough for now."

"I'm working on getting you a safe house. In the meantime, no credit cards, and do everything you can to stay out of sight. I promise I'll do whatever I can, but I know they're watching me as well. The good thing is, I don't think they've been able to track where you're staying."

"We're also going to have to dump the car," Josh said. "The windows have been shot out and there are bullet holes in the side."

"That's going to make it hard to disappear, especially if the car's how they've been tracking you. I think I can come up with something. I'll try to have a plan worked out in the next hour."

She caught the hesitation in Josh's voice as he spoke to Quinton. "You're sure running is the best option?"

"I'm serious enough to risk my own career for your neck. Dump anything that might be bugged or that they can trace you with."

"What about Caitlyn?" Josh asked. "I don't want her involved in this—"

"Except I already am involved," she said.

"She's right," Quinton said. "Keep her with you, but out of sight, so she doesn't have to deal with their interrogation. Rumor is that you're with a woman. As far as I know, she hasn't been identified, but that could change. I'll call you with details on this number as soon as I can."

Caitlyn's heart rate rose with the adrenaline pumping through her body as Josh hung up the call. She wasn't sure if it was because of what they'd just learned or because she was going into shock from the gunshot wound. All of this because she started asking someone the wrong questions.

Josh pulled out a flashlight from the glove compartment, then got out of the car.

"What are you doing?" she asked.

"Just give me a minute."

She laid her head back against the seat and tried to slow her breathing, while trying to take her mind off the pain. She was tired, both emotionally and physically, and yet this was far from over. The last rays of sunlight had almost disappeared, leaving shadows surrounding them. Engaging an enemy was one thing. Fighting an enemy you couldn't see was terrifying.

Josh slid back into the driver's seat, then showed her the thin metal disk.

"What's that?"

"A tracker. They haven't had to follow us, because they've been tracking our car. I found it attached to the underside of the car. If I hadn't been looking for something specific, I would never have found it."

Josh shook his head, then threw the device out the window, before starting the engine and heading out of the neighborhood. "Quinton's right. We need to dump everything they could possibly trace."

"I agree."

"We also need to get you to a hospital, but now—"

"Forget the hospital. We'll use what you have in the first-aid kit, and keep an eye on it, but it's only a graze. I'll be okay. Some pain meds would be nice though."

His voice rose a notch. "They shot you, Caitlyn. This isn't just going to end. Not until they have us pinned down and in their sights. And now, not only do we have both sides of the law after us, you need medical help."

She laid her hand on his arm. "I'll be fine. It just means we've got to be smarter than they are. I have the information from the lab to go through. I'm going to need your help to see how it compares to the notes Helen has."

"Do you think you got what we need from the lab to do that?"

She nodded. "I found the file, and what I suspect they did is run two sets of data from the results in order to hide what they'd discovered, giving them time to continue with the project. I need time to test my theory, but with everything that we have so far, it fits. And it definitely seems to be what Helen was trying to prove. And more than likely, Olivia and Dr. Abbott as well."

"So on paper the reports look like legitimate research with normal findings—"

"But in reality, the results have actually been manipulated," she finished for him. "We're going to need to go through the data sets and get as much information as I can on who created it, what versions are out there, along with any information that can clarify the discrepancies I'm finding in Helen's notes. If we can prove that with what I found at the lab—and then if we can nail down who's behind this—we'll have enough to go to your captain, the DA, and anyone else who needs to know. And with that kind of evidence there will be no way they can dispute that something was going on at that lab."

"But that doesn't prove me innocent of murdering my wife."

"Not by itself, but if we can tie the project to the three deaths, they'll have to look at the evidence we have."

"I'm still waiting to hear back from Eddie, but once we get an ID on those photos, that will give us a direction to follow as well as who is behind this."

He stopped at a red light, then glanced at her. "How's your arm?"

"Let's just say I can't even imagine how painful a gunshot would be if it had done more than just graze me, because I feel as if my arm is on fire. But I'll be better once some pain medicine kicks in."

Josh nodded. "We need to dump the car and wait for Quinton, but I'm going to need to stop by a convenience store on the way and make sure we have everything we need to treat your arm."

Traffic pulsed around Caitlyn as they hit the crowded freeway. The surrounding buildings started to close in around her. Every car and every driver was a potential threat. Josh had gone to his boss with evidence that Beckmann hadn't murdered his wife, and now someone wanted to pin it on him? That didn't seem possible, but it had happened.

She'd heard what he said earlier. Understood to a degree what it was going to mean if they tried to figure this out on their own with a warrant out for his arrest. They'd have to cut themselves off from the circle of friends they each had. No technology, no phones, no computers, nothing that could leave bread crumbs back to them. *They'll anticipate where we're going next. And every time we order food, or catch a ride, or stop at a store like I'm doing right now, we're taking a chance. And this time, we'll have the authorities looking for us.*

She stared out at the skyline. Lost in a city of millions, one would think she'd be safe. But she didn't feel safe. At all. And yet neither was she ready to give up.

He pulled into the lot of a strip mall, found a parking spot, then turned off the engine. "You know you don't have to do this with me—"

"Yes, I do. You need me as much as I need you. I don't want to be another murder that goes overlooked because I asked too many questions, and on top of that, I don't want you to take the fall for something you didn't do."

Josh took her hand and squeezed her fingers. "Are you sure about this?"

"I am."

"They will find us. Eventually. And we're going to have to be ready."

"My life is on the line as much as yours. All we have to do is find the truth."

*And the truth will set you free.*

The verse from John she'd read recently surfaced. That was all they needed. The truth. She knew that sometimes evil men prevailed. That good people sometimes suffered in the hands of evil men. History proved that over and over again.

And yet history also proved that when good men stood up for truth, evil could be thwarted.

"Besides," she said. "We don't need long. Just enough time to get the evidence so we can go to the DA and prove our case. If the answers are on that drive, we can show them what we have."

"I pray you're right, because if this plan doesn't work"—Josh undid his seat belt—"I'll likely be facing the death penalty."

# 22

Josh grabbed the Houston Rockets cap sitting in the back seat, tugged it on so the bill sat low, then stepped out of the car and headed toward the sidewalk. The strip mall—one of thousands across the city—housed the typical eclectic mixture of stores, including a nail salon, an insurance broker, and an Indian restaurant. It also had the pharmacy and secondhand clothing shop he needed.

He headed toward the pharmacy and breathed in the scent of spicy curry takeout, wishing they had time to stop for dinner. As if anything was normal about his life right now. They needed to get out of there as soon as possible, and chicken curry wasn't exactly on the menu.

Neither was spending a relaxed evening with the beautiful woman sitting in his car with a gunshot wound.

He glanced back at the car before stepping into the pharmacy and letting the reality of what was going on rush to the forefront. Where it should be. Being distracted right now wasn't an option. Because no matter how he looked at things, being dropped back into Olivia's murder investigation and then suddenly becoming the main suspect in her murder had sent him reeling. He wasn't supposed to be running from the law. He was one of the good guys who protected his community from criminals like the thugs who'd killed his wife and the ones who'd been waiting in his living room.

*How did this happen, God?*

Questioning why, though, wasn't going to change anything. He'd done the same thing when Olivia had died. Questioned everything from why God had let her be murdered to why he—her husband and a cop—hadn't been able to stop it. It wasn't the first time he'd asked the questions about life and death and the evil in this world. His work as a homicide detective had forced him to work through the reality of the fallen world they lived in and to eventually conclude with certainty that Christ's death was the only way for redemption of this lost world.

But that didn't make it easier. Especially when the dark realities of his job hit so close to home.

He headed toward the back of the pharmacy, searched through the shelves, and finally found some antiseptic, antibiotic ointment, pain medicine, gauze, and tape. He started to the counter, then stopped at the food aisle and grabbed some trail mix, a box of granola bars, and four waters. It definitely wasn't going to be as good as the takeout next door, but the fewer places he showed his face, the fewer chances he would have of being recognized.

He grabbed two prepaid cell phones with air time as backup, then headed toward the bored cashier. He just needed to make it seem like he was another customer. Not a fugitive running from the law.

A fugitive.

The whole idea was ridiculous. A year ago, he'd watched his wife's coffin drop into the ground. There had never been any question at the time about who'd murdered her. He had a perfect record on the force and had received a handful of commendations. No one had even hinted he'd somehow been involved.

Until now.

Now someone had decided he was going down for the death

of his wife, and he had no idea how to stop it. Which was why he was buying first-aid supplies and burner phones with cash at a random pharmacy. At least with the phones there would be no personal data logged, making them hard to trace. Which is what a guilty person would be worried about. Someone who'd killed his wife.

He stopped in front of the counter with his purchases, thankful no one else was in the store. Since becoming a homicide detective, he'd worked more cases than he could remember of domestic incidents where husbands murdered their wives. The thought that someone believed he could actually kill his wife made him ill.

He set everything on the counter, keeping his hat pulled low across his forehead and hoping the cameras wouldn't get a good shot of him. No doubt, if he was still being followed, detectives would be scouring the camera for clues about where he was heading next. He might know how criminals' minds worked, but it wasn't an advantage. So did the officers who were after him.

The cashier, who didn't look like he was a day over sixteen, rang up his bill. "Who are you running from?"

Josh glanced up at the television running behind the counter and felt his stomach sour. Surely there hadn't been enough time to get his photo out to all the news channels yet.

He swallowed hard and forced himself to meet the man's gaze. "Excuse me?"

"A couple burner phones, medical supplies, and your jaw's been messed up. Just figured you'd gotten yourself into some kind of trouble. Don't worry, dude. I see it all the time."

Josh touched his face, then winced at the stab of pain. "It's nothing. And these phones might be cheap, but they're made like tanks. Seemed like a smart thing to have on hand. You know, for emergencies."

He stopped talking. He was rambling, and that was going to make him memorable.

"You've got a point there. I have one, actually. They're great for online dating. You know. When it's time to swap numbers. Having a second number allows me to keep my privacy if the woman turns out to be some crazed stalker."

Josh laid the cash on the counter, not believing he was actually having this conversation. "I can't say I've ever tried online dating, but I'll remember that if I do."

"If you're looking for a good time, you should try it, dude. I've met some crazy chicks out there, but I've also met some pretty hot ones."

Josh let out a low laugh, like he understood what the kid was saying, and glanced at his left hand. He'd stopped wearing his wedding band a few months ago.

"Thanks," he said. "I . . . I'll keep that in mind."

He kept his head low as he walked out, so that if the surveillance camera did catch him, it wouldn't get his face. He should have gone to three separate stores. Now the guy would remember him if anyone came by and asked. How often did someone walk out with a burner phone and first-aid supplies, and hold a conversation on online dating? But he didn't have a lot of time to worry. He glanced over at his car before walking into the secondhand store that smelled like his grandmother's musty attic.

He needed to get something for Caitlyn. He had no idea what her taste in clothes was, let alone her size, but at the moment that didn't matter, considering they were going to have to lay low for a few days. He frowned. She was close to Olivia's size, so he'd go with that. And something simple. He pulled out a pair of jeans, then grabbed a long-sleeve green shirt, a denim jacket that didn't look outdated, and a warm scarf. Another couple T-shirts and he called it good. She might not like his taste in fashion, but it was the best he could do at this point.

A nagging thought pressed on him as he started for the counter. They'd been tracked more than once. He had no idea if the people after them were somehow monitoring the car or maybe even their clothes, but they couldn't afford to take any chances.

Shoving aside his thoughts, he headed straight toward the men's coats. At the end of the metal rack was a lined bomber jacket. He pulled it off the hanger and held it up. Not exactly fashionable, but not bad either. And he wouldn't stand out wearing it, like he probably did in his suit jacket. He grabbed a pair of brown casual boots, jeans, a white T-shirt, and a plaid shirt, then headed toward the dressing room.

Inside, Josh pulled off his shirt, stopping when a loose thread got caught on his watch. If someone had bugged it . . . He quickly pulled off his watch and stomped on it, then paused.

He was losing it. Paranoia had taken over, but if there was any chance that Quinton and Caitlyn were right—he didn't have a choice. He exited the dressing room and dumped his own clothes into the donation bin before heading for the cashier. He was thankful that the woman behind the counter seemed more interested in her phone than making conversation. He paid cash for the clothes and a cheap backpack to keep their things in. If anyone was trying to follow him, he was going to do his best to make sure it wasn't possible.

He headed back outside, then felt his heart stop. A Houston PD squad car was parked in a spot between him and his car. Adrenaline rushed through him as two officers stepped out of the Indian restaurant and headed his way, carrying bags of takeout.

There was nowhere to go. If he ducked back into the thrift shop, they might notice he was trying to avoid them, but if he went to his car and they recognized him . . .

He tugged again on the brim of his hat, shoved his free hand into his pocket, and started walking in the opposite direction of his car. He was just another shopper, trying to catch up on errands after work. Nothing more.

Or at least that was the act he had to sell.

The officers laughed as they headed toward him. Close enough now he could hear their conversation. Close enough they would be able to recognize him if they were looking for him.

"I can't believe you've never tried this stuff. It's by far the best Indian takeout around."

The tall blond officer laughed. "At least it adds something interesting to an otherwise dull shift."

Josh walked past them, trying not to hold his breath. He didn't recognize them, but neither did they seem to recognize him. He was simply a customer coming out of the secondhand shop with a bagful of purchases. Another slow night. No mention of a fugitive. He had no idea how public his arrest was going to be. Or how widespread the captain's search was for him. Until Quinton had more information for him, he was going to assume that they would put out a widespread BOLO for both him and Caitlyn. All of Houston's finest would be looking for them. But thankfully, it looked like that information was taking its time trickling down the chain of command.

Thirty seconds later, he stopped in front of an insurance office, already closed for the night, and watched them drive away. He waited until they were out of sight, then hurried back to the car.

"Sorry it took so long." He dumped his purchases, minus the coat, pain meds, and a water, onto the back seat, then switched on the overhead light. "You okay?" He handed Caitlyn a water bottle and a couple pills.

She downed the ibuprofen. "Thanks. A little cold, but yeah."

Blood had yet to soak completely through the gauze on her arm, which was a good sign. But he was still worried.

He checked her pulse. "Do you feel any nausea or dizziness?"

"No. I'm fine."

"You were just shot."

"Seriously, Josh. I'm fine."

"I got you a couple things to change into. The bleeding seems to be under control, so for now you can put on the jacket. At least it should help warm you up, and no one will notice the gunshot."

"Thank you."

He pulled the belted denim jacket out of the bag and held it up, catching her smile. "You might not thank me when you see it."

"I love it."

"Right." He laughed.

"I saw the cops."

The laughter vanished. "They didn't seem to be looking for anything, which means that the warrant probably isn't out yet." But he knew it was simply a matter of time. "I'd like to change your bandage again, but I think I should wait. We need to get out of here. There's pain medicine in the bag and a bottle of water. Go ahead and take two of them. It will help."

She did what he said and swallowed them.

He'd been a cop for fifteen years. Constantly on the trail of a suspect. Hunting down clues. Waiting for the criminals to make a mistake. Gathering evidence that would send them behind bars for their crimes. He never imagined the day would come when he'd be forced to think like one of them.

The phone Eddie had given him rang as he started up the engine, and he grabbed it off the dash where he'd set it.

"Josh?"

It was Quinton. "Yeah."

"Where are you?"

"On our way to dump the car now. I stopped to get some medicine and bandages for Caitlyn, along with some clothes."

"Good. I'm going to send you a location for a car. You can take a taxi to the address. There'll be a Honda Civic there with the key in a magnetic box under the bumper. I also found a secure house for you in Galveston. I'll text you that address as well."

"You're sure they can't trace either back to you?"

"Both should be safe. In the meantime, go through the com-

puter files and see what you can come up with. I'll keep you up- .
dated on my end."

Josh let out a sharp sigh of relief. "I can't tell you how much I
appreciate your risking your own neck for us."

"You'd do the same for me." There was a pause on the line.
"Just be careful. Please."

"You know I will be."

"We'll give us both a couple days to see what we can come up
with. If we can find enough proof, we'll take it to the captain."

Josh voiced out loud the question he hadn't been able to shake.
The question he needed an answer to. "You think he's clean?"

"He's getting pressure from somewhere, but if we come to him
with enough evidence, I think he'll support us."

He hung up the phone, needing to believe that was true. Needing to believe there really was a way out of this.

# 23

Caitlyn glanced at the television in the beach house's living room, then grabbed the remote and turned up the volume.

*"Authorities in Harris County are looking for a fugitive believed to still be in the Houston area and have issued a warrant out for Joshua Solomon in order to bring him in for further questioning on the death of his wife a year ago. During the investigation of the highly publicized murder, Solomon claimed he saw two men leave his house as he was arriving. Rudolph Beckmann and Larry Nixon were arrested and then convicted of Olivia Solomon's murder, and at the time it was believed that the two men were also involved in a string of burglaries that had plagued southeast Houston for several months. But startling new information surfaced today that points to Solomon as a key suspect in his wife's murder. Solomon is believed to be on the run with Caitlyn Lindsey, an employee of MedTECH Labs. It's rumored he has been having an affair with Lindsey. The police consider this a possible motive for his wife's brutal murder."*

Her driver's license photo popped up on the screen.

*"Anyone with information on the location of Joshua Solomon*

*or Caitlyn Lindsey, please contact your local police department immediately."*

She muted the sound, but that did nothing to alleviate the fear seeping through her. They'd obviously figured out who she was, and now fear was playing with her mind, something she couldn't allow to happen.

She turned back to the laptop Quinton had left for them under the front passenger seat. Between Quinton and Josh, they'd thought of everything. She and Josh dropped the car in the corner of a crowded parking lot, then walked a couple blocks to catch a taxi. The jacket Josh had bought her had covered her wound, and no one had given them a second glance.

The safe house Quinton had arranged for them was directly across from the beach, with breathtaking views of the water she'd be soaking up in any other situation. Instead, waves of panic pulsed through her as she opened the flash drive. She knew her erratic emotions were coming from sheer exhaustion. She'd barely slept last night, and when she had slept, the nightmares followed her into her dreams. Add to that, her arm still throbbed.

She'd spent her life going with the flow. Working hard to get through school but never rocking the boat. Staying invisible was what had kept her out of trouble all her life. But now? Asking questions meant she was no longer invisible, which had her terrified. She wasn't even sure Josh was going to be able to keep her safe. Not if there was a warrant out for his arrest. She'd be a fool to believe this situation could have a good ending.

She looked up as Josh stepped into the living room.

"I just made sure everything's locked up and the alarm's set."

"Good." She glanced at the TV. "We both made the news cycle and they know who I am."

"I'm not surprised. I just received a text from Quinton. The warrant for my arrest was just filed with the DA. They're going to officially start looking for us now."

She shook her head. "I'm still trying to take in the fact that I just saw my face on the evening news."

"You're not the only one." He sat down across from her on the couch. "How are you feeling?"

She touched her arm, thankful for the shift from their too-personal conversation. "It's starting to hurt again, but the pain medicine definitely took the edge off."

He glanced at the clock on the wall. "It's probably time you took some more."

She nodded. "You're right."

"And I know you need to figure out what's in those files, but your priority is to get some rest. Both of us need that right now." He grabbed the first-aid supplies off the table. "I'll clean your arm and change the bandage before you go to bed."

She stood and pulled off her jacket. "I am tired, but I was wanting to keep going through these lab reports. There are definitely two sets of results. Right now, I'm trying to isolate the original data, so I can decipher exactly what they were trying to do with the virulent virus."

He finished taking off the old bandage, then started cleaning the wound while she tried not to wince.

"I have a question for you. Your work at the lab—the projects you work on. Does it ever clash with your faith?" Josh asked.

The personal nature of his question surprised her. "Honestly, biology has only managed to strengthen it. I've seen God in his creation . . . seen his creativeness. It's like the psalmist says: 'The heavens declare the glory of God.' My work has given me an incredible glimpse into who he is." Her eyes watered from the pain, and she bit back a groan. "What about you? You're a homicide detective. You see the worst in people. I don't think I could live seeing that day after day."

"It's not easy." He took a step back, then reached for the bandage material to cover her wound. "Sometimes I'm afraid I've seen too much evil in this world. I know God is there, but when you look into the eyes of a person who's just lost someone they love . . . it's hard. It leaves me questioning my faith sometimes. Like this entire situation has."

"You've been through a lot. I think God understands."

"I hope so. You're exhausted," he said, changing the subject. "You need some sleep."

She yawned, then looked at the clock, surprised it was almost midnight. "Yes, but I'm not the only one."

"We can get back to work in the morning."

"I still have so much to go through."

He finished bandaging her wound. "I know, but for tonight, you're going to take a couple more Tylenol and go to bed." He shot her a smile. "Doctor's orders."

"Yes, sir." She smiled back at him, wishing her heart didn't do a nosedive every time he was near her. She took a step back.

"You take the main bedroom," he said. "There's a Jacuzzi in there that might help your achy muscles."

She weighed her options but knew he was right. As much as she wanted to continue working, without sleep she wasn't going to be able to do anything. "You're right. I don't think I'll get anything else done tonight. My brain feels like mush."

He reached out and took her hand. She studied his face, how his eyes had flecks of gold in them, how his five-o'clock shadow made him look rugged and strong. He made her feel safe. Made her believe they might really be able to put an end to this.

Made her want to listen to her heart.

Josh caught her gaze. "I know we have a lot to uncover, but I'm also trying to figure out what's going on here. Between us."

Her breath caught as he bridged the gap between them and cupped his hand around the side of her face. Forcing her to confront what she'd been trying to ignore. Josh Solomon needed to be someone she could walk away from and forget. Because no matter how close she was to falling for him, she couldn't go there.

"Tell me I'm not the only one feeling something," he continued. "I know it's something I shouldn't be feeling right now, but no matter how much I try to ignore it—to ignore how you make me feel—I can't."

Her heartbeat quickened in response to his confession. She'd done everything in her power to do exactly the same thing, and yet something about him had her thrown off-balance. "No. You're not the only one."

Her words came out barely as a whisper as he took one more step toward her. He pressed his lips against hers, and all the pent-up feelings she'd been hiding shot to the surface. His kiss brought with it a wave of reassurance she desperately needed, shoving away all the terror and fears that had threatened to drag her under.

Josh Solomon had stepped in and rescued her and, in the process, had managed to steal a piece of her heart. His arm spanned her waist as he pulled her tighter against him, leaving her breathless.

The heater clicked on with a loud creaking noise, pulling her back to reality.

She'd been shot.

Josh's wife was dead.

And they were running from the law.

This—*this*—couldn't happen. Josh wasn't just some guy who'd managed to capture her interest. They were investigating his wife's murder, and she . . . she couldn't do this.

She stumbled backward a couple steps, searching for the right words. "I'm sorry, but I can't. Even if you weren't about to be arrested for the murder of your wife, things would never work between us."

She knew she was right. She wasn't going to fall for someone for the wrong reasons. Someone who was still seeking closure for the past. Closure for losing someone he'd loved. She couldn't be that person.

He shook his head. "No. I'm the one who's sorry. My father recently told me I needed to move on. I don't think I'm ready for that, but something about you makes me want to explore that option. Made my heart want to feel again for the first time in a very long time. But that doesn't give me the right to cross the line."

She started cleaning up the first-aid kit, needing something to do with her hands. "Forget it. I'm to blame as much as you."

But the lines had blurred between them, and she wasn't even sure at this point what she wanted.

"You're right. I'm supposed to keep you safe," he said. "And whatever . . . this is . . . it's only going to complicate things."

"Exactly."

She knew if she walked away, she'd never know what could have happened. But a distraction could prove fatal. She told him good night, grabbed her stuff, and headed for the master bedroom, willing her heart to quit pounding. Inside the bathroom, she studied the new bandage he'd put on, thankful that the bleeding seemed to have stopped.

She hadn't missed what had been brewing between them. Part of her felt like she was stepping into forbidden waters. Falling for someone when their lives were at stake. Falling for someone she knew wasn't emotionally available. She couldn't afford a broken heart. And besides, when all of this was over, more than likely anything that now simmered between them was going to cool down. They couldn't base a relationship on an intense situation that had dragged them into the deep end together when they had no idea if they were going to get out alive. Any expectations she had of romance were nothing but fairy tales, and she knew how those turned out. Men left. She'd seen it in her father. Seen it in her fiancé. Why did she think Josh would be any different?

She never should have lowered the guard she'd always kept in place. Not even for him. She'd stopped believing a long time ago in love and valor.

She stared into the mirror. There were dark circles under her eyes. Worry lines across her brow. Running from the police terrified her, and there were no guarantees they'd get the evidence they needed to clear Josh. But without that evidence, the authorities would never listen to them. She moved back into the bedroom. She didn't remember the last time she'd had a good night's sleep.

*Are we doing the right thing, God? I just don't know anymore.*

She trusted Josh. That was the one thing she did know. She believed God had brought him to her. Knew he would do everything in his power to keep both of them safe. But there were no guarantees. If they couldn't find out who was behind this . . .

She started to pull back the comforter and saw the handwritten notes from Helen that still lay on the bed. The answers had to be in there somewhere. The truth about whatever had been going on at the lab and why three people were now dead. She was missing something. Something key.

She picked up the file. Some sort of research had been going on. Research that someone wanted to cover up. She tried to focus, but her mind refused to process the information. She set the notes on the nightstand and gave in to the fatigue. She needed a good night's sleep and then maybe she'd be able to put the final pieces together. Until then she'd pray that whoever was after them didn't find them.

She pulled the blanket around her and closed her eyes, praying for strength and wisdom until she fell asleep.

# 24

Josh cracked a third egg into the bowl, then grabbed the whisk and started beating them together with the milk. The sun was barely up, and he'd only slept a couple hours. Every creak of the old beach house had been a potential intruder, as far as he was concerned. Quinton had assured him that tracking them to this house should be almost impossible, but he knew there were still no guarantees they wouldn't be found. Plus, now he was worried he'd put his partner's life at risk. Someone was clearly willing to do anything it took to stop them. Which meant the closer they got to the truth, the more dangerous this nightmare became.

He glanced down the hallway, glad Caitlyn was getting some sleep. Or at least he hoped she was. At three o'clock, when he'd come out for a glass of water, her light had been on. He wasn't sure if she'd fallen asleep while reading through the files, or if she'd just stayed up, but either way, he had a feeling she hadn't slept much either.

He turned down the gas on the stove, then poured the beaten egg mixture into the hot pan. While he was grateful for the safe house, being here wasn't getting them any closer to finding out who was behind this. But then, what was he supposed to do? His face was on the evening news, so going around interviewing people was going to be difficult, if not impossible. He was still waiting to hear from Eddie, and while Quinton had promised to do as much digging as he could, it was only a matter of time before someone caught on to the fact that he was on their side. And that would put his partner's entire family at risk.

*I'm not sure what to do next, God.*

He looked up as Caitlyn walked into the room, set a thick file folder and the laptop down on the bar, then shot him a sleepy smile. "What are you making? It smells delicious."

"I hope you like eggs and bacon."

She was wearing the jeans and one of the T-shirts he'd bought for her, her hair was mussed, and she looked half awake. Maybe she actually had slept a little.

"Are you kidding? I'd never turn that down. Breakfast has always been my favorite meal of the day, and for some reason I'm starving this morning."

"Good. I always like it when a woman enjoys her food."

He added cheese to the omelet, realizing how stupid what he'd just said had to have sounded. He was completely out of practice talking with women, and certainly wasn't used to flirting with them. Not that he was trying to flirt with Caitlyn. Not at all. Especially after last night. That kiss had totally thrown him for a loop.

"Sorry," he said. "That came out completely wrong. I already told you, most of my family are farmers, so that means we always enjoy eating. Big breakfasts are the norm. Biscuits, gravy, bacon and sausage, hash browns, pancakes, and real maple syrup . . . That's all I meant."

Her sleepy smile only managed to shoot another hole through his heart. "You're fine."

"Toast?" he asked.

"One, please."

He dropped a slice of multigrain bread into the toaster. "Did you get any sleep? Your light was on late, and I was hoping you weren't still working and had just fallen asleep."

"To be honest, despite your orders, I ended up tossing and turning, so I went through the files again." She shot him a sheepish grin. "I think I finally dozed off around two, until I started smelling bacon sizzling and decided I was hungry."

He laughed. "And your arm? How is it feeling?"

She slipped into the bar seat. "It's a bit achy, but I took some more Tylenol before coming out here. Hopefully that will keep the pain under control."

"I can change the bandage as soon as we're done with breakfast. We're going to have to really watch for infection until we can get you to a real doctor."

He was enjoying the small talk between them, if only for the fact that it helped him avoid the topic of last night's kiss. He'd crossed a line, and even though it wasn't something he could take back, he'd spent most of the night wishing he could.

The toast popped up and he pulled it out and buttered it before setting it on the plate in front of her. "There's jam to your left."

"Quinton outdid himself," she said, reaching for it. "He managed to arrange everything, and the ocean view's not too bad either. I just wish we were here to enjoy it under different circumstances."

"He's a good man. A good partner."

"Something I'm extremely grateful for."

"Me too." He hesitated, looking for the right words. "Listen . . . I feel like I need to apologize again about last night."

She looked up at him. "Let's just forget the whole thing happened, Josh. Seriously. Stress is already high enough, and we don't need to add to it by worrying about an innocent kiss. It's fine. We're fine."

"You're sure?"

"I am. Really. I don't want things to become awkward between us. There are too many other things going on that are far more important."

"I agree." He wasn't sure it was possible to simply forget what had happened, but he decided to take her at her word and let the subject drop. For now, anyway.

He slid her omelet onto a plate, added three pieces of bacon out of the microwave, then pushed the food in front of her.

"I'm impressed," she said, picking up the fork.

"Don't be." He started making an omelet for himself. "For the most part, my cooking skills are limited to omelets, pasta, and the grill. Oh, and I can make a killer batch of chocolate chip cookies."

"I would never turn down a chocolate chip cookie. You'll have to let me sample yours someday."

He let out a chuckle, but the thought of them seeing each other once this was over was heading into dangerous territory.

She held up her fork. "This really is delicious."

"Good. I was hoping you'd approve."

He watched his own eggs sizzle. If he was going to forget about what happened between them, he was going to have to keep their conversation strictly business. "Were you able to find out anything else?"

"I was, actually." Her smile vanished. "Between Helen's notes and the files I downloaded from the lab, I'm pretty sure I've figured out exactly what's going on."

"Okay . . ." He felt a surge of adrenaline spike through him. If she'd managed to come up with concrete evidence of what was going on, they were going to be that much closer to ending all of this.

Caitlyn started slathering on a thick layer of raspberry jam. "When I first read through Helen's lab notes, I mentioned to you the problem with a virulent virus she wrote about and how that could potentially be the base for a bioweapon."

"Right."

"Most of the vaccines we have today work because not only do they keep an individual from getting sick, they also stop the virus from being transferred to someone else, which is a crucial part of the development. The problem comes when a new vaccine might protect the host, but instead of stopping the virus from being transferred to someone else, it still allows transmission. Researchers call this a leaky vaccine." She took a bite of bacon, giving him time to process the information. "With a leaky vaccine, you can end up with a virulent virus that continues to survive and spread, often evolving into an even more deadly strain that could be fatal for anyone not protected by the original vaccine."

He worked to wrap his mind around what she was saying. "So the vaccine could itself actually generate a more lethal strain of the virus and make things worse."

"Exactly. And one of the greatest risks would be toward those who are not vaccinated. An example would be one of a number of diseases like HIV and malaria that already cause problems with the body's immune system. Or a disease like Ebola that already has an extremely high fatality rate. If a leaky vaccine is created for these—one that doesn't stop the transmission of the disease or ensure any resulting virulent strains are not eradicated—you have a recipe for a very serious situation."

"So it sounds like this is as bad as we first feared."

"Unfortunately, yes."

"And could something like this be used as some kind of bio-weapon?"

"Combined with a corruptible researcher and the right buyer . . . definitely."

He added cheese to his eggs, folded them in half, then waited a few more seconds for them to finish cooking. "That's a lot to take in."

"I agree." She rested her fork against the plate. "Often when misconduct cases surface, they center around fabricated data and inconsistencies in the methods, but the motivation behind this seems different."

He glanced up at her. "Meaning?"

"Meaning scientific fraud and misconduct usually stem from financial greed, or because someone wants recognition in a competitive field, but they're not necessarily out to hurt someone. This is a whole different ball game. It's clearly financially motivated, of course, but it could be politically motivated as well. And what scares me is what will happen if this research is misused and whoever's behind it doesn't care." She pushed her plate away and looked up at him. "This goes way beyond Olivia's and Helen's deaths and even our safety."

He tried to fight the sick feeling in his stomach. Trying not to wonder what he could have done differently that might have changed this outcome.

Caitlyn leaned forward. "This has to go to the authorities, Josh. Because while I still haven't found out exactly how far their research has gone, it's clear to me that the potential is disastrous. If implemented, whoever is backing this could kill thousands of unvaccinated people in a short period of time, and if it in turn evolved into an even hotter viral strain, the fallout would be devastating worldwide."

He stared out the window overlooking the ocean. The tide was out, exposing a long strip of sand where a family was playing in the water. How many could be affected by this? Hundreds? Thousands?

"Are you okay?" she asked.

"Yeah . . ." He shifted his gaze back to her. "I'm just trying to process all of this. I've spent the last year trying to accept the fact that Olivia wasn't coming back. That she was killed in some horrible burglary gone wrong. But to finally understand exactly what she stumbled into and why they killed her, it's just . . ." He let out a sharp breath of air. "I feel like I'm having to relive her death all over again. I just have so many questions. Like why Olivia didn't go straight to the authorities over this if she knew what was going on."

"I'm not sure it was that straightforward for her. We dove into this after a pattern emerged, but she would have only seen the inconsistencies she questioned. On top of that, there are certain protocols set in place for situations like this before you even go to a colleague or supervisor."

"So when she started asking questions, she probably wouldn't have had any idea what she was dealing with."

"I don't think so. In order to protect herself, she would have first made sure she had enough information before she started throwing out accusations. Once she believed she had enough information, she probably would have gone either to the person she believed to be behind this, or the research integrity officer."

"I just wish she would have come to me."

"I know and I'm sorry. The fallout of this—all because of someone's greed—has already hurt so many people."

Josh's phone went off and he wiped his hands on the dish towel before picking it up and reading the text, his appetite gone. "It's Eddie. Looks like he found out a few things about Jigsaw."

"Anything we can use?" she asked.

"I think so. He found out that a couple years ago, four men were arrested and charged for brokering sales of black-market prescription drugs. Authorities never arrested the fifth man—their leader—but Eddie's sources confirmed it was Jigsaw—Shawn Stover. He's trying to track him down right now."

"So Jigsaw has ties to the black market."

Josh nodded. "Eddie said if you need a buyer, he's your man. And here's the other thing. Turns out that Stover was the other man in the photos with assistant DA Hayward."

"So he's also that man who was following us." Caitlyn's eyes widened. "Does he know how Hayward got involved in all of this?"

"I don't know, but he was the state prosecutor in Olivia's case."

She glanced at the computer and notes lying next to her on the bar. "Well, all we have to do now is track down a vaccine that can be used to create a lethal human virus and sold on the black market and figure out Stover and Hayward's connection to all of this."

His phone rang, and he checked the caller ID before answering. "Quinton?"

"Josh . . . I don't know how, but they found you. You need to get out of there—now."

# 25

Caitlyn's stomach lurched. From the look on his face, whatever Josh had just been told wasn't good news. "What's wrong?"

"That was Quinton." He grabbed the car keys off the counter. "We need to leave. This place has been compromised."

Her body froze, like a deer caught in the headlights, as she tried to process what he'd just said.

But she couldn't fall apart. Not now. She'd do that when this was all over.

She closed the laptop and headed for the room where she'd slept. "How much time do we have?"

"I don't know. Grab anything essential. Don't worry about the rest. I'll do the same. Meet you in the car."

"I'm right behind you."

She dropped the computer into her backpack, along with a few other personal items. When she turned to leave the room, she hit her arm against the bed frame. She winced at the pain shooting up her arm. Her jaw tensed. She'd noticed some redness at the site this morning and had planned to have Josh rebandage it for her. She was worried about an infection without antibiotics, but there wasn't time to deal with that now.

She glanced around the room to make sure she hadn't forgotten anything, then ran after Josh. There were still so many unanswered questions. How had they been found? And who had found them? The authorities, or someone else? Breakfast sat in her stomach like a rock, bringing with it a fresh wave of nausea. All Josh's warnings about what could happen if they decided to run had been right on track. This had been a mistake.

She slid into the passenger seat. Exhaustion settled around her, and instead of thinking straight, all she could feel was panic. At the moment, she saw no way out.

"Where are we supposed to go?" she asked.

"Quinton texted an address in southeast Houston," Josh said, pulling out of the drive. "We'll meet him there, then reassess the situation together."

"I don't understand how this happened." Her mind couldn't stop scrambling for an explanation. For anything that made sense in a world that had totally collapsed around her.

"He didn't take the time to give me any details." He turned left at the first corner away from the ocean and headed back toward Houston. "It's going to be okay."

"Is it?"

She studied the side-view mirror, searching for signs that someone was following them. Nothing seemed ominous beyond the gray rain clouds hovering above them, but they were out there. Somewhere.

"Do you think we need to turn ourselves in?" she asked.

"I don't know." He turned onto Interstate 45 and started across the bay. "Do you think we have enough evidence from the computer files to give to the authorities? Anything that would definitively prove what was going on in that office?"

"The evidence is coming together, but there are other questions. Who is the inside person in the lab? Helen mentions Carmichael, but we don't have any hard evidence connecting them. And it's the same with Hayward and Stover."

"And not only do we not have all the evidence we need, the au-

thorities somehow have evidence against me," he said. "How do
I prove that I didn't hide the murder weapon in my house, or that
I never signed divorce papers? How am I supposed to do that?"

She stared out the window while he maneuvered through traffic. It didn't matter what time of day, Houston traffic was always
a challenge. She studied the cars that passed. Each one a potential threat out to silence them. What happened to innocent until
proven guilty?

He reached out and squeezed her hand. "I still meant what I
said. We'll find a way out of this."

"I think I've heard that before, but we're still running."

"We're alive, aren't we?"

She couldn't help but smile. "I'm not sure for how long, but yes."

"The three of us will come up with a solution, I promise."

She hesitated before asking the question she hadn't been able to
shake. "I know you don't want to hear this, but what if Quinton
isn't on our side?"

Josh dropped her hand and gripped the steering wheel. "He's
the one who set up the safe house and now he's warned us—"

"I know, but if there's a chance that he's been turned, or compromised . . ."

"I know it's hard for you to trust him, but I know him. He's
saved my life more than once. He would never betray me."

She was treading on thin ice and she knew it. "Maybe he would
if they threatened his family?"

His jaw tensed, and he flipped on his windshield wipers as rain
started falling. "So you think this is a setup?"

"I'm worried it could be. I know you trust him, but I don't want
to walk into this blind."

"I know you're right to be concerned, but what choice do we
have? We have to trust someone."

Trust had always been an issue for her. As a child she'd wanted to
trust her father, but then she'd seen what he could do. Her mother

should have been an ally, but as an abused spouse, she'd never been able to fill that role. Which had left Caitlyn with no defender. In the end, she'd learned to do things on her own. That was one reason why her going to Josh in the first place had been such a difficult leap of faith.

Problem was, she was pretty sure she was going to feel vulnerable no matter where she was. Being inside the walls of a locked safe house hadn't erased the fear. Or the threat, obviously. It was going to come down to a choice. She had chosen to trust Josh. Which meant she had to trust the people he trusted—including Quinton—and the decisions they made.

They pulled up at the address, and Josh hesitated before exiting the car. "Why don't you stay in the car until I know it's safe."

"I'll be just as safe in there with you as out here on my own."

He caught her gaze. "You're not going to change your mind, are you?"

She shook her head and grabbed her backpack with the computer. Quinton was going to want to see what they had. They dashed up the sidewalk in the drizzling rain to the apartment, then knocked on number 42.

No answer.

"Are you sure we're at the right place?"

Josh glanced at his phone. "This is the address he gave me, plus his car's parked outside."

Worry gnawed at her. Something wasn't right.

"That's strange." Josh tried the door handle of the apartment. "It's open."

He walked into the room in front of her. Quinton lay in the middle of the living room carpet.

She dropped her bag onto a chair as a wave of nausea swept through her. Josh crouched down beside his partner and checked his pulse before stumbling backward. "Caitlyn . . . He's dead. Quinton is dead. They killed him."

But there was no time to grieve. This was a trap.

He started pulling her toward the front of the apartment. "We need to get out of here now—"

The bullet missed his head by inches, then slammed into the wall.

Josh shoved Caitlyn out of the way, then lunged at the armed man running toward them. Josh grabbed the man's wrist and spun the gun away from him, then twisted the man's arm, flipping him to the ground. He snatched the gun out of the man's hands and stood over him.

But it didn't matter.

"Drop the gun. Now."

Caitlyn struggled to breathe as she looked across the room at another man aiming a gun at her head. Sirens whirled in the background. The police were coming.

The man Josh had taken down looked at his partner. "We can't get caught. We need to get out of here."

"You'll never get away with this," Josh said.

"Really?" The man walked closer to Caitlyn, his gun never wavering. "Because here's the ironic thing. Even if we don't take you down, they will. They'll find evidence here that you murdered your partner."

"If you hurt her, I'll shoot him," Josh said.

"I believe you. That's why we're leaving." He took another step toward Caitlyn. "Let him go."

Josh hesitated, then nodded, his gun still trained on the man as he got up. "This isn't over," he said.

The sirens grew louder as the men ran out the back door.

"Caitlyn . . . we need to get of here too." He pulled the cash he had out of his pocket and shoved it into her hand. "It's safer if we split up. Get out of the city and find a place to stay off the grid."

"What? Wait . . . No." She stopped, her heart pounding. He couldn't be serious about them splitting up. "We're not going to win this."

"My partner's dead. They don't just want me in prison, they want me silenced. And there's someone in the department involved in this. I have no way to know who to trust. If we turn ourselves in, this is over."

"Josh—"

"We'll still find a way to convince them we're innocent, but in the meantime, we need to split up and run."

"No." She didn't even try to mask the terror in her voice. "I'm not going to leave you."

"In about forty-five seconds, they're going to surround this place, and they'll be looking for both of us. We'll have a better chance if we're not together. Trust me."

She could hear the sirens now, growing louder in the distance. "Where am I supposed to go?"

He grabbed her backpack and handed it to her. "We talked about running. You know what to do. Head west from here, then get on a bus out of the city and lay low. Cash only."

Caitlyn stared at him, desperate to pull herself out of what was happening. He couldn't be serious.

"Trust me," he said. "Go now."

He pulled her against him, kissed her for a brief moment, then nodded toward the back door. "Keep the burn phone you have. I'll call you as soon as I can. I promise."

Josh waited a moment to make sure she'd followed his instructions, then threw the gun on the couch and headed for the front door as the team of officers pulled into the driveway and stepped out into the yard. Turning himself in might be a death sentence, but it should also buy her the time she needed to get away. Then maybe—just maybe—he'd be able to figure out a way to save her.

Unlike Quinton.

Guilt raged inside him, reminding him that he was the one who should be dead. Not his partner. This was all his fault, and now Quinton's family was going to have to pay the price. And no matter what he did to try to make up for his death, it would never be enough.

"Detective Solomon . . . Put your hands in the air."

Josh stopped in front of the cop he'd once played golf with, praying he'd given Caitlyn the time she needed to get away. "Detective Acevedo—"

"Get down on the ground. Now."

Seconds later, he was prone on the ground, arms extended outward, legs spread, while an officer confirmed he didn't have a weapon. A second officer handcuffed him, letting the metal dig into his skin.

"Where is she?"

"She's not here."

"You're lying."

One of the officers stepped out of the house. "Detective Acevedo, we've got a body inside. Lambert's dead."

Josh felt a boot dig into his back, pressing him hard against the ground. "You killed your own partner?"

He didn't say anything. Just lay with his face in the grass. He was never going to get out of this. He'd played right into their hands, just like the fool they'd assumed he was. He never should have gotten Quinton involved. Never should have believed he could circumvent the authorities while trying to solve things his way. How many more lives were going to be lost because of him? Quinton was dead. And if they caught Caitlyn . . .

*I'm sorry, Olivia. So, so sorry I couldn't save you. Sorry that your killer is going to get away with murder. And Caitlyn . . . what have I done?*

Somehow in all this mess, he'd found himself falling for her. But none of that mattered because, while she might be able to run for a while, he knew they'd find her eventually.

. And they'd both pay the price for his foolishness.

They jerked him up, wrenching his arms in their sockets. He bit back the pain. He'd done all he could to give Caitlyn the chance to escape. The only thing he could do now was figure out how to get out of this and save them both.

Detective Acevedo avoided his gaze. "Joshua Solomon. You're under arrest for the murder of your wife, Olivia Solomon, and your partner, Detective Quinton Lambert. You have the right to remain silent. Anything you say can and will be used against you in a court of law . . ."

The officer continued giving him his rights as he led him to the car. He'd memorized the words over a decade ago. Said them while arresting dozens of murderers.

And now they were being said to him.

A reporter stood in the rain, holding an umbrella over himself and recording the drama. He'd be on the news again tonight, this time not as a wanted man, but one charged with multiple murders.

He glanced back at the house where Quinton's lifeless body lay. Bile burned his throat. The ME had just pulled up, ready to take his friend to the morgue. A fresh wave of guilt battered him. Had they found Caitlyn, or had she been able to evade them? She was smart, but that didn't mean she'd be able to succeed in the impossible task he'd just handed her. He'd seen it as her only chance. He knew that if they found her, they'd use everything in their power to turn her against him. He slid into the back of the squad car and breathed in the rank smell of vomit. He knew what they would do because he'd do the exact same thing if he were in their shoes.

They'd convict her as his accomplice in murder, then hand him the death sentence. That was, if he managed to survive the first week in prison. They wanted him silenced, which meant no matter what happened next, things were not going to end well.

# 26

Josh had no idea how much time had passed since his arrest. He paced the tiled floor of the interrogation room, trying to make sense of everything that had happened. He'd been arrested, but he still had no idea if Caitlyn had managed to escape detection or if they'd arrested her as well. But his arrest wasn't the worst thing that had happened. Quinton was dead. Shot in the back of the head execution style. His partner's death had been a trap to catch him.

He stopped in front of the mirrored wall, desperate for a plan that would get him out of this. He still had dozens of questions, but the pieces of the puzzle were slowly beginning to come together. And the emerging picture terrified him.

How well did people—including the officers in this department—really know each other? After all, one of them was a traitor. One of them wanted him dead.

Still, whoever was behind this didn't have control over the entire precinct. That would be impossible. He still had a chance to talk to whoever was going to come in and question him. He had to find a way to protect Caitlyn.

He started pacing again. The worry was back, full force. He

wasn't sure anymore that this was something he could fix. Like Olivia's murder. And now Quinton's. No matter what he'd done, he hadn't been able to save them. What if he couldn't save Caitlyn?

*God, I've got to find a way out of this . . .*

With options limited, and circumstantial evidence in abundance, the only way out was to convince them he'd been set up. But was that even possible? He drew in a breath, needing to slow down his heart rate. Whoever came through the door, he'd appeal to them as fellow officers. Hopefully they would know him enough to at least question the evidence.

He turned around when the door to the interrogation room finally opened and Adams and Sanchez walked into the room.

"Detectives . . . I'm not sure what's going on here, but you need to know—"

"Sit down." Adams's frown deepened. "Because here's what *you* need to know. You're not in charge here anymore."

Josh started to respond, then stopped himself as he sat down. The walls started to spin and press in around him. His chest felt heavy and his brow was sweating. He'd just been put in his place. So that was it? This wasn't going to be a discussion between colleagues. He wasn't just a person of interest. From the look in their eyes, they were two detectives looking at a suspect they were convinced had murdered two people.

"Detective Solomon." Adams dropped a file folder onto the table, then pulled back one of the chairs and sat down. "I hardly know where to begin. When we pulled you over, we wanted to talk to you because we were concerned about a fellow officer. But now . . . Let's just say I never thought I'd see the day when you'd be sitting on the other side of the table. You were always at the top of your game. Dozens, if not hundreds, of convictions over the past decade, and even a couple commendations. And now you're facing double-murder charges."

Josh's jaw tensed at the stark reminder of why he was sitting in the suspect's spot. "Nothing's changed. I didn't kill Quinton, and I certainly didn't kill my wife. You of all people should know that. Someone is trying to frame me."

"You think you're being framed?" Detective Adams glanced at his partner and let out a low laugh. "Even for you that seems a bit of a stretch. I'd hate to be your defense attorney, because coming up with a defense to get you off with the evidence we have is going to be complicated, if not impossible . . . We're not just talking about a cop killing his wife, but a cop killing another cop. You know as well as I do that neither will go down well with a jury."

Josh ran through his limited options. He could argue with them, or he could lay all his cards on the table, but at the moment, he didn't like the odds of either option. More than likely, Adams and Sanchez were nothing more than pawns in this case, doing exactly what they were told, but he wasn't going down without a fight.

"I need you to listen to me," Josh said. "Please. I didn't kill them, but you need to understand that something bigger is going on here. And if you let me, I can prove it."

"I'm not sure—"

"Just give me the benefit of the doubt for a minute." He fought to keep the frustration out of his voice. "Sanchez, three months ago, I was at your daughter's birthday party, and Adams . . . I watched your son receive his high school diploma at his graduation last spring. Don't tell me you're going to put everything you know about me aside and buy into these lies."

"Trust me, I don't want to." Adams braced his elbows on the table and leaned forward. "But here's what we know is true. They found your wife's murder weapon stashed in your attic with your fingerprints on it. We also know you were filing for a divorce. Is that why you and your girlfriend killed her? Because she refused to sign the papers?"

"No."

Adams sat back in his chair. "We have one more thing. Caitlyn Lindsey is in custody, and she just hung you out to dry."

Josh's jaw tensed. Someone had already convinced them that he was guilty and had been ordered to find out what he knew and take him down, and now they'd found Caitlyn? He wasn't sure he believed him. Because even if they had found her, she wouldn't have turned on him. He'd bet his life on that.

He also knew all the tricks of an interrogation. He'd used them every time he walked into this room with a suspect. He'd used them because they worked. He looked for signs of deception, nonverbal clues. He would leverage personal connections to get a confession.

This had become a game of chess for both sides, and he was going to have to watch every word. For a suspect, the goal was to appear innocent and cooperative, as if there was nothing to hide, while at the same time not offer up anything that would be incriminating. For the detectives, the goal was to sow doubts and uncover inconsistencies that gave the suspect enough rope to eventually hang himself.

He needed to prove to them that he was innocent without saying something they could twist and use against him. Not reacting to their claim about Caitlyn seemed the better option at the moment.

"Nothing to say?" Detective Adams tapped his fingers on the table. "Well, I have plenty I can say. You had an affair with your wife's coworker, and when Olivia wouldn't grant you a divorce, you killed her."

Josh fought to stuff down the anger bubbling in his gut. "I've already told you, I didn't kill my wife."

"You were smart about it though. You thought you'd get away with murder by tying it to a string of burglaries." Adams pointed at him. "And you know what? That actually worked. For a while. But not anymore."

"You're wrong. And besides, none of this makes sense. If I killed my wife and someone else was convicted for the murder, why would I have started asking questions again? Why would I do anything to draw attention to myself? Why would I do anything at all to try and prove that the men convicted of my wife's murder were innocent?"

"It doesn't make sense . . . unless perhaps your partner discovered the truth and decided he wasn't going to keep your dirty little secret."

Josh tugged on the collar of his shirt. He couldn't breathe. Couldn't believe what they were saying. He tried to calm down. He couldn't forget that their plan was to spin him in circles until he couldn't stand up anymore. He couldn't let that happen.

"What you're saying isn't possible," he said.

But the panic refused to let go. When the detectives had first walked in, he believed he'd have a chance of convincing them he was being set up. Had thought they'd believe him, or at least give him a chance and listen to a fellow officer. But none of that was true.

And how was that even possible? He'd worked with these guys for years. Surely someone would give him the benefit of the doubt. Surely someone would walk through that door and realize that things weren't adding up. But instead, they were coming at him like they actually believed he was guilty.

"I've known both of you for years," he said. "You can't actually think I could have killed Olivia. And Quinton . . . he is . . . was . . . my partner."

"Then tell me why you were there."

"I was there because he asked me to meet him." Josh leaned forward and caught Detective Adams's gaze. "Think about it. You know I didn't do this, Adams."

Adams opened the folder and pulled out a photo of him and Caitlyn laughing and pushed it across the table at him. "You say you weren't having an affair, but this was taken from security footage at Bistro 17 three weeks before your wife was murdered. The two of you look pretty cozy."

Josh shook his head. That wasn't possible. Or was it? He worked to place the photo. "There were four of us. Olivia and I went out with Caitlyn and her date. Dinner and then some event at a museum. You can talk to her date. Gary . . . Greg . . . I don't remember. He'd just told a joke, I think."

"You have an explanation for everything, don't you?" Adams pulled out another photo and pushed it across the table, this time of Olivia's body at the crime scene. "Looking back, I'm actually shocked that you never were on the suspect list after she was killed. Of course, you're smart. Just not smart enough. Because we know now what happened. You and Caitlyn Lindsey were having an affair and decided to murder your wife. When your partner found out, you killed him as well. It will take very little to convince a jury of that."

Josh looked straight ahead, avoiding the image of Olivia's dead body that was already forever imprinted in his mind. "We don't have to go over it again. I've told you what happened."

"We'll go over it until you tell us the truth," Detective Adams said. "Because here's the thing, Solomon. Everything you've told the authorities so far has been a lie. You didn't return home that night to burglars ransacking your house. No, you killed your wife, then called 911. The neighborhood burglars were the perfect scapegoats, weren't they? Everyone immediately had their eyes focused on them instead of you. And all you had to do was say you'd seen them fleeing your house. You even went as far as to say you chased them down the road and lost them, and then returned so you could be there as your wife took her last breath. The grieving husband, with his bloodstained shirt from trying to save her would—just as you thought—make for the perfect alibi. It was quite a performance."

"Except none of that really happened, did it?" Detective Sanchez took his turn. "You killed your wife and watched her bleed to death in your bed."

"And then I hid the murder weapon in my attic?" Josh shoved the photos back across the table. "Do you actually think I'd be that stupid?"

"Then how would you do it?"

"How would I do it?" Josh drew in a deep breath. "That's the point. I didn't do it. I wouldn't do it."

He stared at the wall behind the detectives. Fatigue and emotion were starting to play tricks on his mind. He was going to back himself into a hole if he wasn't careful. After pinning his wife's murder on him, they could easily guarantee his silence. It wouldn't be hard to pay someone to kill him behind bars.

The perfect murder.

He shifted his gaze to the one-way window, wondering who was standing on the other side. Wondering if Caitlyn really was sitting in another room right now, like him, being interrogated. He had no way of knowing whether she was here or still on the run. Either way, she was in trouble. Whoever was behind this had long arms. And he'd played right into their hands.

"There's more behind this than you realize," he said, needing them to understand what had really happened. "It's true that the wrong people were convicted for Olivia's murder. I know that. But I didn't do it. There was something going on at her lab . . . they were working on a killer virus worth millions of dollars . . . and Olivia wasn't the only one killed for it."

Adams glanced at Detective Sanchez and chuckled. "So now you're actually going to spout off some crazy killer virus conspiracy theory."

It did sound crazy. He sounded crazy.

"Are you done?" Adams asked. "We know there was no robbery. No armed men who entered your house that night. And definitely no conspiracy at your wife's lab. Your fingerprints were on the gun that killed her. You killed her."

"No!"

Josh pressed his hands on the table. He was getting caught up in their game. Playing the hand they wanted. He'd been set up. All the evidence pointed at him, and even the truth he'd discovered had been twisted. Somehow, he'd thought because they were friends he could explain the truth. But the truth was that it didn't matter what he said. They were planning to take him down no matter what he did.

"I've said enough. I want a lawyer."

"Fine." Adams scooted back his chair. "You can call your lawyer, but in the meantime, you might want to start praying for your soul. Because according to rumors out of the DA's office, they're planning on going for the death penalty."

# 27

Josh glanced down at the smear of red on the sleeve of his shirt and felt his stomach roil at the reminder. Quinton's blood. Why hadn't he seen that before? The police would say it was more proof he'd been involved in his partner's murder. His attempts to convince them he was innocent had failed because there was a greater force working against him out there. But no matter how this looked, he wasn't ready to stop fighting. Not yet.

He rubbed the back of his neck, knowing he looked guilty. And he couldn't really blame them. The evidence was there. His guilt obvious. They truly believed he'd killed his wife and then his partner who'd gotten too close to the truth. But they were wrong.

*How do I make them believe me, God?*

The door opened, and a brief sense of relief washed over Josh at the familiar face. Eddie stepped into the room before closing the door.

"I'm trying to decide if this plan of yours is brilliant, or just plain crazy." He set two coffees down on the table, then slid one of them across to Josh.

"At this point, probably a bit of both."

"How are you doing?"

"Let's see." Josh frowned at the question. "I've just been accused of murdering two people, including my wife. Everyone here seems to have turned against me, and even if I do manage to get out of this, my career is over. If I don't get off, I'll either be executed or I'll spend the rest of my life in prison if, that is, I manage to survive the first forty-eight hours."

"I guess that wasn't the right question." Eddie dropped his leather messenger bag on the table, then sat down across from him.

Josh reached for the coffee. "I've never seen you in a suit."

"I'd actually forgotten I even owned one, but I thought I should at least try to look the part of a lawyer."

"I appreciate your coming, because I need your help," Josh said, jumping straight to the reason he'd called Eddie and not a lawyer. "At this point, you're the only person I know I can trust. They killed Quinton."

"I heard it on the news on the way over here. I'm so sorry."

Josh didn't miss Eddie's gaze stopping on his bloody sleeve. He wanted to shower and change. Wanted to walk out the door like none of this had happened. But none of those things were going to happen anytime soon. He needed to find Caitlyn and make sure she was okay, and on top of that, find the evidence they were innocent.

"First let me say that I've read through the file they have on you, and I still believe you."

"I was hoping you'd say that."

"You saved my life, and I'd trust you with mine again, but that said, this doesn't look good." Eddie had never been one to beat around the bush either. "The DA has some pretty incriminating evidence that's going to be hard to refute. And if this ends up going in front of a jury . . . I can promise you, those twelve men and women aren't going to be sympathetic to the idea of a cop who killed his wife and then his partner."

Josh managed a sip of coffee. "That's exactly why I need your help, starting with finding a way to get me out on bail."

"The DA's pushing for no bail, and more than likely the judge's going to agree."

The confirmation that he wasn't going anywhere felt like a punch in the gut.

"I guess that makes sense. If the assistant DA's involved in this, he's going to make sure I'm not going anywhere." Josh stood up, feeling like a caged animal. "Here's the other problem. I won't last a day in prison. Someone wants me dead, and whoever that someone is, I'm pretty sure they decided this was the cleanest way to take care of me."

Eddie frowned. "I have to admit the same thing crossed my mind. The problem we have right now is that the evidence against you is pretty solid. The murder weapon . . . the signed divorce papers . . . And there's also Caitlyn Lindsey."

"I'm assuming they told you she confessed that we were having an affair, and when Olivia wouldn't sign the divorce papers, I killed her."

"They did."

"Do you really think they brought her in, or are they just playing me?"

"Honestly, I think anything's possible at this point." Eddie leaned forward. "I tried to call her like you asked but haven't been able to get ahold of her. I'm thinking either she ditched her phone, or they're telling the truth and she's here."

He was second-guessing his decisions. He'd turned himself in so she could get away. Now everything had backfired against him.

"First of all, the two of us weren't and aren't having an affair. I'd hardly spent any time with her until the past few days. And even if they have her, she wouldn't have confessed to any of that, because it isn't true."

"There's something else you need to know," Eddie said.

Josh felt his chest tighten. "What?"

"As I was coming in, the detectives told me they'd just been given new information. Caitlyn had been afraid someone was after her, and she'd been run off the road."

"That's true. The night I met with her for the first time, she had a bruise on her face. She'd been checked into the hospital for observation, but she left." Josh struggled to draw in a breath, waiting for the next bombshell. They'd managed to twist everything that had happened so far. This was clearly not going to be any different. "What did they tell you about it?"

Eddie pulled a file from his bag. "According to the information I was just handed, your car was found. They believe that the paint marks on her car match the paint on your car. On top of that, a witness to the accident gave a description of your car."

"A witness. Of course." Josh ran his fingers through his hair. "But that doesn't even make sense. Why would I try to run her off the road?"

"Because she found out you murdered your wife and decided she was going to go to the police. They're saying you kidnapped her from the hospital and have been holding her until today."

The room was closing in on him. He wasn't going to win this. That virus was worth millions, and someone had already made it clear that anyone who got in their way was going to be eliminated. Framing him for the murder of his wife was actually brilliant. Because proving he didn't do it was going to be far harder than proving he did.

Josh pressed his fingers against his temples. His head pounded like it was in some kind of vise. He sucked in a deep breath. He knew what the detectives were doing. This was nothing more than a mind game. They were trying to play him and Caitlyn against each other, but it wasn't going to work.

"When you were at my store you mentioned a bioweapon. Is that still what we're looking at?"

Josh nodded. "Caitlyn found Helen Fletcher's lab notes and was able to confirm that they'd discovered a virulent virus where the vaccine could generate a more lethal strain of the virus that would spread instead of stopping it."

"That sounds nasty," Eddie said.

"Combined with the right researcher and buyer, it would be deadly. We were trying to find out who was behind it and in particular who might be trying to sell the virus."

"I'm assuming you have a plan?"

"You are my plan. First of all, I need to know she's safe," Josh said. "Can you confirm that the police have her in custody?"

"I can confirm that's their story. Whether it's true or not, I don't know."

"Then I need you to find out if she was arrested, or if they're lying to me."

"Okay, what else?"

"If she is still out there, I need you to make sure she's safe. I did what I could to protect her, but I'm worried about her on her own. I also need evidence." He knew it was a tall order, but if anyone could pull this off, Eddie could. "Concrete evidence that will trump anything they've got against me."

"Where do you want me to start?"

"We know there are at least three people involved in this," Josh continued. "The assistant DA Nigel Hayward, Jarred Carmichael from the lab where Olivia worked, and Shawn Stover, aka Jigsaw. The problem is, we don't have any solid evidence that ties them to Starlighter."

"Seems like the DA's office would be a good place to start. I have some contacts there." Eddie nodded, then pushed back his chair. "We're going to figure out who's behind this, Josh."

A wave of relief washed over him. "Thank you."

"Like I said, I owe you, but you need to be careful. You know how this works. I will do everything I can to get the evidence you need to clear you, but in the meantime, think twice before you say anything. They've already proved that they're going to do whatever they have to in order to take you down."

# 28

Caitlyn shifted in the hard, wooden chair in the back of the library as she accessed the building's Wi-Fi on the computer Quinton had given them, then felt her heart stop as she clicked onto Channel 13 news. The featured story showed a photo of Josh handcuffed in front of the house where Quinton had been murdered.

HOUSTON COP ARRESTED FOR THE MURDER OF HIS WIFE AND FELLOW DETECTIVE. JUDGE DENIES BAIL.

She quickly scanned the article that included statements from the assistant DA, who had been involved in Olivia's case, with strong wording that justice would be carried out. There was no mention of her involvement, but this . . . this had to be wrong. She glanced back at the photo. If Josh had been arrested at the house, he hadn't planned to run. He'd planned to take the fall.

The realization brought with it a wave of nausea. Turning himself in was a death sentence. He'd said it himself. And he'd done it all in an attempt to save her. Which meant she had to do everything in her power to put an end to this. And that had to start with a plan. Not taking any chances, she'd ditched the burn phone she had and bought another one where she'd transferred some of the numbers. Two bus rides and a taxi had brought her to a community library on the other side of Houston, ready to implement the rest of her plan.

She sat back in her chair. Josh had wanted her to leave Houston, but this article only confirmed her decision to stay. He was being set up and she needed to find a way to help him.

Her head pounded as she tried to remember everything they had talked about when they discussed running. No credit cards. No cell phones. No communication with friends. They were going to expect her to contact people in her circle of friends. Her friends on Facebook, Twitter, and Instagram.

Somehow it had turned into a game of cat and mouse. She had no idea what the rules were, let alone how to win. Where was she supposed to run? She'd hesitated going too far on her own, which was why she was still in the city. And now she was glad. In the end, she had no doubt that they would find her. She planned to have solid evidence to back up her story when they did.

*I really need your help, God.*

Shoving aside the mounting fear, she ran through her options for help. Quinton was dead. He'd been the one person Josh had completely trusted. Which left her where? She couldn't go to anyone she knew. It wasn't worth the risk of putting their lives in danger. She wanted to call her pastor or Amber, her best friend, but she couldn't do that. It would only be a matter of time before the authorities went to them and started asking questions. Communicating with them would be too risky. If they didn't know where she was, they wouldn't have to worry about lying.

Eddie was her best option. Josh trusted him. He already knew about the situation and might have an idea of how she could help Josh.

Decision made, she pulled out her phone, then looked around the room. She didn't want to call attention to herself, but there were only a couple people in her section of the library, and they both had earbuds in their ears.

A dozen rings later and no answer, she hung up the call.

Biting back the frustration, she sent a text message, leaving her name and praying he'd get back to her.

We need to talk. Urgent.

She started to log out of the internet, then hesitated again at the news article. Eddie had mentioned a connection between assistant district attorney Nigel Hayward and Shawn Stover. That had to be significant. Scrolling back to the top, she found the name of the journalist who'd written the headline. Ben Northridge. She typed his name into a google search and waited for the results to pop up— his Twitter account, LinkedIn, and lists of articles he'd written, including dozens of human-interest reports and humanitarian stories.

She hesitated, knowing she should reject the idea beginning to form in the back of her mind. But if she could talk to him and find a way to get him to at least listen to her, he had to have connections. The only problem was that he'd more than likely turn her in if he knew who she was.

But what if she could get him to help her without giving up her identity? What if she could motivate him with the promise of a bigger story? If he could get her some of the information she needed, and she gave him exclusive rights to the story once everything was all over, it would be a win/win situation.

She opened up Google again and read through his bio and Twitter feed. A bit more searching and she found a Facebook profile. Five minutes later, she'd set up a new email address. Now she just needed to throw out the bait with her first message to the email address she'd found for him.

Mr. Northridge. I have information proving Joshua Solomon's innocence. Please contact me ASAP.

Next, she needed a secure place where they could talk online if he responded. An encrypted chatroom where she didn't have to register, that would keep their conversation private, and that would give her a place where she could send a file with evidence if it came to that. As soon as she'd finished setting up the chatroom account, she clicked back to her email account to see if there had been a response.

Nothing.

And nothing yet from Eddie.

The clock on the wall ticked behind her. A public place probably wasn't the best location even if it did provide her a space to figure out her next move and provide her with free Wi-Fi. More than likely, her face was going to be plastered on the local news channels before long as a person of interest at the very least. Which meant this had probably been a foolish move. The reporter wasn't going to answer a message from a stranger. She opened up another window and started looking through the local news reports to see if there were any updates on Josh's arrest. Nothing yet, but it was still early.

She glanced at the files she'd been going through. Maybe the smarter thing to do was find another cheap motel and keep going through the files.

A message popped up on her opened email account.

Who is this?

She felt her heart pound as she typed in her response.

Don't feel safe giving out personal information at this point, but I've set up a secure chatroom where we can talk online.

She gave him the connection information, then went back to the chatroom and waited for him to show up. Three minutes later, there he was.

**User2308:** I'm here, but I need to know who you are.

**Cyberborg5528:** Sorry, but can't give any personal information right now. Too much at stake. Need to talk about the story you recently broke. There are things I know that will make this a huge breaking news story once the truth comes out.

**User2308:** Like Solomon's innocence? That's a big promise. Why should I believe you? Right now, the latest news is that Josh Solomon has been arrested for not only the murder of his wife, but his partner as well. I was there at the scene of his arrest. Evidence is solid.

**Cyberborg5528:** I'm putting together evidence that proves Solomon is being framed.

**User2308:** Most of the people in prison claim the same thing.

**Cyberborg5528:** Look into connections between convicted felon Shawn Stover, aka Jigsaw, and ADA Nigel Hayward, who's been assigned to this case.

**User2308:** I need to know who you are.

**Cyberborg5528:** Just look into it, then get back to me. Don't have a lot of time.

**User2308:** Not good enough.

**Cyberborg5528:** Look into what I told you, then get back to me as soon as you can.

Caitlyn logged out, not waiting for a response.

Her fingers shook as she erased the browser history in case she ended up getting caught.

She had no idea if she'd made the right decision in contacting the reporter, but there wasn't time now to second-guess what she'd done. Her next move was finding a cheap motel.

*You can't lose it now, Caitlyn. They don't know where you are, and there's no way they could have followed you here.*

On top of that, stressing was only going to make things worse. But trying to convince herself she was safe wasn't working.

She grabbed her bag and headed toward the front of the library. Two police officers walked into the lobby and started talking to the librarian at the front desk. Caitlyn felt the hairs on the back of her neck stand up. Surely it wasn't possible for them to have tracked her down here. She slipped down the nearest aisle between two bookcases, trying to stop the panic, as she grabbed a book off the shelf and pretended to skim through it.

"You're interested in Italy?"

"Italy." Caitlyn glanced at the older woman who'd appeared next to her then looked at the cover of the book she was holding. "*A Traveler's Guide to Italy* . . . well . . . it is a fascinating place."

The woman's smile broadened. "We have a group that meets here once a month and discusses different travel destinations. You'd be welcome to join us."

She looked back at the front desk to confirm that the officers were still there. "Really? I . . . I appreciate the invitation."

"The information is on the board near the front desk."

"Wonderful." She set the book back on the shelf. "Listen . . . I noticed a couple of policemen just came in. Do you know what's going on?"

"I overheard them say something about a drug bust."

"Really?" That wasn't the answer she was expecting. Unless they were using a drug bust as an excuse to search the library for her.

No. She was being paranoid.

"It happens every once in a while, the police coming in here. Drugs, or sometimes they get called in for people sleeping."

"Wow. That's sad."

"It is."

The officers headed toward the other side of the building, but that didn't mean they weren't looking for her.

"If you'll excuse me, I need to go."

With the front exit clear for the moment, she rushed out of the building. There was a bus stop a couple blocks away. All she had to do was get there. Then catch the bus and ride to a motel on the other side of the city. Josh's money would hold her over for at least a few nights while she laid low and went through the files. It was no different than coming up with a plan to process the raw data she collected at work. She was used to planning experiments, then collecting the research. There were always protocols and maintaining a database to track the projects. This was nothing different. She needed to stay organized if she was going to figure this out.

Two buses and an hour later, she slipped the key into the lock and stepped inside her motel room. The decor was out of date and the furniture worn, but she tried to convince herself it could be worse. She took a quick shower, careful to clean the wound on her arm before struggling to put on a fresh bandage.

Next, she flipped on the television while she opened up her computer, praying she wouldn't see her picture on the evening news. There was still no message from Eddie on her phone and no message from the reporter.

She turned up the sound, then sat down on the edge of the bed.

*"Detective Josh Solomon was arrested today for the murder of his wife, Olivia Solomon, a year ago, as well as a fellow police detective who has now been identified as Quinton Lambert."*

There was still no mention of her, but they must have already informed Quinton's wife that her husband was dead. Another family changed forever because of her questions.

She muted the sound, then pulled the Gideon Bible out of the drawer next to the bed. Growing up, she'd struggled to understand what a relationship with Christ truly meant, but over the past few years, she'd worked to make her faith a priority. Today, though, all she could hear was silence. What was she supposed to do when she couldn't hear God's voice? When she had no idea what to do next?

Part of her wanted to hop on the next bus out of town and get as far away as possible, like Josh had told her to. But something stopped her. She missed Josh, and not just because he made her feel safer. He'd made her laugh and smile and stirred something inside her completely unexpected. And then there was the kiss that she had no idea how to interpret. But the bottom line was that she didn't know how to do this on her own. And until she found out the truth about who was behind this, she couldn't help him.

She started reading Psalm 138.

*Though I walk in the midst of trouble, You will revive me; You will stretch out Your hand against the wrath of my enemies, and Your right hand will save me.*

The words of the psalmist worked like a salve on her spirit, calming her mind and helping her see things clearly again. There would be troubles, but she wasn't alone.

*He will protect me from my enemies.*

*His hand will save.*

Her phone buzzed beside her and she picked it up. It was a message from Eddie.

Are you okay?

Safe for now.

Out of town overnight. Meet me @ ice rink, Galleria, 2 tomorrow. Be careful.

# 29

Josh kept his head down as he ate lunch, a reminder of his college cafeteria days. He'd survived the first night in the general population, but he wasn't sure how much longer he'd be able to stay out of trouble. He'd observed several prisoners watching him, circling like vultures, as if they were looking for an opportunity to take him down when the guards weren't looking. Maybe it was just his overactive imagination, but the steady feed of adrenaline that had kept him awake most of the night had left him exhausted. The reality was, he was convinced he wasn't just paranoid. A confrontation wasn't a matter of if, but when.

He wanted to believe that someone from the precinct would decide to dig deeper into the case. Or that Eddie would discover a compelling piece of evidence that would once and for all prove his innocence. But he knew he couldn't depend on either of those things happening. Someone had framed him for murder—someone with the resources to do so—and with all the evidence pointing toward him, he wasn't sure anymore that there even was a way out.

He ate another bite of his bologna sandwich, purposefully avoiding eye contact with anyone except for his new cellmate, Snyder, who sat across from him. He needed to avoid being alone, but socializing didn't seem like a good idea. He knew he needed to keep his head down and stay out of trouble, which hadn't been difficult to do so far. His cellmate was anything but talkative, but at least he'd been decent enough to sit with Josh at meals and answer his questions—primarily about who to watch out for and how to stay out of trouble.

Josh dropped his half-eaten sandwich back on the tray, not sure he could force himself to finish it. "Got someone waiting for you on the outside?"

"Like a girlfriend?"

Josh nodded.

"Nah. She left me months ago. Didn't like the idea of a felon for a boyfriend." Snyder shoved the last bite of his sandwich into his mouth. "What about you?"

"No. No one's waiting for me."

Josh tried to push away the image of Caitlyn that surfaced, but he couldn't get her out of his mind. He had no idea where she was. He still had no idea if she'd actually been arrested, or if she'd managed to run. Either way, he missed that smile of hers that had managed to make its way into his heart, grab on, and refuse to let go. He'd decided that if this wasn't the end—if he did manage to get out of here alive—he was going to tell her how he felt.

But there wasn't time to think about how she'd captured his heart. All that really mattered right now was finding a way to make sure she was safe. Whether or not the authorities had found her, he was pretty certain everything they'd told him was nothing more than lies and scare tactics. But that didn't keep him from worrying. If they could continue using her to get to him, they would. He'd made Eddie promise he'd find out the truth about where she was, knowing he couldn't do anything to help her while he was sitting in prison.

Two inmates sat down at their table on either side of him. He felt their stares as he picked his sandwich back up.

"Rumor is you're a cop," one of them said before taking a drink.

"Not sure where you heard that." Josh shrugged off the comment. "I'm not looking for trouble. All I want to do is serve my time and get out of here."

"Don't we all, but if you're not a cop, maybe you're a snitch—"

Josh caught his gaze. "Seems to me that would be even worse. I'm not that stupid."

"Leave him alone."

Snyder defending him surprised him, but he was grateful. The last thing he needed at this point was for anyone to find out he was a cop. While he was being processed, he'd convinced himself that the chances of running into someone he'd incarcerated were slim, but he couldn't dismiss the fact that he was a detective who'd put criminals away.

But what scared him the most was that he'd always been a defender of justice and the legal system. He knew there were flaws in the system and those who weren't in it to fight for justice, but now he'd been caught in this nightmare scenario and he couldn't find a way out.

They'd all been right. The detectives and his lawyer. The judge had deemed him a flight risk, and because of the severity of his suspected crimes, he'd been ordered to remain in custody until his trial. Eddie had promised he'd fight the decision, but Josh knew it wouldn't make a difference. Whoever was pulling the strings had a tight grip on the case. He wasn't going anywhere.

He glanced at the men who'd started harassing him, who now seemed to have already lost interest in him. But it was a reminder of just how alone he was. He didn't want to know what his family's reaction would be. His mom had never liked the idea of him being a cop and had told him more than one time that she wished he'd move back to Kansas and run the farm with his father. At least she wasn't alive to get the news that her son was in prison. He had no idea what this news was going to do to his father.

Snyder stood and picked up his tray. "I'm heading to the yard."

He grabbed his own tray. "I'll come with you."

Josh followed Snyder, realizing just how much he'd taken his life—and freedom—for granted until it was all stripped away. He missed his morning run. Even missed Houston traffic and waiting in line for his morning coffee. Things he'd always complained about. Right now, he'd do anything to be fighting traffic at the I-10 and I-45 interchange. Instead he was fighting for his life.

Someone came at him from around the corner, a sharp right jab to his rib cage, then a second punch to his nose before he could even react. He looked up to see the inmates who'd sat down next to him at lunch. Josh struggled to catch his balance as Snyder deserted him and hightailed it to the yard. Years of training kicked in and he responded by slamming his fist into the second man's throat. He could hold them off for a while, but the odds were against him taking down both of them. He ducked again as the man came at him with a shiv, then struck the shorter man's nose with his elbow and heard the crack of cartilage, before ramming his fist into the man's rib cage. He fought to catch his breath as he shifted his feet, trying to outmaneuver the two men who came at him from both sides.

He hit the ground with a thud and rolled over, anticipating another blow.

It never came.

Josh opened his eyes. One of the guards hovered over him.

"Get up and come with me now." He offered his hand, then nodded toward the empty corridor. "You need to get as far away from this mess as possible."

Josh winced at the wave of pain shooting through his right side as he followed the guard down the corridor. His eye was starting to swell shut, but he wasn't going to argue with the man. He stepped over the two guys who'd attacked him, both passed out on the ground.

"You gave those guys a run for their money," the man said, "but there's a price out on your head. You won't last another twenty-four hours in here, and I might not be here to save you the next time."

Josh wiped the blood off his lip with the back of his hand as they stepped inside the laundry room. He didn't think anything was broken, but he was going to be sore for a few days. And at least the other two hadn't gotten away unscathed.

"Why would you help me?"

"I have my own reasons."

Josh studied the uniformed guard. He looked familiar, but he couldn't place him. Six foot two, maybe three, two hundred thirty-plus pounds, who clearly spent his free time at the gym. The kind of guy he definitely wanted on his side. But what he didn't understand was why he would come to his rescue.

The man folded his arms across his chest. "We've got about sixty seconds until someone notices I'm talking to you, but I can help you out of this mess."

"I still don't understand why you'd want to do that. You could lose your job."

The man's expression softened. "You saved my life three years ago."

It took a second for Josh to pull up the name from his memory. "You're Reagan Bray."

The man nodded. "I was a beat cop working the streets at the time. There was an ambush and you and your partner showed up and saved me."

Josh glanced behind him at the bins of laundry and industrial-size washers. They were running out of time. "I'm being set up."

"I believe you, because someone clearly wants you dead. If you were guilty, why would someone want to keep you quiet?"

"I wish you could help me, but I've been denied bail. I'm not going anywhere."

"You need to get out of here before they kill you, and I have a plan."

"To get me . . . out?" Josh hesitated, his mind spinning. Surely he wasn't about to contemplate escaping. "If they find out, you'll lose everything."

"Then we better make sure no one finds out."

Escape.

He still couldn't say the word out loud. He was the one who followed the law and sent guys to prison. He still wanted to believe the system would work. That justice would prevail. It was why he did what he did.

"How?"

"The less you know, the better."

The decision was easier than he thought. "What do I need to do?"

A couple inmates were walking toward them. "We're out of time. Go to the yard or sit and watch TV, I don't care, but keep your head down. Make sure there are people around you. I'll give you a signal once I'm ready."

Josh left through the side door, then slipped into the dayroom, where a couple dozen men were watching a flat-screen TV or reading. He prayed he hadn't somehow called attention to himself. Prayed he didn't look as terrified as he felt. A week ago, he never would have imagined he'd be staring at some mindless reality show. There was no sign of Snyder. No sign of anyone familiar, but that was fine. He sat down in a plastic chair and gazed at the screen, attempting to look interested.

This was insane.

He reached up and touched his nose, thankful it had stopped bleeding, but his body ached all over. He had no idea what he'd do if he ended up running into the thugs who'd done this and decided to finish the job. Bray had been right. He might not have anyone come to his rescue a second time. Which was why he was still contemplating the risk. But if he couldn't trust the system, what was his alternative? Either way, he was probably going to die. If he stayed, he was certain to. If he did manage to get out alive, then what? Quinton was dead. He didn't know where Caitlyn was, and they still had no idea who was behind this. No idea who to trust . . .

Another show came on, but he wasn't paying attention. A couple dozen more inmates had filed into the room. Most seemed bored, staring at the TV like he was. There was no way he could do this day in and day out.

Someone handed him a magazine. "There's a good article on chess in there."

"Thanks." Josh flipped open the magazine and found the page. A message had been scrawled on the bottom.

*2:30. Laundry.*

His jaw tensed, but he'd made his decision. He would be there. It was his only chance of staying alive.

# 30

She'd come close to not showing up, and on top of that, she'd heard from the reporter right as she was leaving and was now running late. But meeting Eddie was a risk no matter how Caitlyn looked at it. Even with burner phones to communicate and a neutral meeting place at the crowded mall, she still wasn't convinced it was safe. But he'd insisted they meet in person, which meant all she could do was hope she'd made the right decision.

She tugged at the ball cap she was wearing, keeping her head low and hoping to avoid the security cameras as she headed down the busy second-level corridor of the Galleria in Houston's uptown district. She'd made certain no one had followed her by taking two buses, then opting to get off early and walk the four blocks to get here. But even that hadn't managed to reassure her she was safe.

When her mother had died, she'd found herself thrust into a world she had no idea how to navigate. She'd ended up living, for the most part, on her own, bouncing from one foster care home to another until she'd finally gone to live with her grandmother. And while that situation had proven to be a far better arrangement than most of the homes before, trusting someone—even family—hadn't come easy.

And now she was having to trust someone again.

Eddie was leaning against the railing that overlooked the ice rink below, looking just as intimidating in black jeans and a long-sleeved black T-shirt as he had the first time she met him. She grabbed a free spot next to him that overlooked a group of kids practicing hockey drills.

"Sorry I'm late," she said. "I had to make sure I wasn't followed."

"I didn't think you were going to show up."

She studied the rows of restaurants and shops around her, trying to shake the sensation that no matter how many precautions she'd taken, she was being watched. "I'm still not sure we should have met in public."

"I'm glad you got ahold of me. I tried to call you—"

"I dumped the phone and got a new one."

"You're here and you're safe, that's what's important right now. I have a couple of things I need to talk about with you, and I thought it would be easier this way."

"I guess you know what happened." Caitlyn lowered her voice. "They arrested Josh for the murder of his wife and his partner."

Saying it out loud sent a chill down her spine and made the situation seem even more real. She'd gone to Josh, trying to put a stop to all of this, and instead, he'd been framed for murder.

Eddie's frown deepened. "I've seen him."

Her eyes widened. "How?"

"He called me in as his lawyer."

Caitlyn couldn't help but chuckle. "I guess I shouldn't be surprised."

"He sent me to find you, and to find the rest of the evidence needed to put an end to this."

"Then I'm glad you're here, but I'm scared, Eddie." She stared down at the rink while a kid slammed the puck into the goal. Why couldn't all of this be that easy? "He told me if he was arrested, he wouldn't survive forty-eight hours in prison. That they'd put a hit out on him."

"We don't know if that's true."

"We don't know it's not." She blinked back the tears that threatened as she looked up at him. "He turned himself in, giving me time to run. If I had known what he was planning, I never would have let him make that decision."

Eddie turned to her, resting his arm against the railing. "I know this is hard, but whatever he did, he did it because he cares for you."

She shook her head. "It doesn't matter. He never should have surrendered."

"Maybe not, but he did what he felt was right at the time. Why don't we take a walk. I don't know about you, but I could use something to eat."

She studied the other shoppers as she followed him downstairs to the food court, wishing she could shake the fear that had settled over her. Sunlight streamed through the skylights above them, but her heart couldn't stop fighting the darkness. She'd learned to put her faith in a God she knew she could trust. But there were still times—like today—that holding on to her faith felt more like she was lost in the pounding waves.

Someone shouted. She spun around, heart racing, then let out a sharp huff of air. It was just a kid, running to catch up with his mother.

Eddie stopped and rested his hand on her arm for a moment. "It's okay."

She nodded, but in reality, nothing was okay right now. And she had no idea how to make it okay.

"I'm here to help, Caitlyn."

She glanced up at the man, surprised at his confession. Josh didn't owe her anything. And Eddie certainly didn't.

"I just . . ." She struggled for what to say. "I don't want anyone else to get hurt."

Deadly Intentions

He cupped his hand around her elbow and started walking again, guiding her through the crowd of shoppers. "It's not the first time I've put myself on the line for someone."

"But people have died."

"True, but I'm used to trouble and have no intention of running from it. We're going to figure this out together." He stopped in front of Chick-fil-A. "Do you want anything?"

She shook her head. He didn't need to know how close she was to losing it, and that the smell of food made her stomach churn.

"You should eat," he said.

"I can't."

She waited while he ordered, then followed him to an empty table. In a few hours it would be dinnertime and the crowds would grow, but for now the setting gave them a measure of privacy, and the background noise would drown out their conversation.

He sat down across from her, then slid a chocolate shake in front of her. "This is for you."

"But—"

"I have three sisters, and from my observation, chocolate might not be able to actually fix problems, but it can make you feel better."

She couldn't help but smile at his crazy logic. "I suppose I can't argue with that."

He bit into a fry. "Good."

But even a chocolate shake couldn't make her fear go away.

"You told me you had information," she said, taking a sip of the milk shake.

"I was able to ID the woman in the photos you showed me."

"Who is she?"

"Her name is Brooke Jennings, and she happens to be ADA Hayward's mistress."

"He has a mistress? So much for the family platform he runs on with a wife, two kids, and a dog."

250

"This is a secret he won't want to get out."

She took another sip of her shake, hoping it would actually settle her stomach. "How'd you find out?"

"Don't ask."

"There has to be a way to exploit that for answers. Especially considering we have photos."

"Blackmail?"

"If it would get us the answers we need."

"I had the same idea. I have someone surveilling Ms. Jennings in case we decide we need to talk to her." He wiped his face with a napkin and shot her a smile. "Josh was right about you."

"What do you mean?"

"You're tougher than you look. And you need to know that he's a good guy. The real deal."

She filed away the information for later, because what he'd said wasn't something she was ready to hear. It didn't matter what she felt about Josh. All she could do now was focus on finding a way to help him. "How is he?"

He took another bite of his sandwich before answering her question. "He's struggling. He was told you were brought in and that you confessed that the two of you were having an affair. Then when Olivia wouldn't sign the divorce papers, Josh killed his wife. You decided to make a plea bargain with the DA for a lesser sentence."

"What?" She pushed away the shake, anger replacing the nausea. "None of that is true."

"I know."

"Why would they say that? They know it's not true. He knows it's not true."

"They're using it as leverage with Josh to get him to confess."

"He can't confess to something he didn't do. He didn't kill his wife. We both know that. Just like we weren't having an affair." She shook her head. "What happened to innocent until proven guilty?"

"This has got to be very hard on you."

It was, but she wasn't the one sitting in jail right now.

"There's something I need to tell you." She hesitated, pretty sure he wasn't going to like what she was about to say. "I wasn't late because I was making sure I wasn't being followed. I was delayed because I was talking to Ben Northridge."

Eddie shook his head. "Who's that?"

"He's a reporter who's been following Josh's case—"

"Wait a minute . . ." Eddie leaned forward. "You've been talking to a reporter?"

"We were using a private, encrypted chatroom, and he doesn't know who I am."

"If he's a reporter who's any good at his job, he's probably already figured out who you are."

"Even if that's true, it's been worth it. I think he might have connections we don't."

"He's a reporter after a story. He probably won't hesitate making promises to you he has no intention of keeping. And if he knows who you are—"

"It paid off."

"How?"

"I received a message from him as I was leaving to come here. Let's just say I clearly got his attention, and he did some digging. Turns out that he has a friend, a fellow journalist, who was researching a possible front-page story about extortion and bribery in local government and linked ADA Hayward and lowlife Shawn Stover together."

"What happened?"

"Her main source went back on her account, and she had to drop the story."

"Who's the witness?"

"Northridge wasn't able to get a name."

"Why not?"

She fiddled with her straw. "His reporter friend died in a car wreck."

She'd clearly caught his attention. "That sounds pretty convenient."

"That's what I thought. And it means we have a pattern emerging here. Similar stories linking Stover and Hayward together and people who know about them conveniently dying."

"But even if you're right, we're talking about government officials who have way more power than we do."

"Hayward has to be behind all of this. He's got to be the one putting pressure on the precinct, including the captain."

"Did Northridge have any kind of evidence we could use?"

"Nothing beyond a conversation he had over a year ago. But it proves to me that we're on the right track."

"Maybe, but we still need more. I wasn't able to meet with you sooner, because I had to go to Dallas to speak with Nigel Hayward's personal assistant." Eddie paused. "I might have told her I was a journalist who'd followed his career and wanted to do a feature on him."

Caitlyn leaned forward. "Why's she in Dallas?"

"She took a couple weeks off so she could take care of her mother, who just got out of the hospital."

"And?"

"According to her, he's a family man, who spends his free time doing charity work."

"Did you believe her?"

"I believe she was scared of something, but I couldn't get anything out of her." Eddie let out a sharp sigh. "Here's the problem. At this point the DA's office and, in fact, pretty much all of Josh's precinct, believe he's guilty, considering the evidence that's stacked against him. We can't walk in there until we have indisputable proof of what's going on."

"So how do we do that?" she asked.

"*We're* not."

"What do you mean?"

"Josh asked me to watch out for you, and it will be safer for you if you leave Houston. I can get you somewhere safe until this is over."

"Forget it. I can't help him if I'm not here."

"I'm not sure you have a choice at this point. If you stay here, one side or the other is going to find you."

"Why are you helping him?"

Eddie shrugged. "I owe Josh. And besides that, he made me promise I'd get you out of here if anything happened to him. I've got cash for you. He wanted you to leave. To get as far away from here as you can, and I think he was right. You're not safe here."

His phone chimed, and he pulled it out of his pocket and looked at a text. His jaw tensed.

"Eddie . . . what is it?"

"I just got a message from Josh."

# 31

The knots in Caitlyn's stomach tightened as Eddie followed US 290 toward Cypress—an unincorporated community northwest of Houston. They were heading to the address Josh had given her after she called him. Eddie drove just below the speed limit, knowing, as did she, that they were taking a big risk being out in the open. All it would take was a routine traffic stop for the authorities to find her. Or one wrong move on their part, allowing whoever was behind all this to track them down. But it was the possible consequences of Josh escaping prison that truly terrified her. She had a dozen questions she wanted to ask him, but for right now, all she really wanted was to see with her own eyes that he was all right.

The uneasiness she'd felt all day continued to grow as she glanced in the side-view mirror, looking for anyone who might be following them. Whoever had killed Olivia, Quinton, and the others wouldn't stop until they'd dealt with all their loose ends. And she and Josh were definitely loose ends.

"What if this is some kind of trap?" She spoke out loud the question that had been niggling at her since Eddie had first received Josh's text. "That's what happened with Quinton. We showed up to meet him, but it turned out to be part of a plan to frame us for his death."

Eddie's jaw tensed. "When you talked with Josh on the phone, did he sound like he was being coerced? Like he was in distress?"

"I didn't think so at the time. But now . . ." She drummed her fingers on the console, feeling like an animal confined in a cage as Eddie took their exit. "All I noticed was the understandable stress of a fugitive who'd just escaped from jail."

"You can hardly blame him for that." Eddie took a left and drove into a neighborhood filled with brick houses and a scattering of tall trees. "This is the street he gave us, but we don't have to stop. We could do some surveillance . . . make sure he's alone . . ."

A crazy idea popped into her head. "Give me a second."

She sent Josh another text.

> Is it safe to visit the state fair this year?

He answered right away.

> Pull into the garage. I've got watermelon for you.

She smiled at his reply. "It's okay. He wants us to pull into the garage."

"Should I ask what he said?" Eddie asked.

She shook her head. "It's a long story."

Eddie pulled into the driveway of a brick house with a large covered front porch as the garage door opened. Once inside, he turned off the motor and waited for the door to close behind them before exiting the car.

Josh met them at the door leading into the house. She tried to hide the shock over his appearance but couldn't stop the sharp gasp that escaped her. His lip had been busted, he had a black eye, and his left cheek was swollen.

She pressed her fingers against her mouth. "What did they do to you?"

"It doesn't matter. I'm safe . . . at least for the moment."

But if he got caught, if he were arrested again, then what? He'd never make it out alive a second time.

He bridged the gap between them, pulled her against his chest, and wrapped his arms around her. "They told me you'd been arrested. Until you answered my text, I had no idea if they were telling the truth or not."

"I'm okay." She looked up at him and took a step back. "Shaken from all of this, but okay."

"And Eddie . . ." Josh reached out and shook his friend's hand. "Thank you for bringing her and keeping her safe. We both know how much you're risking being here with me."

Eddie brushed off the comment. "We were meeting when your text came through. Thought it would be safest if I brought her myself, and that you might need some help coming up with a plan to get you out of this mess."

"That's what I'm hoping. Come inside where we can talk."

She walked in behind Josh, whose uneven gait made it obvious that all his injuries weren't visible.

"I've been so worried about you," he said, turning around. "How's your arm?"

"It's fine. Forget about me. You're the one who's hurt."

"It's nothing."

"Nothing? That's debatable. Do you know if there's a first-aid kit in here?"

"I don't know. I haven't looked."

Caitlyn started opening up cupboards until she found a small first-aid kit under the sink. "At least let me clean up your face and put on some antibiotic cream."

"Really, it's just a few scrapes."

She walked up to him and pulled up his shirt to reveal a nasty

<2>

bruise across his rib cage that was already turning a bluish purple. "A few scrapes? This is way more than that. You've been in a fight."

"She's right," Eddie said. "You really should be in the emergency room finding out if anything's cracked or broken. What happened?"

"Apparently, I was right that I wouldn't last long in prison. There was a hit out on me after someone decided to spread a few rumors and offer a bit of cash."

Eddie frowned. "I'd hate to see what the other guys look like, because I'm pretty sure they didn't know about your ninja skills."

Josh chuckled, but Caitlyn wasn't laughing. Instead, relief mixed with anger flooded through her as she blinked back tears. She pressed her lips together, wishing she didn't fall apart so easily.

"I just don't know how to deal with this," she said. "Don't know how we're supposed to get out of this. But for now, sit down and let me clean you up while you tell us what happened."

She motioned for him to sit on the bar stool while she got out what she needed to clean his face.

He grimaced as she started washing his cuts. "Turns out I had a friend who's a guard on the inside."

"A friend on the inside isn't exactly what I would have expected for a cop in general population to encounter," Eddie said.

"Agreed. But long story short, a few years back my partner and I saved his life when he was on his beat and got ambushed."

"And his escape plan?"

"Let's just say it was the only way I was going to get out of there alive. I realize I'll have to deal with breaking the law, but if I hadn't gotten out when I did . . . I have no doubt I'd be dead right now."

She avoided his gaze as she dabbed antibiotic cream across the cut on his cheek. She didn't want to think what might have happened if he was still in there, though she wasn't convinced that the worst wasn't yet to come.

Eddie leaned against the kitchen counter. "There's got to be someone in your precinct we could go to."

"I'm sure there is, but who? Someone there is calling all the shots, and if we were to go to the wrong person . . ."

"I'm done," she said, gathering up the trash and putting the first-aid kit back together. "But I still wish we could get you in to see a doctor."

"Seems like I said that to someone not too long ago." Josh squeezed her hand. "Thank you."

She smiled at him, wishing he didn't stir up her emotions the way he did. All she needed to focus on right now was finding a way out of this current mess they were in.

"Why don't we take this to the living room," Josh said.

She glanced around the kitchen to make sure everything was put away, then followed the men into the other room.

"Whose house is this?" Eddie asked, sitting down in one of the recliners while Caitlyn and Josh took the couch.

"Belongs to a second cousin of my mom and her husband, who I also have to thank for the plaid shirt and jeans I'm wearing, by the way. I check in on them every once in a while and have a spare key. They're out of town for the weekend visiting her sister, so we should be safe for now, though I know I can't stay long without involving them."

"What are you planning to do?" Eddie asked.

"The only thing that will put an end to this. Find the evidence I need to clear myself, then turn myself in."

Caitlyn glanced at Eddie before turning back to Josh. "We have an idea."

"I'm listening."

"We believe we now know at least some of the key players involved in Olivia's death. And now we need to prove it."

They spent the next few minutes bringing him up to date with the connection between Shawn Stover and ADA Hayward, his mistress, and Ben Northridge, the journalist.

"I've also been going through the rest of Helen's notes and was able to decipher most of them," Caitlyn said. "I'm convinced she wasn't planning to kill herself. She was planning to go to the police with her own concerns. She figured out what was happening, just like Dr. Abbott did. But there's something more. The last entry she wrote was the day she died. She found out about an imminent attack and confronted someone."

"Then they killed her."

Caitlyn nodded.

"Where was the attack supposed to take place?"

"I don't know where, but the date in her notes mentions an event taking place tonight. Which means we're out of time."

"And Olivia?" Josh asked. "What was her part in all of it?"

"I believe she was a part of the original team that discovered the virulent vaccine strain. According to Helen's notes, Olivia discovered that Carmichael was working on a strain of the virus that had the potential to wipe out the immune system in a human being."

"And like Helen, they killed her for it."

Caitlyn nodded.

"Sorry to interrupt." Eddie stood up. "But do you mind if I use the restroom?"

"Of course not," Josh said. "It's the first door on the left down the hallway."

"Can I get you some tea? Or painkillers?" she asked, once Eddie had left the room. "You've got to be in a lot of pain."

"I took some when I got here, and will take more as soon as I can, but it's still too early. What about your arm?"

She glanced down at the bandaged spot beneath her jacket. "I almost forgot about it. I cleaned it this morning. It's a little red, but I think it's okay."

"Good." He let out a low laugh. "We make quite a pair, don't we, between all our scrapes and bruises and gunshot wounds."

"Yeah, we do."

He reached for her hand. "I thought I lost you, Caitlyn. And I realized that scared me more than going to prison."

A surge of emotions she didn't know how to handle erupted inside her at his confession. But what she felt toward Josh Solomon wasn't something she could examine right now. Maybe not ever.

"I know my timing is crazy," he rushed on, "and I know you're scared, but I have no guarantee that I'm going to get another chance to talk to you."

"I'm sorry. I just can't, Josh. Not now."

She knew she was going to have to work through her feelings, but not now. Not when everything could come crashing down around them again at any moment.

"That's fine." He squeezed her fingers. "We'll figure out this part of the equation—where we are—later."

She nodded. When their lives weren't hanging in the balance.

"Then let me ask you this. Do you think Olivia was ever a part of Carmichael's plan?"

"No. I think she just didn't get time to tell you before she was killed. I don't think she realized the gravity of what she was dealing with until it was too late. But Eddie and I have a plan that might work to finally catch her killer."

Eddie walked back into the room and sat down across from them. "We found out that ADA Hayward meets his mistress at a hotel every Sunday afternoon," he began. "His wife thinks he's playing squash with one of the guys."

"Today's Sunday, isn't it?" Josh asked.

Eddie nodded. "I hired a buddy of mine to do a bit of surveillance on Hayward. He's going to let me know when he arrives at the hotel."

"So, what are you thinking?"

"We have photos of the two of them together—Hayward and his mistress," Caitlyn said. "You've seen those, but there's nothing compromising about them. Nothing that couldn't be explained away as a casual meeting."

Josh shook his head. "So what are you proposing?"

Caitlyn leaned forward. "We're going to get the photos we need and force Hayward to confess."

# 32

Josh cupped his hand around Caitlyn's elbow as they crossed the hotel lobby, praying they simply looked like another couple who belonged there. The decor, with its marble flooring and modern furniture, was a stark contrast to the seedy motel they were holed up in a couple days ago.

He kept his head down, aware of the security cameras, but he wasn't too concerned about them. By the time the authorities went through the footage, he would either have already been arrested, or would have turned himself in.

In another hour or so, he'd know which one.

Caitlyn matched his stride as they passed Eddie, who was sitting in one of the plush lobby chairs, reading a newspaper, ready to inform them if the authorities showed up.

"I'm having second thoughts about this plan," she said.

"Just smile and keep your head down. No one will know we don't belong here."

He slipped his hand down and took hers as they walked toward the elevators. An arriving group was talking with the concierge while the woman at the front desk was busy checking in a couple. No one was paying any attention to them.

He punched the button for the fifth floor, hoping Eddie's information on Hayward was accurate. He'd insisted on keeping Caitlyn out of any confrontation with the ADA, but she'd only shot down his worry. Both Eddie and Caitlyn had objected to the idea of him being involved in the actual confrontation with Hayward, but he could be just as stubborn as she was. In the end, they'd settled on a plan with the two of them going to see Hayward and Eddie watching the lobby.

He touched his wireless earbuds. "We're heading up the elevator now, Eddie."

The tension around them was palpable as the elevator doors closed and they traveled upward. They were laying everything they had on the line in a last-ditch effort to get what they needed to give to the captain.

He squeezed her hands as the doors opened. "You okay?"

She nodded. "I just want to end this."

They started down the paisley green and blue carpet toward room 531. Black-and-white photographs of Texas scenery hung on the walls. For the moment, there was no one in the hallway, and no signs of a maid. Which was good. The fewer people they encountered, the less chance they would have of being recognized.

They stopped in front of the door. He was used to grilling suspects in the controlled environment of an interrogation room, but today they had the disadvantage. And it was going to take far more than luck to get Hayward to give them what they needed.

He nodded at Caitlyn, and she knocked on the door. "Housekeeping."

Ten seconds later the door swung open. "Wait a minute. You're not—"

"No, we're not." Josh shoved his way into the room, taking Hayward by surprise, backing him onto the bed.

Caitlyn shut and locked the door behind her.

"Nigel—" The blonde in the bed wrapped the bedspread around herself and scooted back against the headboard. "What's going on?"

Josh quickly snapped a string of photos of the compromised couple and sent them in a text message to Eddie.

Hayward lunged toward Josh. "You're going to give me your phone, then get out of this room. Both of you. Right now."

Josh easily blocked the man's punch and shoved him back onto the bed. "It's too late. I just sent the photos to a friend. If you don't want them going to your wife—and going public—you'll do exactly what I tell you. If anything happens to either of us, I've left strict instructions with my friend on what to do."

"You can't do that—"

"It's already done. In the meantime, I want you to sit in that chair." He pointed to the chair beside the desk.

"Do you know who I am? You'll never get away with this." Hayward let out a low groan, then paused. "Wait a minute . . . You're Josh Solomon."

"Get up and sit in the chair," Josh repeated. When Hayward complied, Josh took a pair of zip ties from Caitlyn and secured the man's hands and feet to the chair.

"You're supposed to be in prison."

"I was, but it turns out that I had a friend on the inside who was able to arrange an . . . early departure."

"You escaped? You think anyone is going to believe your word over mine after what you've done?"

"Doesn't matter at this point, because here's what's going to happen." He turned to the woman, still cowering against the headboard. "Caitlyn's going to check the bathroom, then you can go in there and get dressed and wait for us. Don't try anything stupid unless you want these photos to hit the front page in the morning."

Caitlyn checked the bathroom for any cell phones and emerged a moment later. "It's clear."

The blonde grabbed her clothes and scurried into the bathroom while Josh took a moment to study the man. Nigel Hayward had always been a bit of a golden boy to the courts. In his late thirties, he was young enough to please the millennials, yet he had more than a dozen years of experience under his belt. In court, he always came out swinging, and there were rumors circulating that he had an appetite for the district attorney's job.

Their research had confirmed that while he was tough on the squash court, he was even tougher in the courtroom. He'd been married for seventeen years to a surgeon, and together they'd had two children, who attended private schools in the city that cost as much as college tuition. The only vices they'd managed to uncover were his love for cars and his mistress, who apparently gave him something his wife couldn't.

Josh was hoping that weakness turned out to be the one thing that gave them what they needed.

"We're going to talk," Josh said, "but remember if you make any noise, or do anything stupid, those photos hit tonight's news cycle."

He glanced at Caitlyn, then sat down on the edge of the bed across from Hayward. "I'm going to get straight to the point. I know you were involved in the murders of Olivia Solomon, Dr. Walter Abbott, and Helen Fletcher. I also have evidence that you were involved in the selling of a virulent virus that has been made into a bioweapon and that there is an imminent attack being planned for tonight, using that virus."

"Wait a minute . . . Bioweapons and murder?" Hayward let out a nervous laugh. "You can't be serious."

"Oh, I'm very serious."

"I'm an attorney. I put people who are involved in things like that in prison. I don't participate in them, and you're insane to accuse me of it."

"Oh, I can assure you that I'm quite sane. You were involved.

And not only were you involved, you were in the perfect position to make sure that anyone who asked questions—like Olivia and Helen Fletcher—were silenced."

Hayward leaned forward. "You know you won't get away with this, don't you? Incriminating pictures or not, you'll be back in police custody by the end of the night, and I'll be back at my job tomorrow."

"I'm not sure what your payoff was," Josh continued, ignoring the man's comments, "but a few million dollars in an offshore bank account would give you enough to afford expensive hotels like this, vacations, and gifts for your mistress. That account shouldn't be hard to track down—"

"Listen to me." There was an edge of panic to Hayward's voice. "I don't know where you got the information you have, but clearly, I'm the victim here. Anyone who knows me will vouch for me. Besides, I'd never compromise my job for a few secrets—"

"We're not just talking about selling a few secrets," Josh said. "We're talking about your involvement in a bioterrorism attack."

"You're crazy. You both are."

"I don't think so." Caitlyn had opened up a briefcase that had been sitting on the desk and pulled out four passports and an itinerary. "This is interesting. Looks like someone's headed to San Juan on the 11:45 flight out of IAH."

"Just a vacation with my family."

"And a separate ticket for Ms. Jennings to Las Vegas at eleven."

"She has a sister there."

Caitlyn glanced at the bathroom door. "Your timing is what is particularly interesting, considering there's a planned attack for tonight. It's risky, but we've heard you have your eyes on the DA's job, so you're probably not planning to disappear. Just staying out of harm's way in case things go wrong, I'm guessing."

"Nothing you're saying is true. Just tell me what you want and let us go. If it's money—"

"I'm not interested in your money," Josh said. "We need to know who's involved in the scheme and who you sold the virus to."

"I've already told you I don't know what you're talking about."

"Problem is . . ." Josh leaned forward. "I don't believe you."

"You don't have anything on me. You're a fugitive who killed his wife. Do you really think they're going to listen to you after everything you've done? And now you can add kidnapping the assistant DA to your list of crimes."

"Actually, I do think they will listen once we're done here." Caitlyn dropped a photo of Hayward and Shawn Stover she'd pulled from her bag on the end table beside him. "I'm sure you recognize Stover. He's an opportunist, connecting buyers and sellers of black-market items." She dropped another photo onto the table. "This is Toni Salazar. She was a reporter looking into your connection with Stover. She died in a hit-and-run before she could finish her investigation. And these . . . are Olivia Solomon, Dr. Walter Abbott, and Helen Fletcher." She pulled out three more photos. "All dead because they discovered what you were doing. We can connect them all to you."

He tried to laugh away her words, but fear registered in his eyes. "You're crazy!"

"Am I? We're waiting for new autopsy results, but I just received confirmation from his wife that someone switched Dr. Abbott's medication, upping his potassium levels and causing irregular heart rhythms that have been connected with sudden death. As for Helen Fletcher—"

"Stop." Hayward shook his head. "Like I said . . . You're crazy. Because if you had real evidence you would have gone straight to the authorities. Instead you're here trying—futilely, I might add—to get information out of me. Which tells me that you're bluffing. So you really should forget whatever game it is that you're playing, because I have nothing to say to you. But I can promise that my office will have plenty to say. As soon as you're done here,

I'll be requesting warrants for your arrest that will send both of you to prison for the rest of your lives."

"In case you've forgotten, I don't exactly have anything to lose." Josh stood up. "I've already been arrested for the murder of my wife and partner. Threatening the assistant DA with blackmail in his hotel room is nothing."

"I hope you mean that, because you will pay."

Josh took a step back in frustration. Hayward was scared. That was obvious, but he was right about one thing. They wouldn't be here if they had the evidence they needed to go to the authorities. And they only had one card left.

"I do have something else to show you." Caitlyn pulled a vial and syringe out of her bag and held them up. "Do you know what these are?"

Hayward shrugged. "Should I?"

"I work at MedTECH, where most of our work involves creating vaccines. Typically, what we work with isn't dangerous, but there is always a very small chance for the genetic makeup of a virus to create a lethal one. And if that were to happen, you have the potential—with someone who knows what they are doing—for it to be weaponized. Now normally, if something like this were to happen, there are ethical boundaries we stand by. Except in this case, someone got greedy and decided to try and make a profit for themselves. Which is why we're in this situation."

"Interesting story, but how many times do I have to tell you that this has nothing to do with me?"

Caitlyn put the vial and syringe on the table beside him. "Then I'm guessing you really don't know what this is."

Hayward squirmed in his chair. "Why would I?"

"And I guess you don't know this man I work with. His name is Jarred Carmichael. He's one of those unethical employees who thought it might be advantageous to squirrel away a little nest egg of his own. I paid his wife a visit earlier today and found this in the refrigerator at his house. He must have pulled aside a few of the vials for a second buyer. Not a bad idea, considering how much they're worth."

"I still don't know what you're talking about."

"Then let me explain. I'm not sure how much you know about this, but vaccines work on the premise of both keeping an individual from getting sick as well as stopping it from transferring to someone else. So you can imagine the problem we'd have if a vaccine not only produced a more dangerous strain of a virus but was also able to spread that virus."

"Why are you telling me this?"

"Take for example, a disease like pneumonic plague or maybe smallpox," she said, ignoring his question. "Pneumonic plague causes the infection to spread to the lungs through the bloodstream. That in turn causes a secondary issue. And here's the problem with that. While the bubonic plague can surprisingly be treated with our basic antibiotics, pneumonic plague is different. Not only does it develop rapidly, the fatality rate is quite high. And it's not a pleasant way to die. Especially when sepsis sets in. There will be organ failure, respiratory distress, hemorrhaging, and then death. Now can you imagine what would happen if something like this was created in a lab, not to stop the disease from spreading, but to cause it to spread?"

She picked up the plane tickets and dropped them onto the bed next to him. "It seems to me as if you believe you could leave the country for a week and walk away unaffected. The problem is, when you let something like this loose, you can't pick and choose your victims. It will continue to spread rapidly without an antidote for days, maybe weeks. That means that the odds of you or your wife, your mistress, or your children getting it when you return are pretty high."

"You're bluffing and you're crazy."

"Am I?" She took the protective cap off the vial, pulled out the syringe, and shoved the needle through the rubber top before moving in front of Hayward.

"What are you doing?" he asked.

"Jarred Carmichael found a way to make this into a weapon, which would mean a death sentence to thousands of innocent people. And since you're so certain that I'm bluffing, I say we try it out on you and see what happens."

"Wait." Hayward turned to Josh. "Stop her. Please."

Josh stepped forward. "Who are you working with, and where are the rest of the vials?"

"I don't know."

Caitlyn drew up the dose with the plunger, then pulled it out and checked for bubbles.

"What are they planning to do with it, Hayward?" Josh asked.

"You're too late. They're gone."

"Then who was your buyer?"

Hayward tried to pull away, but couldn't. "Don't . . . please don't . . ."

Caitlyn swabbed his arm and injected the needle, her thumb hovering over the plunger. "I wouldn't move if I were you. My finger might slip and accidently inject our little vaccine sample."

"Tell me who it is."

Hayward winced, and his hands shook in his lap, but he refused to answer.

"In case you hadn't thought of it," Josh said, "you and your family will be missing your flight tonight. If this virus gets out—"

Hayward was sweating bullets. "His name is Angelo Braddock."

"Who else is involved?"

"Carmichael was our genius in the lab . . . Stover found us our buyer. He tried to get your wife involved, but she refused."

"And so you killed her." Josh frowned. "What about the precinct? Who was your inside person there?"

"No one. I put the pressure on the captain and fed him the evidence we planted."

"If you're lying—"

"I'm not."

"Where can we find Braddock?" Josh asked.

"He didn't exactly tell me his plans—"

"Hayward . . ." Josh glanced at Caitlyn. "All I have to do is say the word and you won't need to worry about the virus getting out, because you'll have it—"

"No! There's a party being held at the Egyptian Consulate tonight. They're planning to release the virus there as a test, but honestly, I don't know any details."

Caitlyn pulled out the needle without injecting the harmless saline.

Josh clicked on his earbud. "You're up, Eddie. It's time to turn ourselves in."

# 33

Caitlyn stepped out of the taxi in front of the police station, her legs feeling as if they were about to collapse. After her stint in juvenile detention as a teen, she'd never gotten in trouble again with the law. And now she was about to turn herself in to the authorities as a wanted fugitive. If things didn't go their way, she'd end up spending years in prison.

Josh took her hand as they walked up the sidewalk toward the precinct, giving her a slight measure of comfort, but it wasn't enough. When she was twelve, she'd asked her mother if one day she was going to end up like her father, certain she carried in her blood the same demons he battled with every day. Her mother had pulled her into her arms and told her to never, ever believe those lies.

But now here she was, facing prison just like he had.

She shoved the taunting thoughts aside. Josh had copies of everything they'd discovered, but she still wasn't sure if it was going to be enough to put an end to all of this and prove that they were innocent. Or make up for what they'd done trying to prove that innocence. All she knew to do was pray that the light would shine through the darkness and the truth would be revealed.

"You need to know what's going to happen once we step inside." Josh paused in front of the precinct's front door. "We'll be surrounded by armed officers, all of whom have been ordered to arrest us. Do exactly what they say. We'll get a chance to explain our side, but in the meantime they will treat us like criminals."

She swallowed hard, then nodded. She'd watched enough cop shows on TV to give her an idea of what was about to happen. Something that did nothing to reassure her. Instead, the thought that she was about to be arrested made her want to throw up. But they were out of options and to keep running would only make things worse.

They walked across the shiny tiled floor toward the main desk. The half-dozen people sitting on benches ignored them, caught up in conversations or their cell phones.

Josh stopped in front of reception and tapped on the glass. "Mary . . ."

Recognition fluttered in the woman's eyes and her face paled. "Detective Solomon, I—"

"I need to speak to the captain." Josh held up his arms while still holding the file. "I'm here to turn myself in."

The receptionist grabbed her phone and called someone. Ten seconds later, doors on either side of them slammed open, and they were surrounded by six or seven uniformed officers, all pointing weapons at them.

One of the officers stepped forward and took charge. "Drop the file, Solomon. Both of you, put your hands behind your head and lock your fingers. Now!"

Caitlyn followed their instructions, her heart pounding as she fought back the tears. All she'd wanted to do was find out the truth, and this is where it got her.

*God, I need you to put an end to this . . . please . . .*

"We're here to turn ourselves in, and we will cooperate." Josh dropped the file on the floor. "But I have information that the captain needs to see immediately. We have evidence that a bioterrorism attack is imminent at the Egyptian Consulate. You can do what you want to me, but you need to look at what we've got. It will tell you exactly what's going on."

The sergeant grabbed the file from his hand, then took a step back. "On the ground. Both of you. Now."

Josh fell to his knees, then lay down prone on the ground beside Caitlyn.

"I need you to call the captain," Josh repeated.

Another man walked into the room. "What's going on?"

"Captain . . . Detective Solomon's just turned himself in."

Josh hesitated, then looked up from the floor. "I have information on a bioterrorism attack tonight—"

The sergeant stepped up next to him. "Shut up and don't move."

Cold tile pressed against her cheek. Tears welled in her eyes, and she struggled to breathe. Josh put his head back down. What were they supposed to do if no one would listen to them?

"Let him speak," the captain said.

"There's a virus with the potential of killing thousands about to be let loose," Josh said, still keeping his head down. "We have hard evidence, plus a recording of a confession from ADA Nigel Hayward that he and others were involved in both the selling of the virus and framing me for my wife's murder. But right now, there is an attack planned for tonight at the Egyptian Consulate. It needs to be stopped."

The sergeant moved next to the captain. "Solomon's a wanted man, sir, who just escaped from prison. I don't think you need to be listening to him."

"That's my call, Sergeant, not yours. Give me the file and the recording." He turned back to Josh. "You mentioned a bioterrorism attack."

"According to Hayward, it's going to be at the Egyptian Consulate. Tonight."

"Explain."

"A lot of vaccines use viruses to transport genes into the body, then those genes are able to alter the immune system's response and eliminate whatever disease the vaccine is targeting. In this case, though, the virus created turns lethal when introduced into the body. And if let loose, this lethal virus will spread like the common cold."

The captain dropped his hands to his sides. "Who's the buyer?"

"Angelo Braddock."

The captain frowned. "He's on the FBI's most wanted list."

"Yes, sir, I believe he is."

"Take them to separate interrogation rooms." The captain headed out of the lobby. "Sergeant, you're with me."

"Yes, sir."

Someone pulled her up off the ground. She groaned at the sharp stab of pain that shot through her shoulder and down her arm, but she bit her lip instead of crying out. She'd do what they said. She was innocent, and surely that was going to be enough in the end for the truth to come out.

It had to be enough.

Caitlyn stared at a long scratch on the metal table in front of her. She had no idea where Josh was or how much time had passed since an officer had brought her here. Had no idea if the captain planned to take what they'd said seriously. What she did know was that every minute that passed was another minute closer to someone letting the virus loose. They'd done everything they could to stop what Braddock was planning, but unless the captain believed them, it wasn't going to be enough.

Numbness spread through her as her mind switched to Josh. He'd gone through so much both emotionally and physically. Seeing his partner's murdered body. Taking the brunt of a prison beating. And now this—the frightening realization that everything they'd worked to fix might be coming unraveled.

She gnawed on the inside of her lip. For a moment she was fourteen again, sitting in the driver's seat, terrified she was going to prison for her father's crimes. Today had become a reminder of just how much there was to lose when you cared about someone. Why she'd learned at a young age how to close her heart so it didn't hurt as much when it was broken.

Which was exactly what was going to happen if she let Josh in. The men in her life always left. She had no desire to repeat the cycle. A cycle that always left her with a broken heart. His kiss might have left her off-balance, but she'd meant it when she'd told him things wouldn't work between them. He'd gotten emotionally caught up in the situation, something she couldn't afford. Not if she wanted to keep her heart intact.

She shifted in the chair, her entire body aching from exhaustion. No. She couldn't think about Josh right now. Just like she couldn't give in to the fatigue or the fear. This wasn't over. Not yet.

The door to the interrogation room swung open, and an officer stepped into the room with a badge and gun on his hip, startling her awake. "Get up. I've been ordered to transport you to a holding cell at the county jail."

She glanced at the door, fear washing over her again. "Wait a minute . . . Why?"

"I'm just following orders."

"I want to speak to the captain first. Where is he?"

"The captain's not available." He cuffed her, then led her out of the room, toward the elevator.

"I want to see the captain before I go. I need to make sure he understands—"

"Do you know how many people come in here with stories of

why they shouldn't be in jail? You're not exactly in a position to make requests."

She felt her heart pounding in her chest as they stepped into the elevator. The doors closed. She was starting to panic. Struggling to breathe. "Then I want to see a lawyer. I have the right to an attorney before you take me anywhere."

He shook his head. "I'm just doing what I'm told."

"I want to see a lawyer," she repeated.

He stopped the elevator midfloor and pushed her shoulder against the wall. "Here's the deal. You're going to shut up and do as you're told. If you scream or do anything to try and get attention, I won't hesitate to shoot you. All I'll have to do is tell them you tried to escape my custody and I had to shoot to stop you. And trust me, they'll believe me. Do you understand?"

A wave of panic swept through her as she tried to take in what he was telling her. Hayward had lied to them. He had a contact in the precinct, and this detective wasn't following orders to transfer her. He was planning to use her as leverage if things went south for him. She pulled against his grip, but he only dug his fingers deeper into her flesh. This was insane. They were at a police station. A place where she should be safe.

She glanced up at the man, and Quinton's image flashed in front of her. Any doubt of this man's intent vanished. For the moment she had no choice but to do what he said.

Once outside the precinct, they started across the darkened parking lot toward his car. Temperatures had risen over the last few days, leaving behind the cold snap that had swept through the area, but she still felt chilled. She tried to slow her breathing while she hunted for a way out. Once she got into his car, her odds of escaping were going to diminish drastically.

"You can't do this. You're only going to make things worse for yourself."

He clicked his key fob and opened the silver sedan to their right.

"I don't think things can get any worse. Just get into the car and shut up."

He handcuffed her to the inside door handle, made sure her seat belt was secured, then seconds later, peeled out of the parking lot and headed north toward the freeway.

"Where are we going?"

"Doesn't matter. I heard the captain talking, and it's just a matter of time before he figures all this out and puts out a warrant for me. You're going to be my insurance until I can disappear."

"And then you what? Arrange to have me killed like you did the others?"

His silence spoke volumes.

"You know this isn't going to work," she said.

"Shut up." He banged his hand against the steering wheel. "You can't just be quiet, can you? If you'd done that in the first place, none of this would have happened."

"What about Dr. Abbott and Helen? Were they murdered because they couldn't keep quiet?"

He glanced in the mirror, then took the next exit. "They were loose ends."

"And the virus they're going to release? Are you planning to just ignore that?"

"What is that supposed to mean?"

"Do you even know what they are going to do with the virus? Once it's out, a lot of people are going to die. And don't think it can't affect you. You have no idea what you've gotten yourself into."

His phone rang. He checked the caller ID, then ripped out the battery and threw it into the back seat.

"Why did you decide to do this?" she asked. "Betray your city. Your country."

"Does it really matter at this point? My wife walked out, left me with a huge monthly alimony payment. I had twenty years of service behind me, and I was left with a broken marriage and bad back. I deserved more."

"So you became a dirty cop?"

He pressed on the accelerator in order to swerve around a blue pickup. Her fingers gripped the armrest, thankful at least her hands were cuffed in front of her, but he was going too fast which made it difficult to keep her balance.

A second later, their vehicle clipped the back end of the truck. Her abductor fought to keep the car upright, but the force of the impact was too strong. The car lost traction, flipped a full 360, then skidded across the pavement. The moment it stopped, a heavy silence surrounded them. Caitlyn opened her eyes. Dust settled around her from the air bag, but she couldn't feel anything. Sirens blared, and someone nearby was shouting, but the sounds around her were muffled.

He reached over and undid her seat belt, then unlocked the hand-cuffs. "You're coming with me."

A sharp pain ripped through her rib cage as he dragged her out of the car. He held her in front of him, with his gun pointed at her chest. Blood poured out of a cut on his head. Her own shoulder throbbed, and her chest felt as if someone was sitting on her.

Two police cars pulled up to the scene. Seconds later the officers exited the vehicles with their weapons drawn.

"Adams . . . put the gun down and let her go."

"No, you listen to me. I'm walking out of here with her as my insurance."

"There's nowhere to go. This is over."

"You're wrong. It's not over. Not yet." Adams shook his head. "I'm walking away with her. If you follow, I'll shoot her."

She stumbled next to him as they crossed the parking lot of a small strip mall.

"They're right." She tried to keep up but was only able to draw in shallow breaths. "There isn't anywhere to go."

"Shut up."

He pulled her toward the entrance of a local coffee shop, located at the end of the strip mall.

"What do you think's going to happen if you take more hostages?" she asked.

"Shut up." He stepped up to the curb, dragging her with him. "I need time to figure things out."

The man was in a panic. And he should be. This wasn't going to end well for him no matter what he did.

"Let me call the captain," she said. "We can work something out if no one else gets hurt."

"What is there to work out? I'm already looking at life in prison."

Another sharp pain shot through her as she tried to take in a breath. She stumbled in front of the coffee shop's entrance, almost losing her balance, then froze at the crack of a gunshot.

# 34

Josh tapped his foot against the tiled floor of the interrogation room and stared at the door as if that would somehow move things along faster. Except for the night Olivia died, he didn't remember ever feeling so out of control. They didn't have the luxury of time if they were going to stop what was going on.

Two detectives had spent over an hour interrogating him on everything from his escape from jail to Caitlyn's involvement in the situation to the file he'd turned over to them, but they'd focused primarily on his accusations of ADA Hayward and the planned attack on the consulate. He had no doubt that they had many more questions for him. Whether they believed him or not, he had no idea. So now he had no choice but to simply wait.

He let out a sigh of relief as Captain Thomas stepped into the room and dropped the file folder onto the table in front of him. "Sorry you've had to wait so long, but things are a bit crazy out there."

Josh didn't respond, just waited for the man to continue, hoping that the apology was a good sign he hadn't decided to dismiss him.

"The evidence you gave us was pretty compelling, and I'll be the first to admit that it looks like you were right." The captain sat down across from him. "Since Braddock's on the FBI's most wanted list, we were obligated to loop them in. And thanks to your intel and a rapid-fire plan, he was arrested outside the consulate about forty-five minutes ago."

"And the bioweapon he had?"

"In the course of our search we found an aerosol container that we believe, once tested, will contain the virus, but the building was evacuated successfully. Another hour and we would be looking at an entirely different outcome."

Josh leaned forward. "Do you believe me now? All the evidence against me was nothing more than a setup. I didn't kill my wife . . . or Quinton. This is about black-market sales of bioterrorism materials—that won't end with this attempted attack—plus corruption in the DA's office—"

"I know, and I owe you an apology. I was facing tremendous pressure from Hayward's office to bring you in. They had evidence that supported what they were saying. If I'd had any idea of what was really going on, and the evidence that was planted . . ."

"Tell me how I can help."

"For now, you're going to have to be patient while we sort all this out. I'm still skating on pretty thin ice here. If we don't do things right, this case is going to fall down like a house of cards, not to mention I keep being reminded that you escaped from jail and in the process broke at least half a dozen laws." The captain shook his head. "You know I can't just ignore that. If I want any charges to stick against Hayward and anyone else involved, I'm going to have to tread carefully."

Josh nodded. This might be far from over, but at least they were finally moving in the right direction.

The captain pressed his palms against the table. "Why didn't you just come to me from the beginning?"

"If I remember correctly, I did come to you, and you told me to let the case go, take a vacation, and in the meantime, get my head on straight."

"Fair enough, but after you found out about Hayward's involvement and the virus? You saw what going rogue did. I know about the hit on your life. You're lucky we didn't pull you out of that jail in a body bag."

"It might not have been the best option, but in looking back, I don't know that I would have done anything differently. Quinton told me to hold off coming to you. He suspected that someone higher up was involved. I didn't know who to trust. But let me help. Please. I know what's going on, and I can—"

"Forget it. I'll make sure all charges are dropped against you and Miss Lindsey, but it's going to take time. You're still technically a fugitive who just escaped from prison, which means no matter what I think, you can't be involved in this." The captain sat back in his chair. "Though you might find this interesting. I just got confirmation that Hayward was found sitting in his hotel room with his mistress, exactly where you said he would be, waiting for the police."

"Really?"

"What did you tell him?" the captain asked.

"I might have given him the impression that there was muscle outside the room and that he would be safer staying inside."

"You threatened him?"

Clearly Hayward hadn't disclosed everything that went on in that room. "I was just trying to save lives, and in the process, I admit, my own."

The captain's phone rang. He took the call, hanging up without saying anything, then turned back to Josh. "I don't remember seeing Detective Adams on your list of those suspected in being involved in this mess."

"He wasn't."

"Security footage has him leaving this building with Caitlyn as a hostage."

Josh jumped up from his chair. "Where is she?"

"There was an accident . . ."

"Just tell me she's okay."

"All I know is that she's been injured, and Adams was shot. I'm heading to the scene now."

Josh braced his hands against the table. "Let me go with you. Please."

"What did I just tell you?" The captain headed for the door. "You can't be involved in this."

"Like it or not, I am involved." He wasn't going to back down. Not now. "But I just want to see her. Please."

The captain stopped, then turned around. "If you promise to talk to her only, and no one else."

Josh nodded.

Twenty minutes later, the captain pulled up at the scene of the wreck. Josh recognized Adams's smashed-up vehicle. First responders were on the scene, including an ambulance and the county medical examiner's van. The ME's van could only be here for one reason. Someone was dead.

But Caitlyn . . . she had to be okay.

He followed the captain to where the officer in charge was standing near the crash. By the looks of the vehicle it was a miracle anyone had survived it.

*As hard as it is, son, maybe it's time to move on. I know what it's like to lose a spouse. Loving someone new will never take away the love you had for her. And Olivia would want you to be happy again.*

His father's words played through his mind. But what if he'd lost Caitlyn before he even had a chance with her?

"Captain Thomas."

"Detective Bower. What happened?"

"Witness says that their vehicle hit the truck from behind, causing it to flip. The detective then dragged his hostage—a Caitlyn Lindsey—toward that coffee shop. Deciding he was about to escalate the situation with more hostages, an HPD sniper took him down."

"He's dead?" the captain asked.

Bower nodded.

"And his hostage?" Josh spoke up, unable to stay silent. "Caitlyn Lindsey . . . where is she?"

"She's on her way to the hospital right now."

"She was injured?"

"Possible broken ribs and internal injuries. They're not sure yet."

No . . . He'd wanted to keep her safe. He thought that turning themselves in would guarantee that, bring this nightmare to an end, but now . . . how had this happened?

"Solomon?"

Josh turned to the captain. "I need to see her."

He nodded. "I'll take you to the hospital as soon as I'm done here."

Josh followed the nurse's directions to room 324, then hesitated in the doorway. Caitlyn lay on the bed, talking to the doctor. She had a nasal cannula for oxygen and an IV in her hand—reminders of how close he'd come to losing her. And of how grateful he was that she was alive.

"Josh?"

He stepped into the room, stopping at the end of her bed. "Hey . . . you've had us all worried."

"I'm okay. Really." Caitlyn nodded at the doctor. "He can explain better than I can."

"She will be fine, but she has two broken ribs and a pulmonary contusion. The main treatment is rest, and barring any infection, the bruising on her lungs should heal within the week. The cracked ribs will heal also but will take longer." The doctor turned back to Caitlyn. "I'll check in on you in the morning, and if your oxygen levels are normal, you should be able to go home."

"Thank you."

Josh waited for the doctor to leave, then sat down on the edge of her bed. "Hey."

"Hey . . ." She shot him a tired smile. "I can't believe you're here. I was worried they'd have you locked up in solitary confinement."

"They're dropping all charges against us."

Her eyes widened. "You're serious?"

He slipped his hand around hers. "Yes, but still I'm so, so sorry you had to go through all of this. Are you really okay?"

"I will be. Especially now. Funny how I was thinking that the only thing I had to worry about in turning ourselves in was going to prison. I guess I was wrong."

He shot her a smile. "You really will be the life of the party with all this to add to your story—"

"Don't." She pulled her hand away, pressed it against her side, and groaned. "Please don't make me laugh."

"I'll try not to."

Her smile faded. "It shouldn't be that hard, really. Adams is dead. They shot him."

"I know."

"What about Hayward?" she asked.

"He was picked up in his hotel room where we left him."

"He actually believed your threat about not leaving the room?"

"Eddie can look pretty threatening. They also arrested Braddock."

"So they stopped the attack?"

He nodded. "There are still some loose ends to tie up, but this is finally over."

She reached up and brushed her finger across his jawline.

"I'm a mess, aren't I?" he said.

"A few colorful bruises of your own, but you're alive. That's all that matters."

"We're both alive."

But the sadness was back in her eyes. "I wanted to tell you how sorry I am about Quinton. I know you haven't had a chance to grieve, but he proved that he was a good man. He gave his life to try and stop this. We owe him our lives."

"Quinton is one of the pieces I've wanted to ignore dealing with until I'm forced to. I just don't know how I'm going to explain what happened to his wife or his two little girls. He didn't deserve this."

"None of them did. Olivia . . . Dr. Abbott . . . Helen . . . At least no one else should get hurt now."

He caught her gaze. "How are you? Really."

"Besides feeling like someone is stabbing me every time I take a breath?" She shook her head. "I'm tired . . . Relieved . . . Sad. If you would have told me a month ago I was going to do even one of the things I've done in the past week, I would have said you were crazy. After today . . . I don't know. I hope I'm never put in a position of feeling like I have to choose the wrong side of the law."

He brushed back a tear from her cheek. "You have nothing to feel guilty about."

"What happens now?"

"Well, for starters, you're not to leave until you're officially discharged."

"What about you then?" she asked. "Have you been checked out by a doctor?"

"Not yet."

"Promise me you will?"

"Fine . . . I promise. As long as you keep your promise."

She rolled her eyes at him. "It's a deal."

"After that, I'm thinking about Chinese takeout, then sleeping for about a week." He tried to read her expression but couldn't. "Does it hurt bad?"

"Just every breath. A week sleeping sounds pretty good, though I have a feeling I'm going to be sick of resting before I'm better."

"I'd say you deserve that. I'd say we both do, actually." He ran his thumb down her cheek, wanting badly to kiss her.

She turned away. "Please. Don't."

"What's wrong?"

She shook her head. "I'm thrilled that Hayward and Braddock and the others will pay for what they did, but as far as us . . . nothing has changed for me. I'm sorry."

He fought to come up with a response that wouldn't push her away further. When he'd kissed her at the beach house, despite her hesitation afterward, he knew he hadn't imagined the longing in her response. "I know what it's like to have your heart broken, but I also know what it's like to love and be loved. What if it's worth the risk?"

"What if it's not?" She looked back at him. "Everything that's happened these last few days—and especially today—has reminded me that sometimes, no matter how hard you try, people get hurt. Hearts get broken. People die. I don't want to go there again."

"Not even to take a chance in finding out that we could be happy together?"

"Josh, this isn't some storybook tale where everything ends when the hero kisses the heroine. What about after that moment? Things don't always work out that way in real life. They get messy. Men walk out, abuse their spouses, or they die. And hearts get broken."

Like her heart.

Which made sense. It was why she was pulling away from him. Not because she didn't feel the same way he did, but because she was terrified of what she might lose. And he couldn't blame her. An abusive father who had killed her mother. A fiancé who had walked out on her. In order to guard her heart, she'd closed it off completely. And there was no way she was going to just let him in.

"You're right," he said. "But I'm not your father or your ex-fiancé—"

"That doesn't matter. Anything that happened between us isn't real. We barely know each other outside all of this. Whatever you're feeling . . . it's not going to last. It can't."

"Why not?" He shifted on the edge of the bed, searching for a response that wouldn't push her away further. And deciding the only answer he could give her was the truth. "It feels real to me. When we drove up and I saw Adams's car, I didn't know if you were dead or alive. But I knew at that moment that I couldn't lose you . . . And I realized how much I want you in my life." He rushed on before she had a chance to interrupt. "I know you've lost a lot in your lifetime and you've been hurt, and I won't be foolish enough to think I would never hurt you. Because I will. Even if I don't want to. But I need you to understand that you are the reason that my heart is feeling again. You've made me want to open up and love again. To step out and take a chance. It's all because of you. And just because your heart is telling you to run right now doesn't mean you have to listen to it. Give it a chance, Caitlyn. Give us a chance. Please."

She was crying now. "I can't, Josh."

He wanted to pull her into his arms. To tell her to fight against the fear that entangled her. To convince her that taking a chance was sometimes worth the risk. But that wasn't his decision to make.

The nurse walked into the room. "I'm sorry, sir, but you're going to have to leave. She needs to rest."

"Caitlyn—"

She avoided his gaze. "Goodbye, Josh."

He hesitated, then walked out of the room. After everything that had happened, he'd been so sure she'd be willing to make a fresh start with him despite all the baggage and hurt they both carried. But he'd been wrong. Instead of healing and moving on, he felt as if his heart had just shattered all over again. What did finding out the truth matter if he lost her in the process?

# 35

Caitlyn sat in her favorite cushioned chair on the back patio of her house, legs pulled up beneath her, and the latest book by her favorite author in her hands. The pain pills she'd taken thirty minutes ago were kicking in, giving her some relief, and on top of that, the Texas sun had finally decided to come back out and warm things up.

But she still felt restless. She found herself reading the last paragraph half a dozen times and had no idea what it said. No matter how hard she tried to tell herself she didn't care, all she could think about was Josh.

"Hope you're hungry." Her best friend, Amber, stepped out onto the patio from the house, balancing two bags of takeout, plates, and a jug of sweet tea. "I picked up barbecue and it smells so good, you're lucky I didn't eat it all in the car driving back."

Caitlyn set the book down, then moved the bouquet of flowers out of the way. "You know, you're spoiling me."

"That's what best friends do." Amber started arranging the take-out containers of brisket, fried okra, beans, coleslaw, onion rings, and corn bread. "Besides, it's not like I went out and smoked the brisket myself. I like taking care of you, even if you are somewhat of a difficult patient who for some reason didn't call me when you were in trouble."

"Do we really have to go there again?" Caitlyn moved too quickly to grab an onion ring from sliding onto the floor, paying for it with a sharp pain that shot through her rib cage. "I did it to keep you safe."

Amber frowned. "I still think I could have helped."

"I know, and you know I love you for coming, but it's been over a week now, and you've been here every day. These ribs of mine will take a while to heal, but I'm okay. I feel guilty you're not with your family more."

"Forget it. I wouldn't be a best friend if I didn't smother you with a bunch of TLC. Besides, my family can survive without me for a few days. And if they can't, they might just realize how much I do for them."

"So I guess it is a win-win situation." Caitlyn popped a piece of fried okra into her mouth. "Seriously, I can't tell you how good it is to hang out with you. We don't do it enough as it is."

"Agreed." Amber sat down across from her and started filling up her plate. "Listen . . . I know you don't want to talk about this, but—"

"If you're referring to Josh—"

"He's left at least a dozen messages, not to mention the gorgeous bouquet of flowers sitting on this table."

"He'll give up eventually." She looked at the food on her plate, her appetite suddenly gone. "And you were right. I really don't want to talk about him."

"Except I think you do."

Caitlyn frowned.

"Listen, I realize you're recovering from a very traumatic situation," Amber rushed on, "but that doesn't mean you should brush him off. Especially when you're in love with the man."

"I'm not in love with him, and besides, whose side are you on?"

Caitlyn's frown deepened at her friend's persistence. Amber never had been able to drop a subject until she was ready. "I thought you were supposed to be on my side."

"I am. Remember, I'm the one who offered to spend time with you this past week even though Noah's in the middle of basketball season and Chloe—"

Caitlyn rolled her eyes. "Please. I know your tactics. Now you're trying to make me feel guilty?"

"Hmm . . . I thought I was doing a pretty good job. But seriously, I just don't understand why you're running from him. I met him when he stopped by. You haven't said much, but he's good-looking, seemed charming, and even though I'm sure you haven't told me everything that happened between the two of you, goodness, girl, the fact that there was something between you was obvious."

Caitlyn knew Amber was trying to help, but there were still times when she pushed too hard. "You don't understand—"

"Really? Is that what you're going to throw at me? Because it won't work. I know this has everything to do with your father and Bryce, and your fear of letting anyone into your heart because you're afraid it might get broken again. But not all men are like them. I'd even say that most men aren't like them. You know, you've come so far over the years since I've met you, but using your father as an excuse not to fall in love is crazy."

"That's not what I'm doing. And besides, that was a long time ago."

"Which is exactly my point. Who else have you let into your life since then?"

"Amber—"

"All I'm trying to do is tell you, that guy's in love with you. At least you should hear him out."

"Just because you're happily in love doesn't mean I have to be or even want to be."

"Since when?" Amber asked.

"Since love makes everything complicated—"

"I'm not buying that. You were always so tough and independent, but it's okay to rely on someone else. To let someone into that closed world of yours."

The problem was, no matter how hard Caitlyn tried to fight it, Amber was right. She wanted to let him into her world. She missed him and couldn't get him out of her mind.

"Caitlyn . . . I'm not trying to hurt you. I just want you to be happy."

"What would you say if I told you I can't stop thinking about him?" She said it before she let herself think about the consequences of her words. She hadn't wanted to admit her feelings to herself, let alone to Amber. But now that it was out . . . "He's the last thing on my mind when I go to sleep and the first thing on my mind when I wake up."

Amber smiled. "I'd say you're finally being honest with yourself."

"You've always had that effect on me."

"Why don't you just tell him all of this yourself?"

Caitlyn caught her friend's gaze. "He's here, isn't he?"

Amber nodded. "He pulled up right behind me and is in your driveway. Just talk to him. You don't have to tell him what you said to me if you're not ready, but the guy's worried sick about you. And after all the two of you have gone through, he deserves that."

Caitlyn nodded. There was no way she was going to win anyway. "Fine."

Amber grabbed her plate of food and headed for the back door.

"But you can stay," Caitlyn said.

"Not this time."

Josh stepped onto the back patio a minute later, looking far too good in black jeans and a black button-down shirt. "Hey . . . sorry if I'm interrupting lunch."

"Help yourself, please. There's plenty to eat, plus tea . . ."

"Tea sounds great, but I've already eaten."

She felt his gaze search hers as she busied herself by pouring him a glass of tea, wishing she didn't feel so awkward around him.

"I just want to know how you're doing," he said. "I've been worried."

She handed him the glass of tea, then sat back down in her chair, making sure she didn't grimace with the pain. "Thankfully, I'm almost back to normal. Still sore, but there's no fluid in my lungs and no additional injuries. What about you? Your face looks almost normal."

"I've been given leave until the investigation is finished, but I'm going to be fine."

"I'm glad." She searched for what to say. "I'm sorry I haven't answered your calls. I just haven't really felt like seeing anyone."

"No one, or just me?"

She glanced away at his question. "It's not you, Josh. None of this is you."

He sat down in the chair across from her and scooted it forward until their knees were almost touching. "Then I'm just going to say what I'm feeling, because I figure at this point I don't have anything to lose. I think you're wrong. Wrong about believing that there isn't a man out there who will love and cherish you and treat you the way you should be treated. I can—I want—to be that person in your life."

She felt her lungs constrict. She couldn't breathe, but this time it wasn't from her injury.

He reached out and took her hands. "Let me show you how to love and how to be loved. I want to be that person who wakes up beside you every morning, who does the laundry with you, takes out the trash, and builds a home and a family with you."

She was crying now, tears streaming down her face as he waited for her to respond. She needed to let go. Needed to finish ripping down the walls she had built to keep herself from getting hurt, but even if she wanted to, she wasn't sure she knew how.

"I'm just so scared," she finally managed. "I don't know if I can take that kind of risk. Scared that if I do, I'll wake up one day and it will all be gone."

"Do you love me?" he asked.

A part of her wasn't sure she truly knew what love was. She'd known the love her mother had for her, even when she hadn't known how to show it. She'd felt her grandmother's love. And Amber's. She'd struggled understanding the love of her heavenly Father and had finally come to realize that it wasn't based on what she did but on what he'd already done for her. The one true sacrificial love.

She studied Josh's expression, the now familiar brown and gold of his eyes, the five o'clock shadow and fading bruises that made her want to reach out and run her fingers across his jawline. As much as she wanted to ignore it, she couldn't deny how she felt. As crazy and irrational as it seemed, she knew she loved him.

She nodded. "Yes . . . somehow in the middle of all this madness, I fell in love with you, Joshua Solomon."

He smiled at her. "Then let's find a way to make this work. Together. We can take as long as you want. There's no rush. We both still have to heal. I just want to do it with you beside me."

He wiped her tears away, then cupped both hands around her face. "I never expected to fall in love again. We might not know what's going to happen tomorrow, but it won't matter as long as we're together."

She smiled at him and nodded. He kissed her lips, now wet with tears.

"I'd like you to meet my family," he said before kissing her again.

"You did promise if we made it out alive, you'd take me to the Kansas State Fair. Funnel cakes, barbecue, watermelon—"

"Yes, but I don't plan to wait until September to take you home with me."

She sat back and smiled at him, feeling as if the world was spinning around her, but somehow, everything right in front of her made sense. Love and life were never easy, but if you could find someone in the midst of the chaos to help give you balance and clarity and support, it was enough to make the journey sweeter. And after a lifetime of running, she felt as if she'd finally come home.

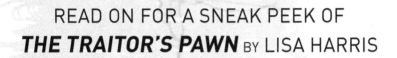

READ ON FOR A SNEAK PEEK OF
*THE TRAITOR'S PAWN* BY LISA HARRIS

COMING SPRING 2020

# 1

*Watch your back . . . this isn't over.*

Aubrey Grayson tried to bury the ominous warning and instead focused on the clear, southern Texas night sky suspended above her. She was safe for now. Lost beneath a million brilliant stars. A rush of happy memories pushed their way to the surface, past the threat, and managed to bring with it the familiar sense of contentment she always found here.

She needed to do this more often. Needed to find time to step away from the frantic pace of life she'd found herself caught up in back in Houston. God had a reason for reminding his people to be still, and three days of trekking through the Texas wetlands in exchange for her high-stress job was exactly what she needed. She took a sip of the steamy coffee she'd brought with her and breathed in the invigorating scent. She'd spend the rest of the morning hunting waterfowl, eating bacon and eggs cooked over a fire in a cast iron pan, and listening to Papps and his boys swap tall tales from previous trips.

But for the moment she was simply going to enjoy the quiet.

Something splashed in the distance, breaking through her thoughts. She turned toward the noise, immediately feeling the spike of adrenaline, but she couldn't see anything. She shook off the instinctual warning. It was probably nothing more than a duck or a frog enjoying the last moments of darkness, broken only by a thin layer of yellow light now along the horizon.

"Aubrey?"

She let out a sharp sigh of relief. "Papps. I was hoping you'd come join me."

"Sorry . . . did I scare you?"

She motioned for him to sit down next to her. "Just lost in thought."

"I'm not surprised. No matter how early I get up, you always beat me." The former senator sat down on the slice of dry ground she'd found overlooking the wetlands. "I'm glad you decided to come down here. You needed a break."

"You're right, and I'm slowly starting to relax."

"Good, because this is the perfect setting for that. I love the hunting, but I also know how much you love the solitude out here at this hour."

"It's something hard to find back home."

He nudged her with his shoulder. "Which is why you should come down here more often. You know there's always a place at the house, and next to this setting, the front porch is the perfect spot to watch the sunrise."

She smiled at the offer. "I do need to take you up on it more often."

"I wish you would. The house gets lonely with all the kids gone. With Gail gone."

Aubrey didn't try to fight the wave of sadness that swept through her. "I miss her too."

The former Senator, Grant McKenna, and his family had been a part of her life for as long as she could remember. And Papps, as she'd always called him, had become like a father to her, taking the place of her absent biological father. His home outside Corpus Christi, her home away from home.

"Ryan told me you were thinking about selling the house," she said.

"I talk about it every now and then, but don't think I'll ever bring myself to actually do it. Too many memories. Too much work. And for now at least it gives you and the boys a place to come two or three times a year."

She reached down and squeezed his hand. "You sound lonely."

"I'm doing okay. Really. Gail's been gone four years now, though it's crazy how it feels like yesterday sometimes. Other times it seems like a lifetime ago."

"How are you doing? I mean really doing?"

"I can't complain. I'm staying busy and that helps. I'm still volunteering on a couple nonprofit boards and am involved in a Christmas fundraiser next month. On top of that I try to catch as many of the grandkids' sporting events as I can."

She let out a low laugh. "Maybe I'm not the only one who needs to slow down."

"I think about stepping down every once in a while, but staying busy helps. Gail and I had so many plans. So many places we wanted to travel to together. I guess you plan your whole life for retirement with the idea to enjoy it with the person you love, but sometimes . . . sometimes life doesn't go the way you think it will."

Aubrey heard the regret in his voice. He wasn't the only one who found it hard to believe Gail was gone.

"But enough about me," he said. "You're the one I'm worried about. You seem tired this trip. More tired than normal."

She stared out across the water as the sun continued to slowly bathe the horizon in yellow and gold. She was tempted to tell him about the threats she'd received, but she wasn't going to add to his worry. "Things never seem to slow down, but moments like this remind me how much I need a break."

"You could always transfer and get a job down here. I understand they're hiring game wardens. It's got to be calmer than what you're doing in Houston."

She took another sip of her coffee. "While it's true my job has its ups and downs, I love it, and can't imagine doing anything else."

"Meaning your promotion to detective?"

She nodded.

"I remember when you first started talking about law enforcement. You were probably ten, maybe eleven. You always had this desire to serve your country."

"And you were one of my biggest influencers. If wasn't for you and your family, I'd be in a different place right now."

"I don't know. You've always been strong, no matter what life throws at you. Besides, I think I'm the one who should be thanking you. I love my boys, but we needed a bit of softness to balance out all the testosterone. We all love it when you're around."

She laughed, loving how he always made her feel like she was one of his own. "You've definitely got that between Ryan and the twins. But now that Kyle and Mitchell are married, it's a bit more balanced."

"True. And don't get me wrong. You know how much I love my daughters-in-law, but you'll never catch them out here duck hunting."

"You do have a point." She watched the rays of light start to edge their way across the marshland and reflect the vivid color across the water. Renee and Kim had no idea what they were missing. "Mitchell told me they made a weekend of it and were Christmas shopping in Houston."

Even her mother had never understood how she preferred camping and hunting to a weekend shopping trip, but she'd choose time out in the middle of God's creation over shopping any day. It always helped lower her stress and calm her mind.

Papps squeezed her knee. "I'm glad you're here, but there's something you're not telling me, isn't there?"

She glanced at him. The morning glow on the water giving her just enough light to read his worried expression. "You always know when something's going on, don't you?"

"It must be a sixth sense. Before, in case you forgot, before I got into politics, I was a father, counselor, and youth pastor."

She let out a slow breath. "I'm just learning how to deal with some of the new aspects of my job, but it's nothing really. Nothing to worry about."

"Were you threatened?"

She closed her eyes for a moment. Wishing she could permanently erase the image of the dead bodies lying on the living room floor. And the chilling expression their suspect had given her when they arrested him. But what she'd experienced was part of the job. Part of her commitment to keep her part of the world a safer place. And nothing anyone could say or do was going to change that.

"Empty threats," she said. "The man's now sitting behind bars and looking at life in prison."

"If you ever feel like you need extra help, please tell me. I've got friends who work in security—"

"I can't run every time someone threatens me." She shook her head. "I've got a partner who watches my back and a supportive captain. It has unsettled me some, but I'll be fine."

Papps let out a sharp sigh. "Sometimes I forget you're not the little girl begging me to take you to the aquarium every weekend."

She laughed. "I still love the aquarium."

"I'm not surprised, but if you change your mind . . . seriously—"

"I appreciate it, but like I said, I'll be fine."

She would. She just needed to shake off the alarm. Nico was in prison and couldn't hurt her. Or anyone else for that matter.

"What frustrates me the most is that while he might be finally behind bars, there are still more out there." She pulled up the zipper of her jacket a couple more inches to block the wind. "The work to get people like him off the streets never ends."

"No, but your job isn't to catch all of them. And everyone you do take off the streets is one less criminal who can hurt someone. That's all you have to do."

"You always know exactly what to say, don't you?"

He let out a low laugh. "I try."

She smiled, reminded once again of how much she enjoyed being with him and his sons. How they'd become like a second family to her after her mother passed away. And how the emotional and spiritual encouragement they gave her was exactly what she needed. And while she was here, surrounded by Papps and his boys, she didn't have to worry about Nico. He couldn't touch her here.

"You ready to get in a few hours of hunting?" Papps asked. "I hear Ryan has challenged me to see who can get their day's quota first."

Aubrey laughed. "Why am I not surprised?"

"You know me. I always like a bit of competition."

They stood up and started back toward the duck hunting blind. All three of his sons shared their father's love of hunting as well as his competitive spirit, and had made this weekend an annual event. Aubrey just enjoyed the feeling of belonging. The familiar sound of the slide action of a shotgun shifted her attention to the right. A second later, a shot echoed off the water, followed by the flapping of wings.

"Bree . . ." Papps sucked in a sharp breath and grabbed onto her arm. "Bree . . . I think I've been hit."

"What?"

He stumbled beside her, then collapsed onto the ground, as she tried to decipher what had just happened. A second later another shot rang out, slicing the air next to her as she knelt down beside him. She stuffed down the panic, needing to keep them both out of the shooter's line of sight. Water seeped into her rubber boots. In this position, there was no protection beyond the tall grass surrounding them, but what terrified her even more was that she was certain this wasn't an accident. Not only had the shot been suppressed with a silencer, it didn't seem to have been aimed at any birds. Which meant it looked to her as if Papps had been both targeted and hit.

But motivation didn't matter right now. What mattered was getting Papps out of here alive. The problem was that they were too exposed and trying to call for help would only expose them further. Staying low, she managed to pull Papps into the outcropping of muddy, tall grass behind them.

"Where were you shot?" she whispered.

"My side."

She pulled back his shirt, but in the low light of dawn, it was impossible to tell how much damage had been done.

"I'm going to try to stop the bleeding," she said, "but you're going to have to stay as still as possible."

She untied his neck bandana, folded it quickly, then pressed it into the wound. But stopping the bleeding wasn't going to be enough. They needed medical help. His son Mitchell was a doctor and only a few hundred yards away, but hunting hours had just started and even if he had heard the shot, no one would think twice. As crazy as the idea sounded, she was going to have to try and take down whoever was out there.

Keeping her hands pressed against Papps's side, Aubrey shifted her position slightly to the right, then raised her head. Marsh grasses rustled around her. Duck calls and shots fired sounded in the distance. A slight flash of sunlight glinted off the gun as she caught site of the silhouette of a man.

Bingo.

She glanced back at Papps. She might have found the shooter, but her options were still limited. She was irritated at herself for not bringing her weapon with her. All she'd wanted to do was catch a few moments of quiet before the sun rose. Now that had turned out to be a deadly mistake.

No doubt the retired senator had a score of enemies, but he wasn't the only one who'd been on the receiving end of death threats. There was simply no way to know at this point. She glanced back down at Papps's side. The bandana was already soaked, but she was unsure how much was blood and how much was water. Her heart pounded. A dog barked in the distance. Butch, Papps's Labrador, was already retrieving ducks at their hunting site, and no one had any idea what was going on.

"Stay with me, Papps," she said. "I'm going to get you out of this. Can you hold this against your side?"

She pressed his hand against the cloth.

"I'll try."

"I'm going after him," she said.

"Aubrey, don't . . ."

She caught the panic in his voice, but she didn't have a choice. She kept low, her boots pressing into the mud as she headed toward where she'd seen the shadowy figure. He was still out there. Waiting. Stalking. She stopped behind a large clump of marsh reeds, not moving, barely breathing, and tried not to shiver. Even with her waterproof gear she could still feel the moisture seeping through to her skin.

*Show me what to do, God. Leaving Papps could mean he bleeds out, but if I go back . . . If I don't stop this person . . .*

Aubrey caught movement to her right and turned toward the figure, but she was a fraction of a second too late. He grabbed her, slamming her backward onto the ground. She groaned as she landed on her back, opened her mouth and tried to fill her lungs with air, but the muscles in her chest refused to work.

"Don't scream." He stood over her, gun pointed at her head. "Don't make a sound, or your friend is going to end up with another bullet."

"What do you want?" she asked.

"You're coming with me."

He dragged her toward the water where there was a small boat bobbing next to the shoreline. The familiar sounds of duck hunting surrounded them while the sun continued to slowly move above the horizon. So Nico had made good on his threats. She had no idea how he'd found her here. She hadn't mentioned to anyone except a couple of close friends where she was going. Nothing on social media to announce she'd be gone. Still, it wouldn't be too hard to find out that this was a trip she made every year. What didn't make sense was his plan. If he was planning to kill her, why not just shoot her and leave? And why shoot Papps? No. There was something she was missing.

She felt the barrel of his gun jab into her rib cage. "Get in the boat, on your knees. Now."

She hesitated before obeying, knowing if she got in that boat and left, she was as good as dead. The bottom was wet with an inch of cold water, but that was the least of her worries. If someone didn't find Papps quickly, he was going to bleed out and die. And if she didn't get away, his family would eventually find her body floating in the water. If she was going to get out of this alive, she was going to have to escape. She spun around and jammed her elbow into the man's Adam's apple. He countered back by throwing a wild punch at her, but she managed to duck, then block his punch. She let out a scream as he swung at her again. This time, she prayed Papps's boys would hear her. She used her weight as leverage to give her an advantage and blocked his punch again, then struck him hard beneath his chin. But she wasn't the only one trained in self-defense. A second later, he swung the butt of his weapon against her temple, and everything went dark.

# *Acknowledgments*

Every time I finish a story, I realize that it takes a village.

To my mother, who used to dictate my stories before I could even write.

To my crit partners over the years, who have made me a better writer.

To my agent, Joyce Hart, and the incredible team at Revell, for believing in the stories running through my head.

And to my family, who continues to support me and the time it takes to pen a story.

Thank you!

**Lisa Harris** is a bestselling author, a Christy Award winner, and the winner of the Best Inspirational Suspense Novel from *Romantic Times* for her novels *Blood Covenant* and *Vendetta*. The author of more than thirty books, including The Nikki Boyd Files and the Southern Crimes series, as well as *Vanishing Point* and *A Secret to Die For*, Harris and her family have spent almost sixteen years living as missionaries in southern Africa. Learn more at www .lisaharriswrites.com.

# meet
# *LISA HARRIS*

---

lisaharriswrites.com

AuthorLisaHarris

@heartofafrica

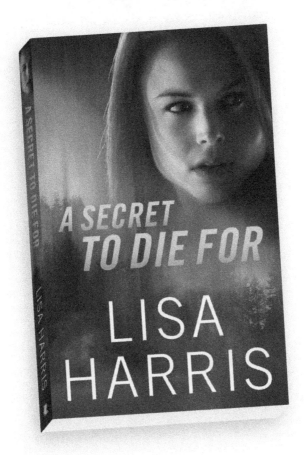

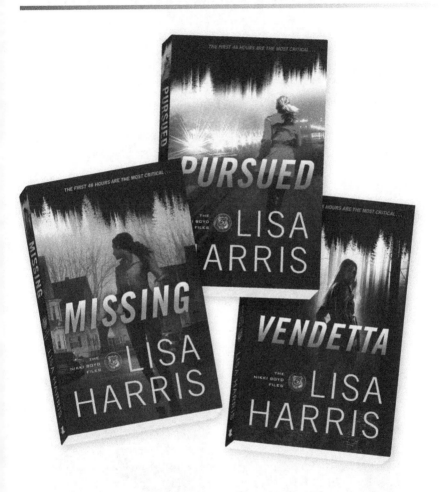

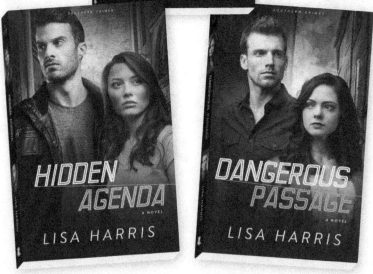